HOPE IN HUNGNAM

David Watts Jr.

This story is based in part on historical events. In certain cases, incidents, characters, and timelines have been changed for dramatic purposes. Certain characters may be composites, or entirely fictitious.

HOPE IN HUNGNAM
Copyright © 2012 David Watts Jr.

www.HopeinHungnam.com

Map of Korea Copyright © 2011 Rasà Messina Francesca
Dreamstime.com

Cover design Copyright © 2012 Karen Haub

ISBN-13: 978-1434829665
ISBN-10: 1434829669

Dedicated to the men of the SS *Meredith Victory*.

You changed the future.

Joseph Blesset, Wiper
John P. Brady, Chief Engineer
Robert H. Clarke, Utility
Russell V. Claus, Messman
Richard C. Coley, Ordinary Seaman
Charles C. Crockett, Oiler
Sidney E. Deel, Assistant Electrician
Andres Diaz, Wiper
Alvar G. Franzon, Third Mate
Major M. Fuller, Steward
Lee Green, Fireman/Watertender
Nathaniel T. Green, Radio Officer
Albert W. Golembeski, Second Mate
Lawrence Hamaker, Jr., Oiler
Edgar L. Hardon, Utility
Morall B. Harper, Electrician
Charles Harris, Able-Bodied Seaman
Leon L. Hayes, Utility
George E. Hirsimaki, First Asst Engineer
Joseph A. Horton, Fireman/Watertender
Lonnie G. Hunter, Able-Bodied Seaman
William R. Jarrett, Able-Bodied Seaman
Kenneth E. Jones, Able-Bodied Seaman
Leon A. Katrobos, Jr., Ordinary Seaman
Alfred W. Kaufhold, Licensed Junior Engineer
James A. Kelsey, Junior Third Assistant Engineer
Leonard P. LaRue, Master
Robert Lunney, Staff Officer
Herbert W. Lynch, Chief Cook

Patrick H. McDonald, Able-Bodied Seaman
Adrian L. McGregor, Messman
Ira D. Murphy, Deck Utility
Willie Newell, Assistant Cook
Vernice Newsome, Wiper
Nile H. Noble, Third Assistant Engineer
Elmer B. Osmund, Boson
Harding H. Petersen, Second Assistant Engineer
Johnnie Pritchard, Messman
Dino S. Savastio, Chief Mate
Henry J. B. Smith, Junior Third Mate
Merl Smith, Licensed Junior Engineer
Louis A. Sullivan, Fireman/Watertender
Ismall B. Tang, Ordinary Seaman
Noel R. Wilson, Able-Bodied Seaman
Wong T. Win, Second Cook and Baker
Ernest Wingrove, Deck Utility
Steve G. Xenos, Oiler

It's hard to think of everyone who has made this book possible. But I'll make my feeble effort. My loving wife, Desiree, is chief among my supporters. Before anyone else, she believed in this story and encouraged me greatly in this work. She read, edited, and made invaluable suggestions along the way. I'm also grateful to my children for putting up with my long hours in front of the keyboard. Special thanks goes to James for reading and rereading this manuscript. Even as a twelve-year-old, he could identify what worked and what did not.

I'm grateful to my mother and father, who taught me that if you want something bad enough, and work hard enough for it, you can achieve it. I was raised with plenty of moral boundaries (and for good reason), but I was raised with no boundaries on what I could achieve. That's a great thing and has surely had a profound influence on my life. My dad passed away in 2001, but his influence continues to live on. I think he would have liked this story.

I owe a special debt of gratitude to J. Robert Lunney, Burley Smith, and Merl Smith. To the best of my knowledge, these three men are the only three surviving crew members of the *Meredith Victory*'s actions in December 1950. I've tried to write about these events, but you lived them. Both the Korean and American people deeply appreciate your service. With my pen, but your insight and gracious sharing of history, I hope we have preserved a small part of this important story for future generations.

I am especially grateful to enjoy correspondence and conversation with D.H. Won. Mr. Won and his father were two of the fourteen thousand refugees evacuated by the *Meredith Victory*. Your first-person account filled my imagination.

It is impossible for me not to think about the terrible price paid during the Korean War so that millions could escape the scourge of Communism and live in freedom. Thirty-six thousand US troops died in combat, and eight thousand remain missing in action. Freedom's price was paid in blood.

To all my friends who helped with diligent reading, to my editor, Rachel Starr Thomson, for the excellent editing, to graphic artist extraordinaire, Karen Haub, for the great designing, and to Clarkston Consulting for flying me all over the world (and thus providing me with abundant quiet time on airplanes to write): my deep appreciation for all of your assistance.

May the wind always be at your back, and smooth seas lie ahead.

David Watts Jr.
June 2012

KOREA MAP

HUNGNAM

INCHEON

PUSAN

KOJE-DO

Prologue

The morning's first touch of light danced gently around the pastures surrounding the small New Hampshire farmhouse— soft, gentle light that caressed the trees and gave them a luxurious glow. It reflected among the red and yellow leaves, shimmered in the still pond, and slowly warmed away the coolness of the morning. Autumn had thoroughly arrived. With it came its gentle breezes, weaving their way among the fading leaves and gently urging them to release their hold on the branches. Some held fast. Others turned loose and took their place in the unyielding course of nature.

On the second floor of the white farmhouse, an old woman stirred in the early morning light. She struggled from her bed and slowly wrapped herself in the old robe she had worn for many years. Sleeping was difficult—rising from sleep even more so. She shuffled painfully from her bed to a small wooden desk. She was losing the final battle with time. Her knees and hips stiffened during what little sleep she could steal from the lonely night. When daylight mercifully came, the pain released its grip only reluctantly, and sometimes not at all.

Undaunted, she sat and worked this morning as she had the previous three mornings. The pace was more urgent now. Her family had all arrived, and the time was at hand.

A gentle tap on her bedroom door interrupted her diligent work.

"Mother," the voice on the other side of the door softly inquired, "do you want some breakfast?"

"Yes, please come in," she said as she closed her work and set it aside. Her daughter, tall, slender, and composed, walked to her desk carrying a tray with a few small breakfast items.

"And would you like tea, Mother?"

"Yes, tea will be very fine."

The daughter smiled in response and poured black Darjeeling tea into a white porcelain cup. Little wisps of steam rose as she added a silver spoon and a touch of milk.

"Mother, I heard you speaking on the phone last night. I don't mean to intrude, but did you invite someone to the services?" The daughter leaned closer, looking intently at her mother's worn and fading beauty. Her mother seemed older today, but it was to be expected.

"My daughter, everything is as it should be," she whispered as she reached to coax a strand of black hair from the younger woman's face—so strong, beautiful, and overflowing with life. "It is all well. Look at all that you have become. You know how proud your father would be of you. You know how proud he always was of you."

"I do, Mother. You tell me often. I will miss him so much."

"I know you will. And I will continue to remind you, each of you children, as long as I'm able. Thank you for my breakfast. Please give me a little more time. My work is nearly done."

"I'll be back for your lunch, Mother. Please tell me if you need my help."

"It is all fine, my dear. It will all be fine."

The daughter retreated softly from the room and gently closed the door.

The crisp latching sound faded across the old wooden floors and left her alone again in the silence. She resumed her writing. The writing helped in ways she could not measure. She wrote words she dared to remember, and some she longed to forget. Since time had taken him and soon would take her, she would see to it that their story would stand in defiance of time. It would be a granite marker, the edges of which time's unyielding winds might soften but never displace.

She wrote carefully in a fine notebook with a sharp pencil. With the formal hold on her instrument taught to her long ago, her now-crippled hands still managed to skillfully direct the pencil, writing in the perfect English she had felt so privileged to learn. In one hand was her pencil and in the other his diary, stirring to remembrance her fading memory. The finality of it all weighed upon her: his life, her life; his story, her story; their story —and the savagery of war that had brought it all together. Tears pooled slightly in her eyes. She dabbed them away and chided herself.

She continued her writing for a few more hours until at last she was satisfied that it was done, and then she laid the pencil on her desk and closed the book.

For a moment she opened her little book again and looked at the words she had written a few days ago:

> This is a love story. Or to be more precise, it is a story of love. It is a story of love in war and hate and conflict. It is not about love among the perfect or the immortal. It is a story of love among the imperfect and the imminently mortal. This is my story of a Marine named Jack, a ship named Meredith, and a captain named LaRue.

She closed the little book, more certain than ever that she had done the right thing. A soft smile brightened her weathered face.

She glanced out the window of her second-story bedroom. Through fading eyes she marveled at the brilliant fall colors. Her mind drifted back to faded memories of her father and a home she once knew far away. She was separated from the past by many miles and even more years. She closed her eyes and could almost smell the place again, see her father's face once more, feel his gentle touch. She paused to consider the strange reality of life: that while the unforgiving crucible of war destroys many hopes and dreams, it sometimes refines the immeasurable pain and sorrow and brings forth the brightest jewels of human hope.

It was time to get ready. The day had arrived. Her work was done.

The children had all arrived.

CHAPTER ONE

Home

Winter is slow to release its grip on the lonely, flat plains of the Permian Basin of Texas, often retreating only for the purpose of advancing yet another day. In early March, 1942, unseasonably warm breezes swept down out of the desolate plains of the Texas Panhandle and swirled dusty and dry around the clapboard farmhouse of Robert and Esther Stiles. The two of them sat in adjacent rocking chairs on the well-weathered wooden front porch of their house on the outskirts of Midland, Texas. The mild air brought with it pleasant temperatures and the pungent aroma of cow manure as the spring winds crossed the six hundred and forty acres of their cattle ranch. Robert sat in silence in his faded rocking chair and fiddled nervously with the letter in his hands, twitching it to and fro.

"Supper nearly ready?" Robert Stiles asked his wife.

"Just about. Made a cobbler too. Should be coming out of the oven in a few minutes." She paused for a moment. "Robert, don't be so hard on him, okay? The country does need young men. He'll make a fine soldier."

"Should've talked to me first. Boy's just barely eighteen. War's no place for a boy."

"But he'll make a fine soldier, don't you think?" Esther asked, laying her sympathetic hand on his shoulder.

Robert bristled. "I made a good soldier too. Even fine soldiers get to live with it the rest of their lives. He might hate me for it, but I've got to try to stop him."

"Look, if anybody should be worried, it's me. But all his friends have enlisted. You can't deny it to him, Rob, he's not a boy anymore. He's a man. He wants to defend our country. He wants to do what you did. He wants to be like his father." She smiled, brushing a few windblown strands of blonde hair from her sun-kissed cheeks. "I can't think of anything more honorable than for him to serve our nation at this time."

"A man, not hardly. Still too much of a boy. But war will make him a man whether he wants it or not. And it may leave him half a man." Robert fumed, staring out toward the main road.

A long, dusty drive connected the house to FM 619, an equally long and dusty road that led the four or five miles back into Midland.

Out on the main road, a school bus slowed to a stop as its brakes sounded a high-pitched complaint. Four figures stepped out of the bus and started walking. Esther watched as Edgar Morrison, her younger son's best friend, said his good-byes to the group and walked back in the direction of the bus and his family's house. The bus hesitated, lurched a couple of times, and then accelerated forward as the driver ground the offending gears into submission.

The young lady in the group, Jessie Nelson, whom Esther often said was one of the prettiest girls in school, smiled and said good-bye to the boys before walking north toward her grandmother's.

Esther watched as her two boys started down the several hundred feet of dirt driveway to the house. Richard was just eighteen, and Jack was fourteen. She smiled and thought about what fine young men they were becoming: strong, fit, and handsome. Both had a pile of schoolbooks under one arm and a bat and glove propped over the other shoulder. Whatever Richard did, Jack did. Richard played baseball; Jack had to play as well. Thankfully, they weren't chasing the same girls—at least not yet.

"They're good boys. Be proud of them, okay?"

"I am proud of them, Esther. Just not ready to send one of my boys to war. Not ready to send either one of them to war. You realize Jack's next, don't you? This war goes on long enough, and you'll have *two* boys getting shot at." The thought had not really occurred yet to Esther. She felt queasiness in her gut and metal on her tongue.

Shaking her head, Esther turned her attention back to her boys. She rose to her feet as Richard and Jack exchanged a few words and then broke out into a footrace for the last seventy-five feet of the drive, arriving in a thunderous crash on the wooden porch with Jack trailing just a second behind.

"One day, runt, maybe you'll catch me!" Richard laughed as he pushed Jack back down the stairs.

"Hey, Mom, dinner ready?" Jack asked as he stumbled back up the porch steps and gave her a quick kiss on the cheek.

"Few minutes, Jack," Esther said. "Go inside and wash up, please. Table needs setting. Plates and silverware for everybody."

Esther waited a moment until the old screen door slammed shut and the sound of Jack's footsteps confirmed he had walked a comfortable distance into the kitchen. Richard started to follow his brother into the house.

"Richard, stay here, please. Your father needs to speak to you."

Richard drew his hand away from the screen door and shifted a bit nervously on his feet as he turned to face his father. "Sure, what's up?"

"Anything we need to talk about, son?" Robert asked. He scarcely shifted in his rocking chair, eyes still staring out toward the horizon. "Anything on your mind?"

"Uh, not that I know of. What's up?"

"Got plans for the future, son? How's school? You serious about your studies?"

"Sure, Dad. I got ninety-five on that math test."

"Good. Glad to hear it. Boy your age should pay attention to math and science. Kinda doubt you want to be a cattle rancher your whole life."

"Yes, sir. I mean, no, sir, I'd rather not be a cattle rancher. I mean, I don't mean to criticize your choice, Dad, I just don't think it's right for me."

Perplexed, wondering where this conversation was going but afraid he knew, Richard watched his dad continue a gentle back-and-forth motion in the faded rocking chair, his right hand twitching badly until he gripped the armrest of the rocking chair. It had been this way as long as Richard could remember. The twitches, the crippled walk. He waited for his dad to reply. The silence burned.

Robert rocked gently back and forth. The only sounds this late afternoon were the creak of the rocker on the wooden porch and the faint rustle of passing traffic on the main road.

"What do you think about graduation?" Robert finally asked. "Looking forward to it?"

"Well, yes, sir. I'll be glad to be done, glad to move on to other stuff." Richard glanced nervously at his mom. Esther stood quietly in her simple gingham cotton dress, barefoot. She radiated a sort of natural beauty, born of a life of equal parts freedom and toil on the West Texas plateau.

"Where do you think you'll graduate?"

"Should be near the top of my class, Dad. Probably not at the top, but near . . ."

"That's not what I'm talking about, son," Robert interjected as he slowly extricated himself from the rocker. He grunted as pain coursed down his right side of his body. With his trembling right hand he grasped his ever-present cane, and with the other hand held the unpainted porch rail for support. His mangled right leg slowly extended vertically but remained viciously bent at the knee in a way nature had never intended.

"You planning to graduate from some place in the Pacific, son?" he asked as he turned unsteadily and glared at his eldest. His left hand abandoned the support of the rail for a moment and fished the envelope from the US Army out of his pocket.

"When were you planning to tell me? Do I not deserve to know? You'd think maybe you might ask my opinion given that I know a little something about the subject."

Richard exhaled, resigned to the discovery.

"You would have said no, Dad. I know how much you hate the idea. But all the other guys have signed up. It's just me and the girls, Dad, and the kids that are too young—we're the only ones that haven't signed up."

"Well, you're signed up now, aren't you? The Army doesn't care what I think—not that they ever did. They think you're old enough to send yourself into combat without my consent. And so you have. You don't really understand what's coming your way, do you?"

Robert shifted his weight away from his right leg onto his left and spread the remaining weight between his left arm on the rail and his cane. "You think it's all fun and games. Got yourself all cranked up with the fever of bloodlust, ready to kill some Japs?"

Richard recoiled at his dad's suggestion. He stood a little taller, took a short step back across the porch, and thrust his shoulders back and his chest out. "I'm going to defend our nation, Dad. You understand that, don't you? They attacked us. We didn't attack them. Three thousand Americans died at Pearl, and now Japan will pay the price. I intend to be there to deliver my share of it. You did the same against the Germans. If was good for you, it's good for me."

Robert steadied himself again, trembling, just barely able to hold the knobby head of the cane. Esther approached silently and rested a compassionate hand on her husband's shoulder.

"Boy, let me explain something very important. I understand what war looks like in a way you never will. Not until you see it, anyway. I understand there are boys your age over there that are being trained right now to kill you." Robert jabbed a finger at his son's chest as he struggled to remain steady. "And I know firsthand they'll do everything in their power to kill you because you'll be doing everything in your power to kill them. I understand that your officers will sometimes send a hundred or two hundred or a thousand boys just like you into certain death because that's what it takes. That's what it takes to win! Except, one of those boys will be *my* son," Robert emphasized as he dropped his voice to scarcely a whisper. "My firstborn."

He paused, catching his breath. "The funny thing is, you don't like this very much, do you? I can see it in your face. Your old man's a little upset with you, and you don't enjoy it. Do you?"

Richard remained silent, seething inside with anger.

"Answer me, son. You enjoy this? You like me getting in your face?"

"No, sir, I do not," Richard said.

Robert leaned back a little. "I didn't think so. You don't like your crippled-up old man yelling at you, but you're quite happy to have the entire Japanese army trying to kill you. Makes a lot of sense, doesn't it? And try to kill you they most certainly will. Let me tell you something: war is for men who have nothing to live for. And when you get killed trying to hand-deliver your wrath to the Japanese, it will be your mother," Robert said, pointing at Esther, who had begun a slow retreat until she pressed her back against the front door, "that gets the news that her boy died fighting over some worthless rock in the Pacific. And maybe, if we're lucky, they'll recover enough of your body to send you home for a proper burial. She carried you, nursed you, cleaned your diapers, and raised you into a strong young man. But look at her!" Robert shouted, and Esther recoiled more.

The crippled man's voice dropped to a whisper, as though the outburst had sapped what little strength he had. "She may end up burying you."

Richard stared blankly at his father, stunned and without response. His mother began to cry, and he watched her quickly enter the house. The screen door slammed hard behind her.

Robert Stiles looked at his son eye to eye now. He did seem taller and stronger than before. Maybe Esther was right, but still, this was *his* boy.

"You're wrong, Dad."

"Excuse me, boy?"

"You're wrong. War isn't for men who have nothing to live for. War is for men who have *everything* to live for, and everything to fight for."

Richard paused and spoke again just as his dad drew a breath to respond. "Maybe you don't want me to fight for you, but I'll fight for Mom, and I'll fight for my little brother, and I'll fight for liberty. I'll fight for the liberty for my generation to live our lives just as your generation fought for the liberty to live theirs. Surely every generation must pay the price with blood. And if I have to make my sacrifice in blood, it won't be too much to pay."

Richard's heart pounded within his chest. He knew what he said was right. But he had surprised himself with the passion of his response. He looked sympathetically now at his dad's broken figure, hobbled in front of him. At his broken heart full of bitterness.

"Son, it will be too high of a price for me and your mother to pay. Just remember that."

"I'll be careful, Dad," Richard said without further emotion as he snatched the envelope from the Army and followed his mother inside.

Inside, the kitchen table was yet to be set. Upstairs, sitting by an open window, Jack absorbed the dialogue and wiped a tear from his eye.

* * *

Richard entered the United States Army in April of 1942 and was quickly assigned to the Seventy-Seventh Infantry Division of the US Tenth Army serving in the Pacific theater. He had the qualities the nation looked for in a soldier: physical strength, courage, integrity. Most of all, he possessed those essential traits of brashness and unrestrained enthusiasm that come with youth. Basic training had been a mere formality for him. It had not served to challenge him so much as it refined his developing muscles for combat.

But it had allowed time for reflection. He spent many dark nights many thousands of miles away from home, thinking back to the moments of his departure. His mother had cried, kissed him on the cheek, and told him she would pray for him every night. Despite her sadness, she never wavered from her commitment—serving in the military would be her son's greatest honor. When it was time to depart, his dad remained seated in his favorite chair in the living room and simply admonished, "Be careful, son."

For Jack, the world back home in Midland functioned much as it had before. He did the same things: played the same baseball games, rode the same bus, went to the same school, chased the same girls. But it often felt to him like he was going through life in a fog. It was the same world. It was essentially the same view, yet it was different—more one-dimensional. He missed his brother immensely. Without Richard, life was disjointed, no more a seamless flow of time. Instead, time moved predictably from punctuated point to point, with those points defined by some new communication from Richard: a postcard, a letter occasionally, some little news from the Pacific to freshen their day.

Jack's time with his buddy, Edgar Morrison, increased. Edgar wasn't a brother, but he was a good friend, and a good friend was a good thing. Through the week, they shared a fairly normal routine: school and perhaps a baseball game or two in the afternoons. On Saturdays, it was usually a matinee at the movie theater. Jack loved the movies for the entertainment, but especially for the newsreels. He always held out hope that he might get a report of some brave, heroic campaign that Richard was part of—maybe even a glimpse of Richard himself as the camera took in the sights and sounds. But the faces were never Richard's.

It was the mail, letters and postcards, that really marked the passage of time. The routine was settled by now. Jack would pick up the mail on his way home from school and deliver it to his dad. Robert would tear into the envelope and read it first, silently, often with a skeptical grimace and a grunt or two. Then he would hand it to Esther, usually without comment. She read every letter excitedly, pausing to offer commentary after each interesting tidbit.

Days rolled into weeks, and weeks into months.

* * *

By the spring of 1945, the battle in the Pacific had pressed Japan back into a defensive posture as the Allies encroached on the Japanese home islands. Spring in Midland not only brought warmer temperatures but the start of another season of baseball for Jack.

"Mom," Jack called out, "I'm heading to baseball. I'll meet Edgar on the way, and when we're done we'll walk back home together."

He poked his head into the kitchen, regarding his mother at her seat at the kitchen table. "Mom?"

She looked up. "Oh, sorry, Jack. I'm just reading the latest. I think the war is really turning against Japan. I hope we can have your brother home soon. Not too late, okay?"

"Should be home by seven. Love you, Mom." Jack patted his dad on the shoulder and walked out the front door, baseball bat and glove in hand.

Edgar was already waiting on the large brick front porch of his family's house a half-mile or so away. As Jack approached on foot, Edgar came down the front porch steps and bounded across the yard. The house was ample evidence of the different lives they lived. Edgar's was a big brick house in town, while Jack lived in a wood-frame farmhouse on the outskirts. Edgar's dad ran the bank while Jack's dad ran cattle. Edgar was an only child, whereas Jack just *felt* like an only child these days.

Edgar quickly joined Jack on the sidewalk, and they turned in the direction of the ball fields. "Hey man, what's going on? You hear from your brother lately?"

"Got a letter today. Didn't read it yet. Mom had it—checking names and places like she always does. She's proud of him. Dad just does his usual grunting thing."

"Any idea where he is?"

"No, just somewhere out in the Pacific. I guess he can't say much about where they're going—he only tells us a little bit about where he's been."

"Any idea of when he's coming home?"

"I hope soon. But I don't really know what to believe anymore. Dad doesn't tell me much. The little bit Dad talks about the war, he says things in the Pacific are turning our way right now. He reads this column in the paper from this reporter who's over there in the Pacific—some Ernie Pyle guy. Dad says we've pushed the Japanese back to their own islands. He said there was

14

a report on the radio earlier about a battle raging on some island called 'Okinawa' or something like that. I don't know. Mom's really hoping we'll wrap things up soon and that Richard will get to come home." Jack brightened. "Hey, I wonder how many Japs he's killed so far. I hope he's killed a whole bunch of those sorry people."

"Mom tells me I shouldn't call them Japs—says it's kind of rude," Edgar said. The boys looked both ways and then crossed the street en route to the ball fields.

"Hmmph. That's funny. No such rules at my house. My mom had this recipe for fruitcake she originally got from her mother. I guess it was called 'Japanese Fruitcake'—Mom showed me the recipe card. Well, she drew this line through the name at the top of the recipe card and called it 'American Fruitcake.' Funny!"

Edgar looked confused—not an unusual expression for him. "I don't get the joke."

"Come on, you big dummy. Isn't it obvious? She doesn't want to call it Japanese Fruitcake anymore—not after what they did to us at Pearl. Anyway, I hope he gets to kill a whole mess of 'em. We should never forgive them for what they did to us."

"Well, if he doesn't, at least we're going to show those Japanese we mean business about our fruitcakes, huh?" Edgar bellowed. The boys laughed, heartily agreeing that yes, at least insofar as the subject was fruitcake, wives across America had really taken it to the Japanese.

"So what are you going to do if the war keeps going?" Edgar asked. "You going in, too?"

"I wish I could. I'm tired of watching everything from the sidelines of dusty old Midland. I mean, war is where heroes are made. That's where the action is. But I don't know. Dad nearly lost his mind when Richard went in. He has this idea that because he was in the first war, he knows exactly what it's going to be like. With him it's all doom and gloom and everything. I tried to tell him that wars aren't fought the same way as back then. I mean, back then they used gas and poison, and now they've got laws and stuff that prevent that kind of thing. They've just made war a lot more civilized. Dad doesn't get it. That's the problem with the older folks. I mean, you can be on a ship now, twenty miles offshore, firing these massive artillery shells at the enemy, and hardly break a sweat." Jack jerked his arms backwards like the recoil of one of the massive guns on a Navy battleship and shouted, "Booooom!"

"Yeah," Edgar said. "Or drop some bombs from a plane." He set about to imitate the screech of an incoming bomb, followed by his best imitation of the resulting cataclysmic explosion.

"Hey, you know the Japs do this stupid kamikaze thing?" Jack said, taking the time to offer his best Japanese accent for the word *kamikaze*. "I mean, how stupid is this? You strap yourself into a plane filled with gas and bombs, and it's nothing but a suicide mission. I mean, you know you're going to die. What kind of stupid people do that? What's wrong with those people, anyway? What'd we ever do to them?"

"Yeah, can you imagine—here's this guy screeching out of the sky toward your ship. And you're manning those big antiaircraft guns we've got. I would be firing nonstop, just this wall of bullets spewing out, and it would be so great to just cut that plane in half and watch it fall into the sea. So much for *kamikaze*," Edgar laughed, offering his own best impression of a Japanese accent. "They would never get through my gunfire."

The boys laughed and carried on the rest of the way to their baseball practice, happily fighting World War II in all its glory. As they arrived at the baseball fields, they transitioned from their combat duties in the Pacific to more serious matters of balls, bases, strikes, outs, and hits.

* * *

16

Twilight hung lightly in the West Texas air as a few stars started peeking out of the eastern sky. Jack and Edgar meandered their way home from practice, reliving their glorious plays and feats of daring sportsmanship. By the time they arrived back at Edgar's house, they had pretty well worked out that Edgar would go to the Yankees and Jack would most certainly play for the Cubs. That was much the same decision they arrived at each time, but they enjoyed the arguments as much the tenth time as the first.

"Want to come in and get some dessert, Jack? Mom doesn't care. She made this incredible pecan pie last night."

"Nah, I better get home. I told Mom I'd be home by seven. See you later, buddy. And by the way, if you drop another one out there, I'm going to come out to center field and smack you myself!"

"Hey—my glasses got all sweaty and I couldn't see. Give a guy a break, okay?"

"Yeah, I'll give you a break!" Jack said, taking a mock swing at his buddy as they both laughed.

Jack left Edgar's house and walked up to the intersection with FM 619. He turned west and ambled along the dusty two-lane road toward his house in no particular hurry. With each passing step, the town receded behind him a bit more and the sky's increasingly inky darkness revealed more and more stars. He walked on the edge of the road just safe of the passing cars and just far enough out of the clouds of dust to avoid choking. The traffic at this time was fairly light—just a few cars heading home from town. On occasion, one of the folks would recognize Jack and pull over to offer him a ride home. But this evening, they just sped by as they hurriedly went on their way.

Jack reached his family's drive and through the fading light saw that one of those cars had turned in and stopped at his family's house. The dust was still settling as Jack walked up the long drive. *Maybe one of Dad's farmer friends,* Jack thought. But he didn't really recognize the car.

With his curiosity piqued, Jack picked up his pace to see who the unexpected company was. When Dad's farmer buddies dropped by, it was always interesting to hear them talk about the latest cattle futures, prices on grain, or problems with water. Jack wondered if farmers ever relaxed and smiled, or whether all they did was complain. Probably nonstop complaining, he had decided. But there was something rather soothing about listening to the men talk. Mom would always be in the kitchen chatting with the women, sometimes making a pie or a cake. He really loved those evenings. All the heat from the day would take flight, and with all the windows open wide, soft breezes wafted through the house. Many summer evenings, Jack would catch a hint of a rumble far off in the distance as big West Texas thunderstorms rolled across the flat plateau. He loved to go out by the barn and watch them make their approach. He loved that about West Texas —the land was flat for as far as you could see, three hundred and sixty degrees of nothing but openness. Jack spent many evenings watching the storms roll in for at least an hour before the first raindrop fell.

As he got closer to the house, he saw two men in military uniforms on the front porch and his mother at the door, hands clutched to her chest.

He heard a bitter wail across the distance and saw his mother fall to her knees. And he knew at once why the men had come.

CHAPTER TWO

Storm Clouds

Just a few years after the shadow of the global struggle that was World War II, the Korean Peninsula erupted in war, and the blood of men flowed freely. One unique group of men did not carry guns into combat, but carried the guns to the men who fought. This was the work of the United States Merchant Marine and the men of the SS *Meredith Victory*.

On the morning of July 28, 1950, just a few hundred miles southeast of Norfolk, Virginia, the *Meredith Victory* plowed roughly through the Atlantic seas en route to the war in Korea. After clearing the tip of Florida, she turned southwest and steamed toward Panama for an expedited routing through the Panama Canal. Ships like her, on urgent military missions, received nearly immediate clearance through the locks while others would wait. Once clear of the forty-eight-mile canal, she sailed north toward Oakland, California, where she took on a load of military vehicles destined first for Yokohama, Japan, and then for South Korea.

The *Meredith Victory* had been mothballed at the end of World War II, so her crew busied themselves working out the kinks and getting her back into peak operating condition. She had seen far more abuse than she deserved. That which didn't creak groaned, in what seemed like a symphony of mechanical misery.

Although weathered around the edges, her design and

engineering were simple and rugged. Huge boilers in the engine room burned standard-grade bunker oil and heated water to the boiling point. The superheated steam was routed to the ship's turbine, which dutifully churned out its assigned eighty-five hundred horsepower and transmitted it through a massive reduction gear into a long shaft and finally to the single screw, which turned at a maximum speed of one hundred rpm and pushed the *Meredith Victory* through the sea at a top speed of seventeen knots.

She was, despite her modern trimmings, essentially a steamship: one of the hastily built World War II transport ships, known officially as a Moore-McCormack freighter. Like the rest of the Victory ships, *Meredith* was built in a marvel of the industrialized assembly-line process in just fifty days in Los Angeles, California. At 455 feet long, 62 feet wide, and 10,658 tons, she was built with no luxuries and just enough of the essentials. Her birth at sea was July 1945, and through the remainder of the war, she and hundreds of her sister ships served their country honorably. Victory ships like her weren't built for combat; rather, they were the ships that made the combat possible. In World War II, the *Meredith Victory* and her fellow freighters hauled countless hundreds of thousands of tons of cargo, equipment, fuel, ammunition, and supplies from the United States to both theaters in the war—often at great peril to her civilian crews. Once the war was over, perhaps like all good war heroes, she was decommissioned and parked in the James River at Norfolk, Virginia, with the rest of the laid-up fleet.

Now, as combat flared in the Korean Peninsula, the *Meredith Victory* had been activated for service once more and chartered to the Military Sea Transportation Service.

The *Meredith Victory* was not outfitted, as some were, for troop transport. She had space for a total of twelve passengers in addition to her forty-six-man crew. This tiny crew attended to all aspects of her duties—each man working four hours and then off for eight. If she had been outfitted for passengers, she could have held three hundred. Had she been converted to carry troops, she would have carried about sixteen hundred. She had armament, but pitifully little. Her sole means of defense was two . 38-caliber pistols locked away in the captain's quarters.

Occupying those quarters, and at the helm as they steamed out of Norfolk, was thirty-seven-year-old US Merchant Mariner Captain Leonard P. LaRue. Like his ship, he was a veteran of running cargo during WWII, having served on the dreaded Murmansk Run—the vast movement of goods and material that kept the Russians in the war against the Germans.

In that effort, he had become a master of evading the enemy, running his ship through zigzag courses to avoid mines and submarines alike. On more than one occasion, he had witnessed firsthand the detonation and sinking of a companion Merchant Marine ship and the tragic loss of her crew. Men don't soon forget the sight of a fellow ship erupting into an explosion of fire. They never forget the sounds of the desperate cries of men plunged into the icy waters. And LaRue would never forget the smell of burning fuel, the waft of sulfur in the air, and the despicable feeling of being utterly unable to help his fellow mariners.

While LaRue never forgot it, he rarely talked about it either. Sometimes others, especially younger crew, asked about such things as though they were the stuff of legend and lore. LaRue usually responded patiently that some memories should be tucked away in a lower drawer and only rarely—preferably never— retrieved.

But history was yesterday. His goals now were simple: integrate his crew and officers into a cohesive group, execute their missions as efficiently as possible, and make a difference in this war.

The journey through the Panama Canal and up to Oakland was uneventful. In reasonably short order, the military loaded the *Meredith Victory* to her maximum capacity with an assortment of military vehicles. She was rated for ten thousand tons of cargo, and she would dutifully haul those twenty million pounds across the ocean. She had five separate cargo holds. Those forward of the ship's house had three levels of decks below the topside main deck. Those aft had just two layers of decks. All the decks, including the topside deck, had been filled with their load of vehicles for the war effort.

Longshoremen in Oakland executed the loading. They carefully lowered her cargo through the open hatches into the lowest deck in the ship, down to what was often referred to as the "tank-top deck" as it sat immediately on top of the fuel tanks holding the tens of thousands of gallons of sea bunker fuel. Her large tanks enabled her to cruise for journeys up to twenty-one thousand miles in duration.

LaRue stood on the bridge wings, surveying the loading process. It was August, yet cold, damp winds blew across the Oakland Bay. He buttoned his coat tighter to seal out the early morning chill. His mind raced through the logistical details of the loading, of their departure, of their soon-to-be first crossing of the Pacific. His heart yearned for the open sea.

LaRue was meant for the sea. He, like his ship, belonged here. But in spite of this, or perhaps because of it, he was also a religious man. He had seen enough conflict and combat in his life to know that man needed a reason to hope. LaRue believed that only God could give man the hope of something better. His love of the sea and love of God found harmony on the deck of his ship.

"Captain?" a young man asked, interrupting the silence.

"Yes, what can I do for you?"

"Name's Wilson, Noel Wilson. Able-bodied seaman. They told me to report to the *Meredith Victory.*"

"Oh, yes. Welcome aboard, son. Catch up with Chief Mate Savastio, and he'll get you up to date on your duties."

"Yes, sir. She seems like a good ship, sir. I'm glad to be here."

"She is a good ship. Even more important, it's a great crew. They're starting to work together like a finely tuned machine. I'm sure you'll fit right in."

"Any words of wisdom for me, Captain? It's my first duty. I just want to make sure I do everything right."

LaRue smiled at the young man, remembering his own early days.

"Best advice I can give you, the first lesson you'll learn is to always give another man a hand with a job he can't do himself."

Wilson looked a bit perplexed. "Is that it?"

"Yes, that is pretty much it. You do that, and the rest will fall right into place. Anything else?"

"No sir, thank you, sir, I'll see the Chief Mate right away, sir." And then he disappeared down the passageway.

LaRue smiled at his own advice. He thought of it as a corollary to that old Bible principle, "Thou shalt love thy neighbor as thyself." He figured some probably found such notions old-fashioned and unnecessary. But he was certain that a man who went to work each day on the unforgiving sea needed an unyielding trust in an Almighty God and a helping hand from his neighbor.

LaRue held his convictions but was determined not to push them. Still, he wasn't afraid to live them openly. A few days before leaving Oakland with their cargo, LaRue stopped by J. Robert Lunney's quarters. His staff officer's quarters were just around the corner from his own.

"You ready?" he asked Lunney. "I was able to borrow a jeep."

"Great, let's go. I was afraid it wasn't going to work out." Lunney shuffled his paperwork into a small stack on his desk and quickly followed his captain.

Disembarking from the ship, the men walked briskly to the tattered old jeep parked near the docks. LaRue tossed the keys to Lunney.

"Your turn to drive," he said and smiled.

Lunney cranked the old engine and babied the throttle until the dark smoke from the exhaust finally receded. Then they were on their way. About twenty-five minutes of driving brought them to their destination: Old Saint Mary's Cathedral. They parked the jeep nearby and then entered and walked silently toward the front of the cathedral. The captain kneeled, bowed, and prayed for his ship and his crew. Lengthy speeches were not his style. Brief eloquence was. He prayed simply, "Lord God, be with us."

Sailing from Oakland, LaRue's first order of business was to deliver his cargo to Yokohama, Japan. The journey, as were most of them, was rather mundane for men accustomed to life at sea. But that was the way they liked it. Most of the men were veterans of World War II, now serving their nation again, but this time as civilians. For some, it was an opportunity for adventure. For others, the objectives were more practical. For Staff Officer Lunney, having served in the US Navy in World War II, the Merchant Marine and the *Meredith Victory* were a simple means to pay his way through law school.

Those means would soon provide him with experiences he would never forget.

* * *

The *Meredith Victory* completed her crossing in about twenty days. In Yokohama, Japan, she dutifully disgorged her cargo of vehicles. She spent a few days in port, allowing her crew some time to stretch their legs on land, and then was again loaded to capacity. She received her orders to depart Yokohama, join a twenty-two-ship convoy, and sail for an undisclosed destination. The convoy of ships was organized to sail in three parallel columns. The *Meredith Victory*'s assigned position was the far right, the last ship in the column.

Along the way, the *Meredith Victory* and the rest of the convoy learned their destination. Staff Officer Lunney found LaRue on the bridge.

"Captain, Green in the radio shack asked if I'd give this to you," he explained, handing LaRue the folded message. "It's from the Navy." LaRue studied it for a moment while the bridge crew waited silently.

"Well fellas, we've got our destination. MacArthur's sending the whole convoy to Inchon. We'll land there the morning of September 15. It's an invasion," LaRue said quietly.

Inchon lay on the west coast of Korea, still in South Korea but now far behind enemy lines and in the control of the Communists. A landing so far behind enemy lines was a bold maneuver reminiscent of the Normandy D-Day landings several years earlier. But before the convoy could arrive in Inchon for the invasion, the men of the *Meredith Victory* would first tangle with the unyielding forces of nature. Their route north through the Yellow Sea took the convoy on a direct collision course with the strongest parts of Typhoon Kezia. In the language of the West, a typhoon is a hurricane—and this was a dangerous category III.

As night fell on September 14, the convoy was overtaken from astern as the huge storm roared north into the Yellow Sea. Kezia's winds howled at speeds up to a hundred and twenty-five miles per hour. Giant waves began to batter the *Meredith Victory*. At 8 p.m., Junior Third Officer Burley Smith Jr. took over the watch for the second officer, Albert Golembeski. They stood on the bridge some fifty feet above the normal ocean level. From their vantage point, they looked out the five portholes of the bridge and watched as the crest of giant waves rolled by at eye level.

The *Meredith Victory* had been loaded to capacity with a full load of tanks and other vehicles, and she rolled severely in the waves. M-26 Pershing tanks were lashed securely by means of large restraining cables and chains, but with each massive wave, the ship rolled precariously and the tanks strained against their lashings. After each large wave, she struggled to right herself and rolled back toward her port side just in time to be battered again. The wild oscillations, the direction of the waves, and the heavy load and so much weight on her deck made control of the ship nearly impossible. As the cycle repeated itself over and over and the storm raged more furiously, the white foaming tops of the monster waves sheathed her in a near-constant ocean spray.

As the crew struggled against the typhoon's power, a particularly massive wave pounded the *Meredith Victory*'s port side and forced her at least forty-five degrees over on her starboard side. Smith and Golembeski had stepped outside onto the bridge wings, and the severe roll forced them to desperately cling to the vertical stanchions to avoid falling into the furious ocean below. They dangled helplessly in midair, looking past their boots at the boiling sea.

For a few eternity-laden seconds, the *Meredith Victory* languished drunkenly on her starboard side in the raging storm. The restraining cables finally reached their breaking point, and two tanks broke free and skittered across the wildly tilted main deck. A heavy truck with GIs sheltering inside broke its lashings and careened across the deck and onto its side. For a few painful seconds, her crew waited to see if the ship would right herself or fully capsize in the typhoon. In the distance, the next massive wave closed in on the stricken ship as though it were moving in on a fatally wounded prey.

Slowly and painfully, the ship righted herself just before the next powerful wave crashed into her port side. Smith and Golembeski got their feet back on the ship and scrambled back into the bridge just before the next impact. Her oscillations deepened as she wildly reacted to the next massive wave.

Captain LaRue was normally content to let his crew work out the challenges at hand while he worked in his captain's quarters. This crew's skills and unity had quickly proven to be unparalleled. But the present situation clearly demanded his presence on the bridge. He struggled from his quarters to the nearby ladder to the bridge. In a frenzied battle against both gravity and the gyrations of the ship, LaRue fought his way up the ladder and finally emerged on the bridge.

Catching his breath and bracing for impact from the next monster wave, he took command. "All right, steady as she goes! Let's get her turned directly into the waves—but not just yet. Wait for my command!"

Peering through the rain-soaked portals, LaRue read the anger of the sea and timed the interval of the waves. Patiently, he let his ship ride the storm. Brilliant lightning illuminated the next series of waves and the ones after that. After another crest, LaRue spotted what he believed would be his opportunity to save his ship. His pulse raced as he prayed silently. His officers and crew saw only an intense, unyielding focus through the portals and out at the raging sea.

"Another minute. Steady as she goes," LaRue insisted as the crew anxiously waited. The helmsman held firmly to the ship's wheel and readied himself for action.

The *Meredith Victory* slipped down the crest of the latest wave and into the resulting valley. LaRue thought there was scarcely a lonelier place to be caught than in the trough between two massive waves: on each side, there was nothing but walls of water towering over the *Meredith Victory* and her crew. He had a quick fleeting thought that it was a bit like the Israelites crossing the Red Sea, minus the dry ground and the certainty of success.

As LaRue waited on the cycle of the waves, a young seaman burst onto the bridge. "Captain!" he shouted. "We've got munitions loose in the holds! They're bouncing around down there like crazy!"

The blood drained out of LaRue's face. *Live shells rolling around below. What else will go wrong tonight?* Most of the ammo was impact sensitive. If it hit something in just the right way and the igniter was struck, one exploding shell would trigger others and result in an out-of-control explosion that would finish what the typhoon had started.

"Dino—get some men together, work your way down there. Let's get those shells secured. Put three men in each hold and work them top to bottom. Find it all, and secure it—quickly, please," LaRue said.

"Yes, sir, Captain. We'll take care of it right away," Chief Mate Dino Savastio replied. His mind flickered through the danger of chasing live shells as they ricocheted around in the cargo holds of a ship in the middle of a raging storm, but he promptly raced off to fulfill his assigned duties.

The next crest rolled in, and LaRue saw his chance.

"Hard left wheel!" LaRue barked over a viciously howling wind and crashing thunder. The helmsman struggled with the ship's wheel as LaRue called for full left rudder. For a long moment there was no response. Finally, the *Meredith Victory* responded, but ever so slowly. Her steel structure moaned under the enormous loads being exerted upon her. With her forward speed limited and the waves hitting her fully exposed port side, the rudder lacked full authority—but after several agonizingly long minutes, she grudgingly began to respond and push back against the fury of the storm.

"Stay with her, son . . . stay with her. She'll respond, just give her time. Patience . . . we've got a ways to go." He stood close to the bridge portals. His hands gripped the thick mahogany rail at the fore of the bridge. The helmsman stood directly behind him, wrestling with the ship's wheel, his young, sweaty hands waiting for the captain's next instructions. LaRue watched and waited. Seconds passed as eternity. A few words of his favorite psalm flickered through his mind: *Yea, though I walk through the valley of the shadow of death . . .*

The *Meredith Victory* approached the top of another crest and slowly began to make the hard left turn so that she could face the full brunt of the waves. Head-on, she could take almost anything the sea could throw at her—but first they had to get her turned. At the top of the crest she languished, almost as though she feared what lay ahead. But as she rounded the crest and slipped down into the trough, her rate of turn increased, and she turned more sharply in preparation for the next wave's crest. The ship's wheel bucked hard against the seaman, but he leaned into it and held her steady in the turn. Agonizingly, she continued her hard left turn until she had finally turned through one hundred and eighty degrees. Now, with an intercept angle of thirty degrees on the massive waves, the *Meredith Victory* plowed nearly straight ahead into the oncoming fury of the storm. The resulting impact sent a massive explosion of water crashing onto her deck and battering the bridge with its spray.

As LaRue and the men on the bridge recovered from the first impact, they looked out through the bridge portals and viewed the crest of the next wave at eye level. She rode down the crest and then closed the gap with the next giant wave. The men braced themselves for another collision.

In an instant, the bow of the *Meredith Victory* pierced the enormous wave, and twenty-five feet of water crashed over the deck and into the ship's house with a deafening roar. It seemed to LaRue as though it took forever for the ship's deck to reappear from the near-total immersion. But finally it did, and the *Meredith Victory* slowly started her climb up the next wave.

No one spoke on the bridge for the next ten minutes or so as they rode hard into each successive wave. Finally, as the crew became more confident that she was holding her own at reduced speed, they permitted themselves to speak.

"Captain, I really thought we had lost her," Smith said. "I really didn't think she was coming back. We went so far over, and it took so long for her to right herself."

LaRue shook his head gently. "Indeed, gentlemen. We're fortunate we were positioned where we were in the convoy. That hard left turn came in handy." A wry grin came over his face for the first time during the storm. "I guess we all have a little more to be thankful for tonight."

With the immediate urgency behind them, LaRue busied himself on the bridge for another half-hour or so as he returned to reading the sea and monitoring the situation. A report came up the speaking tube from the Chief Mate that the hastily assembled work crew had found all the loose munitions and stowed them securely. LaRue counted his blessings again. Before retiring back to his quarters, he consulted briefly with the navigator, checked his watch, did some quick mental calculations based on their current position and heading, and reflected quietly on what they had just experienced.

"Steady on this course, gentlemen. Give it several more hours on this heading, and then when the sea calms, we'll turn back north and rejoin the convoy—or at least what's left of them."

"Yes, sir, Captain. And thanks again, sir," Third Officer Smith said.

LaRue gave a quick nod of his head, flashed his junior third mate a quick smile, and stepped off the bridge.

* * *

After the fierce battle with Kezia, the *Meredith Victory* rejoined the convoy and arrived at Inchon for the landing just a few hours late on the morning of September 15, 1950. The other twenty-one ships in the convoy had also emerged from the typhoon relatively unscathed.

In Inchon, amphibious craft used the assistance of the high tide in the harbor to assist their landing. Soldiers stormed ashore and met with stunning success. During the invasion, the *Meredith Victory* remained well offshore in the harbor. Under protective fire from the Navy's Seventh Fleet, she unloaded her cargo into large LST crafts and contributed her supplies and materiel to the retaking of the Korean Peninsula. After a full day of offloading cargo, just as she prepared to sail back to Yokohama, LaRue was summoned to the bridge.

LaRue stepped onto the bridge from his quarters one deck below. "What have you got?"

Chief Mate Dino Savastio had his faced pressed to a pair of binoculars. "Captain, we've been watching a small boat in the harbor for the last twenty minutes or so. Now she's approaching. Looks like some sort of sailboat or even a fishing boat. And get this, Captain—I'm pretty sure its crew is waving a white flag. It's obviously some North Korean sailors, if you can call them that, and I think they're trying to surrender to us."

"White flag? Somebody is surrendering to us?" LaRue asked. He shook his head in surprise. "They must think we're a Navy ship. Whatever you do, don't tell them our total firepower is a couple of .38-caliber pistols!" He laughed. "Can you count how many they've got aboard?"

Savastio took up position on the starboard-side bridge wing, and with the binoculars still pressed to his face, hollered his reply. "I'm counting about thirteen, Captain. They look pretty ragtag from what I can see. Not even in uniform. They look like regular

Korean civilians, all men, of course."

LaRue joined him on the bridge wing for his own look. The vessel was hardly more than a wooden fishing boat pressed into desperate service. It made a laughable contrast to the powerful ships of the US Navy. The men wore tattered clothes, were half-shaven, and actually looked desperate to be captured by the Americans. "All right, gather up fifteen or twenty of the men and get these Koreans aboard. I think one of our Japanese stevedores speaks some Korean. Get him to go with you. I'll have the radio room talk to the Navy to find out what they want us to do with these guys. I'd like to get rid of them here, but let's see what they want."

"Will do, Captain."

Chief Mate Savastio moved quickly down a couple of ladders to the deck and gathered sufficient men from the ship's quarters as he went. LaRue's crew waited patiently at the rail as the disheveled old boat did her best to pull up alongside the *Meredith Victory*. The men looked just like Savastio had reported: ragged clothes, dirty, not in uniform. Two of the men feverishly continued to wave a couple of white scraps of fabric as if to make extra sure the Americans knew of the certainty of their giving up, while the others put their hands high above their heads in the universal symbol of surrender.

Savastio saw it first: two rifles. "Sasai-san," he hollered to the Japanese stevedore.

"Yes, Savastio-san?"

"Tell 'em 'no guns.' We're going to throw a line over. They are to tie it to the weapons and we'll haul them up. Every gun. I see two, there may be more. Understand?"

"Yes, Savastio-san. I understand. I will tell them now."

Sasai leaned over the railing and shouted almost directly down at the men in broken but functional Korean. There was a reply from the men below. A nervous conversation ensued, back and forth with much pointing and gesturing. Finally, Sasai returned to Savastio.

"Chief, they understand. You can throw the line now."

"Great, thanks much. Drop the line, fellas."

The white line snaked its way down the side of the *Meredith Victory* and landed on the deck of the small boat. Savastio watched closely as they tied it around the strap of the rifle. He wanted to make sure their soon-to-be prisoners didn't get tempted to do something foolish. Finally, they waved up at the Americans, and the first weapon made its ascent. Three more weapons were recovered, and then another conversation with Sasai assured Savastio that all weapons had been turned over.

The crew threw a couple of rope ladders over the side and onto the deck of the old boat. Without delay and full of smiles, the Koreans scrambled up the rope, over the rail, and onto the deck of the *Meredith Victory*. In five minutes, it was over. Savastio and the crew shuffled the new prisoners off to the forecastle in the bow of the ship, closed the hatches, and locked them in.

Savastio dismissed the crew back to their regular duties and hustled back up the ship's ladders to the bridge. LaRue was still attending to a few remaining matters on the bridge. "We got 'em all taken care of, Captain. Thirteen of them. Four weapons. Poor guys were probably forced into the North Korean military and are desperate to get out. I reckon we'll treat them better as prisoners than they've been treated as soldiers. I put them in the fo'c's'le for now. Ought to serve just fine as a temporary brig. Any word back on what we do with them?"

"Yeah. Not the word I wanted, but we heard back."

"And . . .?"

"Interestingly, the Navy brass wants us to take them back to Japan with us. It's not a huge deal, I just don't want anything to interfere with the efficiency of this crew and the cohesiveness we've built. We've got a mission to accomplish."

Dino raised his eyebrows. "Really? So now we're a POW ship? Well, we need to move the stevedores elsewhere if you want to keep the prisoners up forward. I can put 'em in the number-two cargo hold. I'll make sure the prisoners get regular provisions and water. Otherwise, shouldn't be a problem, sir."

"Yeah, that will all be fine." LaRue quirked a smile. "It even gets a bit more interesting, Savastio. Apparently, we just captured the first POWs of the entire Inchon landing. Us, a little old merchant ship. If we keep this up, they'll try to put guns back on her," he laughed.

With their prisoners properly secured and all the cargo holds empty, the *Meredith Victory* steamed out of the Inchon harbor and set sail for Japan. Her crew sailed in the satisfaction of playing a key role in what was considered the boldest and most successful naval landing since D-Day. The stunningly bold move to land US troops far behind enemy lines was a classic MacArthur tactic, and it changed the course of the Korean War.

* * *

After arriving in Japan, LaRue and his crew very happily turned over their prisoners and their rifles to the US Navy, then settled into the routine common to the Merchant Marine. They replaced their stevedores with new men fresh for experience and good pay. Then they resumed their mission. They shuttled cargo and equipment back and forth between Japan and Korea, hauling countless rounds of ammunition, mines, and other explosives; tanks, trucks, and transport vehicles; or handfuls of Army troops or other military personnel along with their loads of cargo. These simpler and quieter voyages gave ample opportunity for the men to continue to refine their tight-knit working relationship and their knowledge of their ship. Each day brought greater efficiency and skill as the crew worked together to accomplish their vital missions. As the months rolled by during the back-and-forth shuttle trips, the hot sun fell lower in the sky, and the temperatures grew increasingly pleasant with each passing week—until the air began to take on the first bite of winter.

Morning and evening often found Captain LaRue standing on the bridge wing of his ship with a camera dangling around his neck or checking weather reports. LaRue loved taking pictures of sunsets and sunrises. He often thought the sky was never so big and bold, and the sunsets and sunrises never so vivid, as on the open sea. Upon each return to Japan, LaRue would venture into Yokohama to develop his rolls of film and buy a few more.

Nighttime brought a special meaning for Captain LaRue as well. It was an opportunity for contemplation and reflection. In his quarters, he often sat at his small desk opposite his bed and read his Bible. On his desk were pictures of his sisters back home in Philadelphia and a small wooden crucifix his oldest sister had given him a few years back. But when possible, LaRue loved spending quiet hours outside in the fresh air. The ship's momentum produced a steady breeze, and the sweet smell of the ocean salt was a welcome relief to the sometimes musty, metallic smell inside the *Meredith Victory*.

Late one evening in October, Staff Officer Lunney found LaRue on the port side bridge wing.

"Captain, mind if I join you?"

"Not at all. Beautiful night, huh?"

"Incredible. Totally peaceful. Totally quiet. Not a cloud in the sky this evening." Lunney searched the night skies. "Folks back home just wouldn't understand how many stars you can see out here."

LaRue nodded in agreement. "I never remember looking at the stars as a kid back in Philly. I think there was too much smoke from the factories and too many lights. Out here, it's just unbelievable." Both men craned their necks back, lost in an ocean of stars cut into two hemispheres by the stunning splash composing the Milky Way—a great band of stars laid down like a great paintbrush stroke from one edge of the horizon to the other.

"You know, Lunney, these kids—we teach them to use the sextant for navigation. I wonder if they ever take time to think beyond the navigational utility of the stars, to see something deeper?"

"Probably not, sir. Maybe we should assign them a little deck time for looking at the stars. Might create a little useful introspection."

"Certainly wouldn't hurt, would it?" Both men fell silent for a few minutes.

LaRue spoke first. "I think I love these nights the best: new moon, sky's perfectly dark, you can't even begin to count all the stars. You never run out of things to look at out here. You see that one in the southwestern sky, about halfway up?"

"The bright one, sitting just thirty degrees or so up from the horizon? What star is that?"

"Not a star—I think that's Jupiter. If we had a little scope we could tell for sure. You know, it really boggles the mind." LaRue paused, deep in thought, and then said in a quiet half-whisper, "What is man, that thou art mindful of him?"

"What, sir?"

"Sorry, it's from the Old Testament. I think it's Psalm 8. I'm guessing the psalmist must have spent many evenings like this. He couldn't help but look at the heavens above, see the handiwork of the Creator, and wonder at how insignificant man is. I like to think that since the beginning of time, all of humanity has looked up at the heavens and had the same thoughts. Maybe it sort of binds us all together."

Lunney chuckled at his captain's propensity to philosophize, but his tone remained serious. "I think you're right. It certainly reminds us that we're really small out here. That typhoon we faced en route to Inchon sure demonstrated that. Really shook some of the younger men."

"It is interesting, isn't it Lunney? Here we are, in the big scheme of things—this little ship, out on this incredible sea, under an even more incredible heavens, and we're going about our little jobs the best we can. Sometimes we do it well, sometimes we make mistakes. But we're trying, the very best we know how."

Lunney nodded. Both men listened for a few minutes at the sound of the passing water split by the bow and funneled off to the port and starboard sides of the ship, the gentle rumble of the ship's turbine, the throaty whisper of exhaust from the ship's stack.

"Did I ever tell you how much I hate this war?"

"A few times, Captain." Lunney smiled.

"Don't get me wrong, I know that war is sometimes unavoidable. This is undoubtedly one of those necessary wars. Nonetheless, I really despise its origins. It's nothing but a war formulated by Communists, undertaken by Communists, waged by Communists, in support of their endless determination to enslave all mankind."

Lunney reflected on LaRue's clarity. He admired that about the captain. His mind was clear and unencumbered by the distractions which for lesser men sometimes blurred right and wrong. LaRue always seemed to know what was right, and he never wavered from it.

"You think we'll win?"

"I certainly pray that we do, Lunney. Things were looking really rough until Inchon. We sent a lot of young, fresh kids straight out of boot camp right into the jaws of an experienced enemy. Lot of 'em got slaughtered. Until Inchon, I thought we might actually lose the whole peninsula. Now, it finally looks like things are moving in the right direction. Seems like we're driving the North Koreans pretty far north. We've got to push them all the way to China if we are to decisively end the scourge of Communism in Korea."

Lunney nodded in silence. The gentle rush of water around the bow of the ship and along its sides filled in the silent spaces.

After a long few minutes, LaRue spoke again. "Lunney, do you think we're making a difference?"

"Absolutely, Captain. We're vital to the war effort. I hate this war as much as you do, but the Communists must be completely pushed back or they'll regroup and enslave the entire Korean Peninsula, and from there—who knows where they'll stop?"

"Well, I know we matter in that regard, of course. We haul these tanks and guns, mines and munitions—certainly every load pushes the war effort a little bit further ahead. But do you think we *really* matter?"

"I'm not sure I follow, Captain. In what sense do you mean?"

"I guess what I mean is: out there in the real world. Out there, in that space between wars where people live their everyday lives, where people have children and raise them and try to live out their lives the best way they know how. Out in that real world— apart from all the fighting and killing and suffering. Out there where normal people try to find some happiness and peace—do you think we make a difference for *them?*"

Lunney thought for a moment.

"I remember a Bible reference about casting your bread on the waters. I believe the Bible says that after many days it will return to you. So I guess my answer is yes. I believe that as long as we are doing the very best we can to help people, then we really are making a difference. I don't know how all the parts and pieces of the things we do might help some particular person down the road. I certainly don't know how it might all fit together in the big picture. I suspect history will never remember what we do here

38

on this little ship. But I do know that every ton of cargo we haul helps slow the spread of Communism. And I know that ultimately, that's one more person living under freedom for one more day. Eventually if we slow it enough, we can stop it. I know every time we stop the spread of Communism, that's one more nation that can choose the opportunities of liberty. I don't know how it all works out in the end, Captain—but I know we're doing good. I know we make a difference, and I'm proud of what we do."

Neither man spoke for a moment as LaRue considered Lunney's thoughts. Finally, he put his hand on Lunney's shoulder. "I do hope history will prove you right. Well, good night. Get some rest."

"And you too, Captain. I think I'll enjoy a few more minutes in the fresh air."

"Very well. We'll see what tomorrow holds for us. You never know," LaRue said as he walked away from the bridge wing, slipped back onto the bridge and headed for his quarters.

Beneath him, in the cargo holds, the *Meredith Victory* carried thousands of rifles and tens of thousands of rounds of ammunition and grenades. One such rifle, an M1 Garand, many hundreds of rounds of .30-06 ammunition, and dozens of grenades would soon complete their voyage across the ocean to Pusan, South Korea, and find their way into the hands of a young Marine named Jack Stiles.

CHAPTER THREE

Chosin Son

United States Marine Private Jack Stiles was drowning in a sea of hatred and brutality, whipped to a frenzy by the winds of war. The road he had traveled thus far in his short life of twenty-two years stretched from familiar surroundings in Midland, Texas, to a bitter place in Korea: the Chosin Reservoir. In this kind of war, there wasn't much opportunity for keeping track of dates. By his best recollection, it was late November, 1950.

He always heard it called "Chosin," by his commanders, who adopted the name from the Japanese map they had at the time. The Koreans called it by its real name, Changjin. To Jack and the other twenty thousand Marines fighting for their lives, it was simply Chosin. Most of all, it was simply a cold, miserable place to die.

As he tried to push back the unrelenting temptation of sleep, Jack remembered how it all began for him at the end of November 1950. "Sorriest piece of real estate we've ever fought for, well, at least since Iwo Jima," the weathered Marine gunnery sergeant had said. He had pointed to a worn-out Japanese map on the wall and traced a pointer along a thin blue line as he lectured the troops.

Jack remembered the old man's speech clearly. "This is the Yalu River," he'd said, gesturing on the map. "It separates North Korea from China. Seems the Chinese can't quite stand the thought of us knocking down their little Communist friends in Korea. Ever since Inchon, the Koreans have been on the back foot. Now the Chinese have joined the fight. They've jumped the 1st Division up at Chosin, and it's our job to send the Chinese home. Men, there's a lot of 'em. I'm not going to lie to you. That's the problem with the Chinese. There's just too many. But they're not well trained, and they're not well equipped. Mostly, gentlemen, it'll be a bloodbath for them. We've got superior infantry skills and equipment. We've got the Air Force in command of the skies. And so MacArthur says we go to Chosin Reservoir, and that's where we're going—and that's where we stop the Communist Chinese! No worries boys, we'll be home for Christmas."

Bravado and gusto didn't take long to become blood and death in the Battle of Chosin Reservoir—a bitter killing field between the UN forces, led by the United States, and the Chinese and North Korean militaries. A far cry from his once-noble expectations, Jack lay flat on his belly in the scant shelter of a crater blasted out of the frozen dirt by the advancing Chinese army and one of their countless high-explosive mortar shells. The relentless cold penetrated his marginally effective winter coat and racked his body with a perpetual bone-shattering cold that never went away.

Jack and the rest of the 5th and 7th Marine Regiments were dug in against a furious effort by the Chinese to overrun their positions at Yudam-ni. Nearly one hundred thousand Chinese troops had poured into the Chosin Reservoir area. They vastly outnumbered and surrounded the twenty thousand United States Marines. Jack thought occasionally about those blustery speeches and how quickly they had all deteriorated into desperate hope for survival and escape.

Winter's nighttime had again settled early on the battlefields around Chosin. In the night, the mortars temporarily ceased but faithfully returned at dawn's first light. Until then, Jack and the rest of the Marines clung desperately to their frozen patch of ground, fighting their way south, desperately outnumbered and bitterly cold.

In this crater, Jack crouched for his life, struggling to conceal his rugged, son-of-a-rancher six-foot-three and two-twenty-pound frame. His long days of working cattle had equipped him with a physical strength that was well suited to war. Jack had laughed at the "rigors" of boot camp. Up at four and in bed by nine seemed like his normal routine back home in Midland.

Lying next to him in the unmerciful cold was his childhood buddy from back home, Edgar Morrison. Buoyed by patriotic fervor and a practical desire to avoid the draft, they had enlisted together in the Marine Corps on the same day. Much to Jack's delight and Edgar's chagrin, they had been assigned to the same combat unit. Edgar had other plans, but he soon learned that men's plans often get revised by the winds of war. While Jack had developed the tall, stout frame of a West Texas rancher's son, Edgar was a wiry, intellectual sort. Jack looked like he could easily kill a man with his bare hands. Edgar looked like he might preach the funeral. Although they were glad to be together, they both sometimes wondered what sort of perverse fortune had brought them together, and kept them together, in this forsaken place.

In the daylight, they fought desperately to reinforce their tenuous positions against the Chinese. In the long, bitter cold and sleepless nights, they tried to hold what little headway they made during the day against the constant threat of being overrun by the Chinese. Jack and Edgar often maintained equal parts alertness and sanity with hushed conversations about politics, life back home, or just the war itself. At times, between encounters with Chinese troops, they waxed poetic—at least, poetic by West Texas standards.

Edgar lay on his back against the frozen ground, exhaling little clouds of frozen vapor into the night air. He wiped a bloodied glove across his forehead, smearing a coating of frozen dirt that had been in place for at least a week. He watched as Jack scribbled notes in a small leather bound diary.

"You think much about dying?" Edgar asked.

Jack turned and looked at him. The left side of Jack's exposed face pressed hard into the dirt. His face was too numb to feel anything. The bite of the cold made his eyes water, and the tears flowed an inch or so down his cheeks through the caked-on dirt until the little rivulets froze in place. Jack wiped the frozen tears away with the back of a dirty, bloodstained glove and tucked his diary into an empty pocket.

"Nope. Try not to. No point wasting my time."

"Why not? You're not scared out here?"

"I'm scared to death, man," Jack answered, loading more rounds into the empty clip of his M1 Garand. "I just try not to dwell on the idea of dying out here. I figure I don't have much choice in the matter, do I? Certainly not going to lay around thinking too much about it."

Edgar didn't figure he could disagree much. Jack pressed the loaded clip into the M1.

"You reload yet?" Jack asked.

"No, still got a few in this one."

"I'd reload now, buddy. They're just waiting for you to run out."

"Yeah, you're probably right," Edgar answered, fishing in his pocket for a few more rounds.

"I reckon it's better to focus on them dying anyway. Way I see it, the more of them I kill, the better my chances, huh? That's one less of 'em that might get me."

Their conversation paused a moment as a nearby machine gun rattled off a hundred rounds toward the Chinese lines. They kept quiet, waiting for the enemy's reply.

Edgar nodded toward the sound of the suppressing fire. "All the killing we do—it doesn't bother you?"

"Edgar, your problem," Jack said with a toothy grin, "your problem, boy, is that your daddy was a banker. You grew up playing with numbers and money and figures. You should have grown up on a ranch. I grew up killing pigs and cattle while you grew up playing Monopoly, for crying out loud."

"Well, fine," Edgar quickly objected as he inserted his full clip with eight rounds back into his M1. As he inserted the clip, he shoved the bolt forward crisply and fed a fresh round into the chamber. "I don't think killing cows back home is hardly the same."

"How so?" Jack asked. His tone thickened with disgust. "These Chinese and North Koreans, they're animals and little else. I'll put a bullet in their brains and kill them before breakfast, and it's no different from the pigs back home."

Edgar recoiled a bit and frowned in revulsion. Jack shook his head.

"Look, Edgar, you've got to wake up to the reality of the situation. These Chinese or North Koreans, they'd be quite happy to cut your throat and watch you bleed to death while you cry for your momma—that's why I say they're just animals. You saw what they did to Roberts and Adams last week. And if that wasn't enough, they pulled the pin on a couple of grenades and put them under their bodies. Nearly killed the medics that were trying to retrieve the bodies. Pigs, that's all they are."

Edgar wasn't quite sure it was so simple, but Jack seemed very certain.

"Edgar, I'll never figure out how you made a Marine, boy," he drawled.

"I was supposed to do the paperwork. Wasn't supposed be in this worthless place freezing to death *and* getting shot at," Edgar said.

"Well, you're here in this sorry place now. You ready to die for these worthless people?"

Edgar's face stiffened at Jack's question. "Jack, I guess I don't see it quite like you do. You always see everything in perfect black and white. I'm not sure the world is that simple."

"What's there to see? These people are trying to kill each other as quick as possible. The Koreans up north want to kill these Koreans in the south. How idiotic can you get? It's the same country."

"Yeah, I don't guess we would ever do such a stupid thing, would we?" Edgar sarcastically replied.

"Well, fine, yeah, but doesn't that tell you how backwards these people are? It's 1950, and these people are making the same mistake we made a hundred years ago. The big problem I've got is these fools at the UN deciding to send us to stand between these people as they shoot at each other. Instead of just letting them kill each other, we've got to let them kill us. Real smart, huh? That's a bunch of politicians for you."

"Well, look," Edgar started to explain, but he was interrupted by the unmistakable whine of a round passing just over their heads.

Jack flinched instinctively, clutched his helmet to his head, and muttered his disdain for their precarious situation. "Stay down, Edgar! Gonna be a busy night, I can see that now. Don't even try to tell me you feel anything for these barbaric animals. These people don't even have *half* a civilization. They've not contributed one thing to the happiness of mankind. I mean, seriously, can you name one contribution the Koreans have made to the history of mankind? My view is simple, Edgar: they want to kill each other —let's get out of their way and encourage them to get on with the job."

Edgar slid further into the crater as he tried to give himself more cover. "I think it's not that simple," he said stubbornly. Jack rolled his eyes as Edgar spoke—as though he was listening to an unwelcome sermon for the fourth time.

"Look, if we can stop an all-out war—isn't that a moral thing to do?" Edgar asked. "Isn't that the *right* thing to do? We're doing good over here. Without us, there would be hundreds of thousands of dead civilians. The Communists up north would enslave all these people in the south. The war could spread to other nations. It would be like the second war all over again. First Korea, then maybe China. Maybe Japan would be attacked. We can't just let countries fight wars without getting involved and trying to do something."

Edgar continued, his voice heating to the topic. "Yes, some Americans will die. But isn't that a worthy price to pay so that hundreds of thousands don't get slaughtered? Isn't that a necessary price to stop Communism? Didn't your father serve in Europe? Are you saying it was wrong to go over and stop Germany in the first war? What about Richard? Don't you approve—"

"Shut up about Richard!" Jack blurted out, and then caught himself talking much too loudly. "That was different. Shut up for a second. Stay down." Jack inched forward slightly to the edge of the crater and looked across the frozen vegetation. Pockets of snow dotted the landscape between him and the Chinese. Jack watched closely. Sure enough, a little patch of snow started moving.

Jack raised his weapon, carefully aimed at the center of the moving snow patch, and fired two rounds into the movement. He immediately heard the cry of a man dying.

"I thought so—trying to play the white-sheet-on-the-snow game again. You think they'd know we've figured it out. Put me down for another one tonight," Jack instructed Edgar as he quickly replaced the two rounds in his clip and reloaded his weapon. "Now, what were we saying? Oh, those other places—

we're talking about innocent Western nations like France, Belgium, England—countries like that, that were attacked by the Germans. Now sure, you can let the Germans rot for all I care— they deserved whatever they got. Same thing goes for the Japs. But what my dad and all the others . . . and what Richard did, that was *right*. That made sense. We were saving a *civilized* people from a *barbaric* people. What's going on here is different." Jack paused, seeing movement in the dark ahead. "Your turn, boy. Get us another one of those Chinese laundrymen."

"Why is it different, because they're Korean? Because they look different?" Edgar asked as he inched his way forward, taking his turn at the edge of the crater. Jack held his answer while Edgar concentrated. They knew that when a Chinese soldier went down, others would come out to take his place.

They waited patiently, as if playing a deadly game of chess. Long minutes passed.

"Nothing yet, Jack," Edgar whispered "They're waiting for us to run out. You still got that empty clip?"

"Everywhere I go. Just say when."

"I'll fire two rounds, then throw it."

"At your service," Jack said as he turned the empty clip around in his hands.

Edgar's rapid shots pierced the frozen air, followed by the soft, metallic *ping* as Jack threw the empty clip to the ground. To the ears of the young Chinese soldier waiting to replace his dead comrade, it was just the sound he was waiting to hear—the sound of an American running out of ammunition and his metallic clip automatically ejecting and falling to the ground. It would be at least a few seconds before the American could reload. It was time to run.

Edgar saw motion against the barren landscape, and then his eyes resolved the outline of a man holding himself low as he ran toward his fallen comrade. Edgar held his breath, steadied himself, and through his thick gloves fingered the trigger and gently squeezed. The fierce report of the M1 shattered the icy air and then faded into the distance. Jack listened carefully and heard the final cry of the bullet's intended target. Edgar retreated for cover. He breathed hard, sending icy plumes of frozen vapor from his mouth and nose. His hands trembled uncontrollably.

"Nice shootin', boy. Empty clip trick gets them every time. At least you didn't just wound him like you did the other guy," Jack laughed. Edgar looked disgusted with his success. "Relax a little, would you? You'll get used to it, I promise."

"I don't think I'll ever get used to it, Jack," he said quietly.

"Anyway, to answer your question, I'm not saying it's because they're *different*. Aren't you listening to me? I don't have any opposition to them being different. I'm just saying they haven't done anything for the good of society since the dawn of creation. Why do we have to die for them? If they want to kill each other —let 'em. Just a bunch of animals anyway."

Edgar slowed his breathing. The conversation helped. He hated the killing. "Not exactly, Jack. They've got a sophisticated culture." Edgar said under his breath, "These people invented a printing press something like seventy-five years before Gutenberg. It was the first of its kind in the world. But Jack, everything else aside—come on, they're human beings. They ought to have the same liberties we enjoy. They were enslaved by Japan back in 1910 and were treated incredibly bad. They've been free from all of that for only the last five years. Now Communism wants to enslave them. Nobody deserves that."

Jack crawled back toward a shooting position again, scanning for more targets, desperately trying to detect a faint hint of motion across the frozen field. "Look, Edgar, I'm sorry about their troubles. Everyone's got troubles. I still can't see why you and I have to come here and die for their troubles. How do you think your mother or my mother is going to feel when she gets the word that we died over here in a fight between some barbaric Koreans and Chinese? How's she going to feel knowing her boy didn't even die for a noble cause? Die at Gettysburg, or die at Normandy—but not in this pit for these people. The world will remember what they did on those beaches, and they'll remember what happened at Iwo Jima, but they'll never remember what we did in this forsaken place: Changjin, Chosin, or whatever nonsense they want to call it. I came here to defeat Communism. I didn't sign up to be a target in the middle of these people's civil war."

Edgar stared into the darkness—not bothering to even look back at Jack. They needed each other and had kept one another safe for the past four months. All had been said that could be said between them, or even that should be said.

"Just shut up, Jack. Let's just do our job and hope we get to go home someday. We'll have more time to argue it then."

Jack planned to take him up on the offer.

* * *

For the crew of the *Meredith Victory,* the shuttle trips and pleasant days of November had faded into their collective memories. The men of the Merchant Marine had a job to do, and they set about to do it just as well as they knew how. On the afternoon of December 5, while docked in Yokohama, Japan, the *Meredith Victory* received urgent orders to be loaded with ten thousand tons of jet fuel and make an urgent run to the North Korean port city of Hungnam. Chief Mate Dino Savastio oversaw the loading activities. Each drum carried 55 gallons of jet fuel weighing about 374 pounds per drum. Four drums were positioned on each pallet. In total, nearly fifty-four thousand drums of jet fuel were loaded onto the *Meredith Victory* on more than thirteen thousand cargo pallets. Japanese stevedores carefully handled the cargo among the different cargo holds as Savastio and his crew worked weight and balance calculations to keep the heavy load within the ship's design requirements.

The jet fuel would serve an invaluable purpose. UN forces led by General Almond were still engaged in a vicious battle up at Chosin Reservoir, and they needed constant air support to hold off the numerically superior Chinese forces. The US Air Force flew countless missions to maintain that air superiority, and jet fuel was in high demand. When she arrived, the *Meredith Victory's* vital load of jet fuel would be taken from the Hungnam port to the adjacent Yonpo Airfield, where it would supply the Air Force's new F-80 jet aircraft.

As the *Meredith Victory* cleared the Yokohama harbor in Japan, LaRue and Savastio stepped out of the bridge and into the adjacent chart room to review the charts. As second-in-command, Savastio worked closely with LaRue on most major activities.

"East coast, huh, Captain?" Savastio asked.

"Yeah. Nothing too difficult—except the Navy is reporting that the harbor in Hungnam is very heavily mined. Before we pushed them back up north, the Koreans put just about every type of mine you can imagine into that place. Let's hope they've got a good path cleared through the minefield. Hey, Lunney, got a second?"

"Yes, sir, what can I do for you?" Lunney asked as he looked up from some paperwork he was reviewing. He stepped out from the bridge into the small map room.

"Here's what you can do for me, Lunney. It would help me sleep a lot better at night. Help me get that jet fuel off my ship in Hungnam, okay? When we get there, negotiate with the harbormaster to get it unloaded as fast as possible. I hate tiptoeing around through minefields while we're loaded to the brim with that stuff. It's just looking for a reason to explode—in fact, it doesn't even need a good reason."

"I'm with you, Captain—I'll do everything I can. I know they need it desperately over at Yonpo. I'll do my best to get you a jet-fuel-free ship just as soon as possible."

"As soon as you can get the clearances, we'll get it unloaded," Savastio added, nodding to Lunney. "You clear it, and we'll empty the ship."

"I appreciate it, gentlemen. I'm feeling better already. Oh, Dino—find all the charts we've got on Hungnam's harbor. Just drop them by my quarters when you can."

"Right, Captain—I'll get them to you in a jiffy."

LaRue glanced over at Savastio. The short, stocky Italian seemed to have a boundless supply of enthusiasm and energy—and always that infectious smile. "You ever stop smiling, Dino?" LaRue asked with a grin. "What is a 'jiffy' anyway? How do you define that?"

"Me, stop smiling? Never. Well, maybe if we hit one of those mines, Captain—but until then . . . why stop?" With that, Savastio scrambled out of the chart room, into the passageway, down the ladder, and off to his next quest.

LaRue and Lunney just smiled and shook their heads in amusement.

* * *

When the size and strength of the Chinese forces became fully known, General MacArthur ordered a full retreat down the main supply route, known by the troops as the MSR, and back to Hungnam. But before there could be a retreat, there first had to be a breakout from the stranglehold of Chinese troops around Chosin. While the top brass may have called it "retreat," the field generals in the trenches chaffed at that description and preferred to think of it merely as "fighting in a different direction." In reality, every step along the MSR meant more blood and death.

51

As the bitter cold nights dragged on, Jack and Edgar fought against fatigue and sleep and talked softly to keep themselves alert. They huddled wearily in their makeshift foxhole. The frozen ground was not only their shooting position and shelter from the enemy, but their bed as well. The frozen dirt around them was littered with spent shell casings, the debris of war.

"So Jack, what's the first thing you want to do when you get home?"

"I don't know."

"You don't know? I find that a little hard to believe."

"Well, I'd rather not say. You'll probably just laugh at me."

"No way, seriously, what's the first thing?"

"Fine. First thing I do is hug my mom. I really miss her. I really miss all the sights and smells of the ranch. I miss those cool summer nights, even the smell of cow manure drifting in through the windows." Jack chuckled. "I know it seems strange, but I really miss that place. Besides that, I worry about Mom. We lost Richard. We lost Dad. She's trying to hold the place down with some hired help. I shouldn't have volunteered. They would have drafted me, I'm sure, but maybe I could've gotten a deferment. Anyway, Mom encouraged me to go. She insisted that she would be okay."

"I hear you, man. There's no shame in that. I miss my mom too. Nobody made dessert like my mother."

"Hey, nobody except my mother!"

"Sure, fine, I'll grant you that," Edgar chuckled.

"Then you know what I'm going to do?" Jack said. "I'm going to tell Jessie how I really feel. I got a letter from her last week. I guess I didn't tell you."

"No, you didn't. Good news? You think you'll marry her when you get back?"

"Not hardly. We're finished, me and her. Seems she didn't like the idea of waiting any longer. She decided to marry that Jason

Baumgartner cheat. You know, that guy's daddy has got huge amounts of money. I guess I shouldn't have been surprised that Jason got himself a nice little medical deferment—flat feet or something lame like that. Guess the Baumgartners can't bother getting their fingers dirty with this war."

"Man, I didn't know. I'm really sorry, Jack." Edgar fell quiet a moment, letting the cruelty of Jessie's news hang in the air. He shook his head. "All those times we hung out—the three of us. Those long bus rides home. So much has changed—it seems like it was yesterday, and then at the same time it seems so far away— like almost completely out of reach."

"Yeah—hey, how many grenades you got left?"

"I got three, no, make it four," Edgar replied as he felt the reassuring form of the grenades under his heavy coat.

"Okay, let's try to conserve them. I went through mine a little quick tonight. Anyway, it's just par for the course, my friend. Here we are, fighting a war that's not ours, a war nobody cares about. What do we get from the folks back home? 'Dear Jack,' that's what we get. 'Dear Jack, I'm sorry to tell you . . .'" Jack trailed off. "You know what I *really* want to do when I get home, Edgar?"

"You want to shoot Jason Baumgartner?"

Jack laughed. "No, although the thought has occurred to me occasionally. Well, maybe daily. Anyway, he's not worth the bullet."

Jack turned and looked directly at his friend. Just the smallest amount of Edgar's face was visible in the darkness of the night, shrouded as it was by his heavy combat jacket and hood. It had been nearly white at some point. Now it bore the marks of combat: heavy permanent stains of blood and dirt and death. Jack wondered if battle stained them on the inside as much as it did on the outside.

"I want to *make a difference*," Jack blurted out. "I want to do something that really matters. Look at my dad. He fought for his nation and then suffered the rest of his life until he died. Look at Richard—dead before his life really began. Think about what all he might have done. Lives just get sucked up and blown away. So I guess, if you want to know what I really want to do when I get back, I want to *matter*. I want to do something worthwhile. I want to live, I want to breathe, I want to amount to something in this world. Maybe find a nice girl and settle down too."

Edgar looked on intently. He looked at Jack as he lay on his back, cradling his rifle like little boys cradle a stuffed animal. With every breath Jack sent a white plume of frozen vapor shimmering into the night air. Edgar had rarely heard Jack so unguarded.

"Is that silly, Edgar?" Jack asked, turning to his friend.

"No way, Jack. I think that's the point of all this, isn't it? We do this horrible stuff so that maybe, just maybe, people like us can live and laugh, and breathe, and yes, so that they can love. Maybe even raise a few kids, enjoy a few summer nights, even smell the delights of cow manure on the evening breezes."

On that, the two friends laughed and agreed.

* * *

The journey up to Hungnam was a short trip of just three days. It gave LaRue enough time to review, review again, and review once more the charts that mapped out the Hungnam harbor. As they approached in the late afternoon of December 8, the *Meredith Victory* slowed, and LaRue's phone rang in his quarters.

"We're at the outer harbor, Captain, and we've got word from the Navy."

"I'll be right up, Savastio," LaRue replied.

In a moment LaRue opened his cabin door, and he ducked his six-foot frame through the doorway and into the passageway. A slight right turn brought him to the ladder which led directly to the chart room and the bridge.

LaRue looked intently out the portals of the bridge toward the bow of his ship. "What do we have, gentlemen?" he asked.

"The sweepers are asking about our cargo. I told them we're carrying ten thousand tons of jet fuel. I don't think they were too pleased to hear that."

"I'm not surprised. Emphasize to them that we realize everybody wants to slip through without any bangs, but remind them that if we so much as brush one of those sorry mines, they're going to hear our bang all the way to China."

"Indeed, Captain," Savastio replied with a little smile.

"All stop," LaRue ordered the engine room, and in just a few minutes he felt the winding down of the turbine in the belly of his ship and the echo of the anchor chains being released.

LaRue quickly looked out over the harbor and assessed the situation at hand. From a distance he could see many ships at the docks and an ant-like scurry of men and equipment on land. Just a few miles adjacent to the port, he could make out the general area of Yonpo Airfield with its flurry of airborne activity. "I don't know whether they'll send us a chart or just have us follow a minesweeper through the swept channel. Either way, let me know when we get word. I'll be in my quarters."

"Will do, sir."

* * *

After a few hours of delay, Junior Third Mate Burley Smith rang LaRue in his quarters.

"Captain, we've got word from the harbormaster. They're going to have us follow one of the sweepers through the channel. We expect to be underway in about twenty minutes."

"Okay, I appreciate it, Smith. I'll be right up." LaRue turned from the phone on the wall of his quarters and sat back down at his small desk. Before him on the left side of his desk was a nautical chart of the Hungnam harbor. On the right side of his desk, his old Bible sat open to the book of Matthew, chapter 5. LaRue folded the map carefully, closed his Bible, and returned it to the small storage unit beside his bed before stepping out of his quarters into the passageway.

As LaRue arrived on the bridge, he saw the minesweeper begin to make its approach for the purposes of guiding the *Meredith Victory* into the harbor. LaRue watched as his crew quickly sprang into action, and within minutes, his ship was moving again. LaRue watched the minesweeper as it proceeded ahead of the *Meredith Victory,* making a final pass to ensure that no mines had drifted into the corridor. LaRue closely monitored their speed.

Well, I've played with danger plenty of times, LaRue thought. The Murmansk Run had seen treachery in the open waters of the North Atlantic and the fearsome wolf pack of the German submarines. But at least there he was in wide open waters. Feeling your way through a claustrophobic harbor full of mines was an unpleasant proposition.

Although the *Meredith Victory* was a modest-sized cargo ship, she still needed a significant flow of water past her rudder to be able to maneuver responsively. Too much speed made course corrections impossible in such narrow channels. Too little speed had the same effect. LaRue sensed exactly the right speed at the right time and gave verbal commands as adjustments seemed necessary.

"What distance did they ask us to follow them, Smith?"

"Well, Captain, they said twenty-five hundred feet, but they're moving so fast, I don't think it's really practical for us to keep up."

LaRue looked for a moment and gauged the distance as significantly more than that.

"Obviously, they're a bit worried about us getting too close to them. Don't guess I blame them. Keep her at one quarter, I don't want to get into any tight spots up here and have things go bad on us. Just watch the edges carefully—about all we've got are those floating markers to identify the edge of the swept channel."

LaRue excused himself from the bridge and went outside to the port-side bridge wing. The bitter cold air raced past his hood and bit at his ears. He leaned against the wind and studiously examined the tiny white plastic floating markers spread every hundred yards or so—scarcely enough to catch one's attention. Together, those on the port and starboard sides marked a clear route, a swept channel through the minefield.

With a few quiet moments and through the fading light of the day, LaRue focused his attention on the minesweeper ahead of them. *Brave little ship,* he thought. Like others of its kind, the ship was only about one hundred and thirty feet long. He marveled at its design and mission. The minesweeper was built with a wooden hull to avoid detonation by magnetic mines. It towed a paravane, a type of underwater glider, behind it, skimming below the surface of the water for the purpose of cutting the cables that held the mines in place. Once the cable was cut, the mines would float to the surface where they could be detonated by gunfire from the crew.

The men who manned such ships were brave. He smiled when he recalled their motto, "Where the fleet goes, we've been." But their help was no guarantee of success. The *Meredith Victory* slowly passed the twisted wreck of a ship on her port side. LaRue looked at what was left of the broken and twisted steel hull of a Japanese freighter, her stern jutting from the water like some rusted grave marker for the men she had taken to eternity.

LaRue swallowed hard at the stark sight before him. One miscalculation, and the *Meredith Victory* would join her as mangled and worthless steel.

Deviation from their narrow channel meant certain death.

CHAPTER FOUR
Night

For the past two weeks, Jack and Edgar had been mired in the great battle up at Chosin with others of the 1st Marine Division: fighting, killing, surviving, or at least trying to survive. Temperatures now routinely plunged to minus thirty-five Fahrenheit. Daytime sometimes reached a balmy zero. Most of the men hadn't felt their feet in weeks.

As the breakout effort from Chosin continued, Jack and Edgar spent most nights hunkered in a bombed-out crater, one of many, about twenty yards apart, that marked this bitter-cold, moonlike desolation. Each crater had two men assigned to it. Runners resupplied each crew with ammunition and grenades. More than two hundred men of the 1st Division were spread out to defend their retreat on the southeast side of Chosin.

Most of these men had only been in Korea a month or two but were already battle-hardened and war-wise. They had learned quickly what to expect of the Chinese nighttime offensives, the deathly whistle or bugle marking their midnight charge. They knew that in the darkest moments of the night, the Chinese would move stealthily across the frozen ground. Jack hated their catlike Asian movements. While Americans ran and grunted, the Chinese moved like a cool wind of death on a moonless night. Only their unavoidably frozen breath, if you could catch a glimmer of it in the starlight, would give away their location.

Each evening the sun dropped below the horizon, and the threat of death by war or bitter cold rose as the sun disappeared. Jack and Edgar lay still and listened. Apart from the occasional explosion, they strained against the dark silence to hear more than their own breathing—to hear the faint, fleeting rustle of the persistent Chinese enemy.

During such times of intense threat, their own conversation now mutually forbidden, they communicated by motioning to each other silently. It almost reminded Jack of their silly, far more innocent days in elementary school back in Midland. They had often resorted to such silent motions and gestures during offensively boring history classes.

Jack watched his buddy carefully and noticed under the slight starlight that something had caught Edgar's attention. He lay flat on the bitter cold ground with his M1 cradled in his right arm and his right index finger nervously trembling on the trigger. Jack didn't know if the tremble was a result of nerves or fatigue or frostbite. He guessed it didn't matter. It seemed to him that all of them, young men alike, shook and shuddered like old men.

Edgar looked over his left shoulder to Jack and motioned with his left arm to the northeast. A little tilt of the head served as a silent emphasis for his urgency. Jack shifted quietly across their crater to join Edgar. He paused to clear the air of sound and listen for threatening movements.

Silence.

They waited for painful minutes, daring not to speak, daring almost not to breathe. Edgar thought that sometimes these moments were the most painful of all. He hated the shock he felt after a major firefight—the sort of stunned disbelief when he realized he shouldn't have escaped with his life but somehow had. But he hated these moments most of all—the anticipation. He knew they were out there. He knew they were coming. *Where are they?* He knew they wanted to kill him. But until those moments of death sprang forth, it was time to wait silently in the dark. And after waiting painful minutes, wait more.

Jack breathed hard. While his mind willed the fear away, his body refused to release. Adrenaline pumped heavily through his body, and his heart pounded in his ears. He tried to ignore his breath and Edgar's. He turned his ear slightly, shifting his winter hood so as to briefly expose his ear to the biting and unforgiving cold. He paused and held his breath, waiting.

Whether the wait was a few minutes or a few hours, Jack could not discern. The night was the same. The cold was the same. In normal circumstances, the passage of time is marked by something changing, something happening. This silent, dreadful darkness and cold—combined with the ceaseless waiting—had a disorienting effect that was hard to resist. And so they waited.

Without warning, it was there. It was just a shade above imperceptible, but it was there. Edgar heard it first, and then Jack: the gentle but foreign noise of footsteps in quick succession. Then it was gone.

Silence.

Without moving his head, Jack shifted his eyes toward Edgar, and he knew they had both heard it. Edgar looked like he had just heard the beating of the ebony wings of the angel of death.

The minutes moved agonizingly slowly, as if time itself had been frozen by the bitter cold. Jack's right ear burned in the brutal cold air until he could feel its pain no more as he strained for the slightest sound that did not belong.

There it is again, Jack thought as he heard the deadly footsteps that he knew belonged to the Chinese soldiers. Last night, they had been early. Tonight, well, he wasn't sure if they were early or late, but he knew they were coming. He allowed himself to breathe a bit harder out of necessity. His adrenaline involuntarily surged, and his pulse accelerated to a rate he'd once believed was not sustainable. Jack knew that soon, the hand of death would appear. Soon, men would die. Lives would be crushed. He prayed they would not be theirs. He prayed that the men about to die would be the Chinese he hated so deeply. Hatred was indeed the right word for it. His hatred for the Chinese ran in every course of his body. Maybe his hatred kept him warm tonight.

Silence again. Jack and Edgar strained to hear yet again, their thickly gloved fingers nervously twitching on the triggers of their M1s. The noise of Jack's pounding heart was almost too much compared to the quiet treading of the Chinese soldiers. He held his breath, trying to slow his heart rate and restore his lock on the encroaching enemy. He turned his head a bit more to the side to try to direct his hearing toward the approaching steps. It was then that he saw the glimmer of the feared Chinese burp gun, spitting fire and lead and fear.

The sight of the Chinese infantryman in midair coming from his left and the sound of his blood-boiling scream of rage released within Jack a near-fatal surge of adrenaline. Before he could swing his rifle around, the Chinese soldier landed hard on Jack in an explosion of fire and blood. Four more explosions rang out in his ears, and he felt the hot flash of muzzle exhaust gases on the left side of his face.

By the time Jack could react, it was over. He turned and looked at Edgar, who was still lying on his side. His M1 Garand smoked feverishly from the barrel in the frigid night air, and the gritty smoke of spent gunpowder burned Jack's nose. Edgar feverishly started reloading.

It was another second before Jack realized that he was lying underneath a dying Chinese soldier. Jack shoved him off his torso and rolled the enemy onto his back in the crater, next to the other dead invader.

Jack saw that Edgar's bullet had caught the Chinese soldier underneath his right clavicle and passed into the chest cavity.

Blood poured out of the dying man, and it reminded Jack of the animals he had slaughtered back home. He knew this routine well. In the dark night, the blood looked like a sick, dark ooze leaving the man. Soon, it too would freeze. Until then, Jack felt the warmth of the man's blood as it soaked the front of his jacket.

Jack stared into the eyes of the Chinese soldier as he lay dying. He felt only rage. He wasn't watching a man die, but a beast. The Chinese soldier made eye contact with Jack and opened his mouth to speak. But his tongue only spewed forth more blood as he sputtered and coughed. His head began to tremor uncontrollably, and his hands shook. Jack looked deep into his eyes. The Chinese man was young. For a fleeting second, Jack wondered if he might have a wife, or a mother or father.

For the half-second that Jack wondered, the dying man slowly moved his trembling right hand toward his waist, and it was then that Jack saw the unspent grenade. Without thinking or feeling, Jack looked back into the dying man's eyes and fired a single round from his M1 directly into the man's forehead. The desired results were instantaneous.

It was 12:30 a.m. on December 9, and there were seven hours until daylight. There was plenty of time left for death and dying before the sun brought relief.

* * *

In the Hungnam harbor, in the early morning hours of December 9, the *Meredith Victory* lay safely docked and tied up in her assigned berth. Captain LaRue waited patiently in his quarters for word that their unloading could begin while Staff Officer Lunney argued with the harbormaster on the docks. The harbormaster, short, squatty, heavily overweight, clung to multiple clipboards which he referenced habitually over the rim of small reading glasses pressed into the fat of his cheeks.

"I don't get it," Lunney exclaimed, his tall, slender frame hovering over the short harbormaster. "You rush us up here, we're loaded to the max with jet fuel, we work our way through that mined harbor—and now you're trying to tell me we can't discharge it?"

"Look, it's a simple thing, Lunney. The Chinese are heading this way. MacArthur ordered a full retreat, and that's the end of it. We'll be out of here soon, and obviously we can't leave the jet fuel for those Communists. In fact, we've got to get *everything* out of here. Look at all this stuff," he entreated as he directed Lunney to the window of the small office.

Lunney couldn't deny the challenge. Tens of thousands of tons of war materiel had flooded into Hungnam, like discarded flotsam ahead of the surging tidal wave of Communist forces. Either it would all be taken down south, or it would fall into the enemy's desperate hands.

"Look, Lunney, our orders are clear. We're supposed to send you back down to Pusan. Unload it there, and we'll get you some more directions then."

Lunney knew there was no point discussing the matter any further. "All right. I'll brief the captain. Maybe I'll see you in Pusan some other time, huh?"

"Sure thing, Lunney . . . unless I see you back here again soon," the harbormaster quipped.

"Don't even think about it—once is enough!" Lunney offered as he trotted back to his ship. "They're going to love this one. Back to Pusan."

* * *

At Chosin Reservoir on the evening of December 10, temperatures crashed to minus forty degrees as the flames of war burned more intensely. Men and equipment failed. As the night

63

and its unceasing cold slowly crept on, the silence was periodically interrupted by other foiled or perhaps successful attacks. Sometimes Jack could tell by the cry of the man whether he was American or Chinese. He thought it oddly perverse that even in the cry of death, an accent could often be discerned. Sing a song, and accent disappears. Cry out in death, and a man's last words are true to his native tongue.

Jack and Edgar huddled against each other in the bitter cold, seeking to preserve some of their escaping body heat and share it with the other. Neither man dared sleep. It was virtually impossible anyway, due to the pain of the vicious cold.

And so they lay together and listened and waited. Without exchanging words, Jack and Edgar pondered how far they had come from their homes in Midland to this frigid place of death. Edgar thought often of his father and his mother. He remembered the days at home and the baseball games. He longed for the simple Sunday afternoon lunches after church. It wasn't supposed to have been like this. He had hoped to follow his father into the banking business. Every Texas town needed good banks—two or three at the minimum. Banking, Edgar thought, not war, was his life. But war, not banking, now held his life in the balance.

Over the past two nights, Jack and Edgar's unit had progressed a mere mile. Every yard brought more suffering and more bloodshed. There wasn't much talk at chow time. Their rations were mostly frozen solid anyway. Every man did his best to thaw out the frozen meals over a fire, content to soften them into a sort of lukewarm slop. But besides the work of eating, most of the men felt little motivation to get acquainted. Getting to know another man just meant more suffering when he died.

Only a few hundred yards from the Chinese line, the night was mostly quiet. "The laundrymen must be taking the night off, huh?" Jack asked Edgar.

"Looks that way. Maybe they ran out of rice and went out to get some more," Edgar snickered.

"More likely they ran out of cats and dogs."

"That's revolting, Jack. You know how to make a guy sick."

"I'm just telling the truth. You don't see many little Fidos around here, do you?"

Edgar had to admit Jack had a point.

While the sky was still black, their hushed conversation was shattered by a grenade blast about twenty yards north of their position. Jack and Edgar instinctively covered their heads with their hands and buried their faces in the broken dirt of their crater. Exploded dirt returned to earth and poured down on them along with pieces of the ruptured grenade. With the falling dirt came the acrid sulfur stench of exploded grenade powder.

As the debris fell around them, Jack and Edgar readied themselves for what they knew from experience would come next. The rapid pace of running soldiers was not subtle this time. A bugle blast signaled the Chinese charge. Despite the ringing in their ears, they heard the men pouring across the open, frozen expanse between them and the Chinese. Jack and Edgar simultaneously rose and pointed their guns toward the sound of the blast.

Chinese soldiers emerged from the suspended dust cloud, and the first shots from Jack and Edgar found their marks deep in their enemies' chests. The high-powered rifle rounds from the M1 Garand imparted such intense kinetic energy that the victim collapsed not from blood loss or trauma caused by the penetration of the projectile, but from the systemic pressure shock from the hypervelocity round overloading the nervous system. The victim collapsed and helplessly bled out over the next few minutes.

After the first and second soldiers fell to the American bullets, other Chinese began returning fire with their burp guns. Jack and

Edgar shrank back into the dirt but rose again to return fire, their timing taught by instinct alone.

The vivid flashes from the guns immediately destroyed everyone's night vision, limiting the ability for each man to see his enemy to about ten feet. The men on both sides fired randomly toward their enemies' perceived locations. The slower but more accurate M1 Garand waged warfare against the faster firing but less accurate Chinese burp guns.

Jack and Edgar crouched between shots and ducked under the incoming rounds. After an instinctively defined period consisting of fragments of a second, they'd rise up just enough to return fire and then press into the dirt for cover. Incoming 7.62 mm rounds screeched through the air just above their heads. Mere inches meant life or meant death.

"Edgar! Grenades! Throw a couple now!" Jack screamed above the noise of gunfire.

Edgar ripped a couple off his belt and edged up a bit as Jack laid down covering fire. Jerking the pin out of the grenade, he hurled it toward the Chinese soldiers with every ounce of his strength. Both men retreated into the crater and waited. In a second, an excited voice in the Chinese language was followed by a violent eruption.

Jack thought it puzzling how quiet it would be after such a blast. It was almost as if everyone in the vicinity was briefly reconsidering the worth of combat—as if they might for a moment be persuaded to put it all aside.

In a moment, perhaps just mere seconds, the Chinese rounds started again. Jack and Edgar repeated their return fire, adding just enough randomness to keep the Chinese guessing. Both men did their best to ration their ammo so that when one man expended his clip of ammunition, the other still had rounds left in his. In this manner, they could maintain constant firing action against their enemy. Never *ping* at the same time, Jack and Edgar had agreed. Of course, other Marines in other foxholes were doing the same. Each weapon made its own distinctive sound, and the resulting cacophony of returning volleys developed a hypnotic effect like some sort of macabre symphony, accented by the occasional *ping* as if the death orchestra's triangle had been gently tapped.

This symphony might go on for long minutes without refrain —perhaps ten or fifteen minutes or longer. But inevitably the song changed, and the beat went a different direction—an instrument in the symphony had been silenced. The cause might be a hundred different reasons, many decidedly grim—a malfunctioning gun, out of ammunition, or worst of all, a bullet that had found its target.

Without warning, the rhythm did change—from close at hand. *Where's Edgar?* Jack ducked for cover again, and then a quick glance to his right told the brutal story. He froze.

Edgar's helmet lay a few yards behind his body, shattered by the force of the high-powered Chinese 7.62 mm round. Even in the pitch of the bitter black sky, Jack could see that Edgar lay motionless, his face turned toward his friend, eyes wide open in shock.

Jack called to him as if he genuinely expected Edgar would shrug it off. Then he called again in desperation. "Edgar—no! No. This can't be happening." Jack jerked him by his heavy coat as if to rouse him from a feigned sleep, but Edgar fell limp. Anger boiled up within Jack. His tongue tasted of metal. His gloves soaked up his friend's blood.

Where normal men in normal times would be incapacitated by shock and despair, Jack erupted with the intensity of rage that turns a man into a beast and a soldier into an uncompromising instrument of death.

He fired once at each of the three remaining Chinese soldiers who were still advancing. Each was within ten or twelve feet, and each cried out and fell to the ground. One man escaped immediate death and lay on his side, groaning. For a fraction of a second, Jack thought better of it, but his intense hatred and grief overrode what he otherwise knew to be best.

Jack flung himself from the crater and raced to the dying Chinese. There was a bullet wound on the left side of the man's neck where the bullet had pierced his jugular artery. He would die soon—but not soon enough, or in the right way, for Jack.

Jack looked deep into his eyes, and the Chinese soldier looked back, terrified yet unable to resist. They both knew what was next. Jack took his rifle butt and raised it over his head. He stared into the man's eyes longer than necessary, and then brought the rifle butt down with every ounce of his barbarous fury.

It was then that another Chinese round found the body of an American Marine. A searing pain exploded through Jack Stiles's right leg. His leg collapsed in a storm of pain that he had never felt before, and he fell helplessly to the ground. Reeling from the impact, he tried to drag himself back toward the relative safety of the crater. As he inched across the frozen ground, he was vaguely aware of fellow Marines shifting closer to his position to provide covering fire. Several called to Jack, but their voices twisted into an indecipherable enigma.

Jack's arms suddenly began to feel as though they were made of water. His face lay hard against the frigid dirt, his body unable to move any further. The stars above and the noise of return American gunfire blurred as Jack lost consciousness somewhere to the southeast of Chosin Reservoir, in a place men came to die.

By the time the UN forces could complete their retreat from Chosin, twenty-five hundred of their soldiers would die, and another twelve thousand five hundred would be injured—the majority of these suffering injuries from the bitter cold. On the other side of the fighting, the numbers were staggering. UN forces killed more than forty thousand Chinese Communist soldiers at Chosin in what history would later consider one of the most savage battles in all of military history.

Only a few would remember it. The battle at "Frozen Chosin" would become known as the forgotten battle in the forgotten war.

CHAPTER FIVE

Recovery

The small village of Oro-ri sat just off a small road that led from the main route from Chosin down to Hungnam. Jang Tae-bok, a young Korean woman, lived here with her family in a small house, a shack really, that sat among a hundred or so other nondescript houses populating the small village in North Korea. She and her family sat on the thin stones that made up the floor of their primitive dwelling. The *ondol* heating system routed hot exhaust from the stove in the kitchen underneath the thin stone floor and across to the crude chimney pipe. The stove provided both the necessary cooking heat and the heat for the small house that was so necessary for survival in the bitter temperatures of North Korea. The heat soaked into the stone floor and provided a comfortable warmth that lasted for several hours after the fire went out.

Next to her sat her aged father, Jang Dong-woo. On the other side of her sat her five-year-old son, Lee Yong-ho, and in her arms, nursing, was her infant son, Lee Kyung-chan. They sat close to each other to share the precious heat emanating from the stones beneath them. The low roof of the little house was adorned only with scraps of tin and other metal, with pieces of a stray tarp here or there. The walls were slanted and crooked and could make no claim to being even close to square. Small gaps in the walls that would otherwise let in bitter cold air had been stuffed with old rags in a vain attempt to defeat the drafts.

Tae-bok fed the fire scraps of wood, little bits of coal, and other waste products to keep the vital flames alive. A flimsy homemade door separated the kitchen and eating area from the small bedroom, the only other room in the little shack. A thin straw mattress lay flat on the stone floor. Tattered sheets gave some marginal comfort, and a few worn blankets kept Tae-bok and the boys warm at night. Mostly, Tae-bok struggled to keep the stove burning with scraps of wood she found here and there. Her life and the lives of her family depended upon the fire. The food might come and go, but during the winter, the fire must always remain.

She was twenty-five years old, but she had experienced enough war and heartache in those few years for someone three times her age. A month earlier, she had labored to dig a shallow grave out of the nearly frozen earth in the nearby hills. Into that hole, she had dragged the body of her husband, a forced conscript soldier for the North Korean Communist forces. He died, she had been told, at a fierce battle with the Americans at a place she had heard of, but never been—a place her people called Changjin.

But in a place and time like the present in Korea, there was little time and certainly no space in Tae-bok's life for grief. She was dedicated to survival. She struggled to feed her aged father and two young boys. Whatever she had, she acquired by bartering. When not bartering for food, she searched for scraps of lumber. When not finding scraps of lumber, she looked for food. A continual search for food and fuel was the extent of Tae-bok's weary life in the small roadside village of Oro-ri.

"Tae-bok?" her father asked as he touched her arm.

"Yes, Father?"

"It is very cold out tonight. Will the fire make it through the night?"

Tae-bok wasn't sure. "Yes, Father, I think it will. But tomorrow, early, I will find more wood."

* * *

The icy wind seemed to howl even more strongly farther up in North Korea on the evening of December 10. A heavy blanket of fresh snow had fallen the previous night with the fast-moving storm. In the deep-valley village of Unchon-ri, in the quiet hours just after midnight, friends and family members had all arrived and were huddled together on the floor of a small hut. Fourteen-year-old Dong-hyuck reclined in the corner with eleven other young men. The late hour and the gentle warmth rising up from the stone floor had coaxed Dong-hyuck and most of the other young men into sleep. His father, Won Byung-soon, and his mother, Lee Go-mang, were also there. Even various aunts, cousins, and a sister who lived nearby had all gathered to discuss important matters.

"Byung-soon," one of the older men said, "I am grateful that you have allowed us to visit with you at such a late hour. The matter is urgent, and it could not wait until morning."

"It is quite fine, my friend. What is it that concerns you at this hour?"

"I shall be very direct, Byung-soon. We are leaving in the morning for the south. You should also leave this place immediately and come with us. We have all seen the American troops heading south. The Chinese and North Korean armies will return to this area, and we fear for your safety."

Byung-soon contemplated the matter. He sat quietly on the floor, cross-legged. "I understand what you are saying, but I am not at all sure they will cause us trouble. We have nothing they want."

The older man spoke again while the others remained quiet. "No, Byung-soon. The Chinese and North Korean armies are a very serious threat. Because we all greeted and aided the South Korean Army and the UN forces, we are now at risk. Each of us took part in the anti-Communist self-defense council. When the Chinese and North Korean armies return, they will determine who worked against them. They will find our names, and they will surely kill us. You know this to be true."

Byung-soon thought silently for a moment. "If it is as you say it will be, then how can I leave my family here? My wife and my children are to be left here all alone? How can I do that?" He gestured to his family. Desperation and reality mixed themselves in his voice.

The older man replied calmly, having already drunk this bitter cup of realization. "Byung-soon, because our women were not active in our anti-Communist activities and their names were not recorded, they will not be at such great risk. The armies are too busy to deal with women and children. It is we, the men, they will search for. They will allow no man of any age to live who worked for the South Koreans or the Americans. Even if we had not worked against the Chinese and North Koreans, they would put us in their army immediately."

"What about Dong-hyuck? He is now fourteen years old. What do I do with him?" He motioned to his son, sleeping in the corner. The boy curled under a blanket, a soft pillow under his head. He had a heart and mind of innocence; he was a child yet untouched by war.

"Bring him. It is true that your son should come with us. He is old enough that the military will take an interest in him. They will either put him in the army or put him in a prison camp. He is a clever young man. He can behave himself. He will not be any problem for us."

Byung-soon looked at his wife, Go-mang. She sat among the

women, and he saw the deep concern on her face.

"When you leave here, where will you go in the south?" Byung-soon asked his friend.

"We hear talk that many are fleeing to Hungnam. There is discussion that perhaps there will be some sort of escape from Hungnam further to the south. We do not know for sure, but that is where we are planning to go. Because the weather has been so bad, we need to leave now so that we can make it to Hungnam in time. We are leaving in the morning, before the sun rises."

Byung-soon sat silently. The room joined him. No one spoke. Outside, the sound of the strong north wind blowing through the village accentuated the silence. His mind wrestled with the magnitude of the decisions before him. Decisions made now might very well affect life and death—the very future of his family.

"Please give me some time to think. I will decide before you must leave."

* * *

In the dead of the cold night, a young black Navy medic named Monroe took advantage of a lull in the fighting to crawl his way out to the scene of the bloody firefight. He had seen so much death that the carnage before him scarcely bothered him. Normally, the recovery tactics for the dead and wounded involved throwing a coil of barbed wire out to the man—or corpse. When the barbed wire snagged on the man's clothing, the medic would literally reel him in, dragging him across the frozen battlefield. If the Chinese had hidden any grenades under the body, at least the medic would be spared.

In this case, the Marines had secured the perimeter quickly, and no Chinese had penetrated further. Monroe crawled his way the last forty yards to the scene of the fight. Inside the crater, he saw a motionless Marine. The ugly sight before him made it clear in stark terms that this Marine was dead. He fished around the man's bloody neck for his dog tags. He pulled them from under his shirt and wiped free the blood and dirt. He read the name: Morrison.

Also near the crater were two dead Chinese soldiers. The medic ignored them. Monroe had often proudly told folks back home that his job was "to take care of our boys." He had long ago determined that the more and the faster the enemy died, the quicker he might get to go back home.

A few yards north of the crater were more dead Chinese and one down US Marine. *Dead or wounded?* Monroe pondered. Half-walking, half-crawling, he worked his way over to the fallen Marine—unexploded grenades were still a risk as well as nearby hidden snipers. Two things became immediately evident: Stiles was the boy's name, and he was alive, at least for the moment.

Monroe planned to be back for the remains of the first Marine. He would put him in the standard government-issue body bag, assuming any were available, and drag him to the road, where a military vehicle would come along and pick up the dead. The bodies would first be taken to a regional morgue, then to Pusan, and then flown home to their families—usually by way of Yokohama. Somewhere between now and then, stateside Marine officers would make another sad trip to the front door of some father, mother, or wife. Monroe didn't let himself think too much about that part. He had to keep his mind on the living, not the dying.

Monroe knew that time was critical for Stiles. He inspected the badly wounded thigh. To the best of his somewhat limited medical skills, he concluded the bullet had not completely destroyed the young man's leg. Nonetheless, he had lost much blood. Pressed down into the frigid dirt and hunkering over Stiles's now still body, Monroe worked cloth strips around and around his leg and fashioned a makeshift tourniquet. There was no time to clean the wound or further treat it. This moment was all about stopping the bleeding.

"Stiles, can you hear me?" Monroe asked with a slow, deep Louisiana Cajun drawl that turned the word "hear" into at least two syllables. "Can you hear me, boy? No, I didn't guess you could. Well, listen, if you *can* hear me, I put a tourniquet on your leg. You lost a lot of blood, okay? I'll get everything fixed, and then I'll get you out of here. Keep you warm as well, okay?"

The Marine didn't answer. Monroe finished his quick preparations.

"All right, now listen to me, Stiles. I'm going to have to drag you out of here. I don't mean to hurt you, but I'm trying to keep my head down and keep it from getting shot off. You see, these Chinese and Koreans don't care nothing about us medics. They'd just as soon shoot me for the thrill of watching me die. So I don't mean to hurt you, but it ain't going to be real pleasant, okay? But it's the fastest way to get you out of here. Okay?"

The wounded Marine didn't answer.

Monroe moved up to Stiles's head and turned his back to him, trying to keep his own head down and permanently attached to his body. He crouched a bit and reached back for Stiles's hands. Hitched up like a crude train, Monroe took off, head low, legs crouched as much as he could as he began the awkward hundred-yard sprint back to safety. Monroe always hated this part. Sometimes the men were awake, and it was torment for Monroe to listen to their screams as he dragged them back to safety. In the end, he reckoned the quicker he got it done, the better for both of them. A dead medic wasn't much use to anybody.

At the road, Monroe wrestled the wounded Marine up and onto a stretcher that was strapped to the back of a worn-out jeep. He strapped Stiles down and tightened the restraints as much as was practical. He then secured the hood of Stiles's jacket, hopped into the driver's seat, and cranked the reluctant engine.

From the main road, it was only a few miles by jeep to a temporary mobile surgical hospital. Within twenty minutes, Monroe had arrived with his injured Marine. There, Jack was given additional treatment. The doctors and nurses helped Monroe bring the stretcher inside the interconnected maze of green Army tents, past men bloodied and broken: some dead, many dying, and a few trying to live.

A flurry of scissors began cutting bandages and clothing off until the wound was fully exposed. The entry wound caused by the bullet was tiny—just a quarter of an inch across. It had entered on the right side of Jack's thigh at a velocity of more than two thousand feet per second and bored its way through clothing, skin, and muscle. As it entered his leg, the copper-jacketed solid lead bullet deformed slightly and began a twisted route through the muscle. In a microsecond, jagged edges appeared in the copper jacket, and those razor sharp edges began to shred muscle tissue as the bullet chose a seemingly random path. Finally, it had reached the left side of Jack's thigh and burst into the open, creating a wound the diameter of a golf ball. The bullet had continued on for another several hundred yards before burying itself in the frigid dirt.

Doctors at the makeshift hospital irrigated the path the bullet had taken through his thigh. Jack had been lucky, as the bullet had damaged only muscle. The femur was untouched, and despite the significant blood loss, the femoral artery had not been pierced. The doctor administered penicillin to protect against the inevitable infection. A heavy dose of morphine was given to dull the brutal pain and keep Jack mostly sedated until he could receive further treatment. Blood of the right type helped replace what Jack had lost. The few times Jack did stir to consciousness, his only semi-lucid thought was that he wished he could cut his right leg off.

Byung-soon sat quietly in the early morning hours of December 11. His wife, Go-mang, sat close beside him. Most of his friends and family slept. In hushed tones, he spoke with the few who remained awake. They debated the possibilities and tried to determine the best choice.

Eventually, the discussions brought Byung-soon to a decision.

"Go-mang, I believe I should go and take the boy. May I take Dong-hyuck with me?"

"Yes, my husband. Why not? I understand there is some uncertainty in this. But if the boy remains here, there is greater certainty of death or capture. Even if the journey is uncertain and the future is not clear, it is more promising than remaining here. Let me get him awake and dressed, and then you can leave with him."

Go-mang immediately rose from her place and stirred Dong-hyuck from his sleep. "Dong-hyuck, it is time to wake up and get dressed for travel."

Dong-hyuck stirred and slowly focused on his mother's words. "My son, put your coat on. Bundle up warmly. Your father will be taking you on a long journey to the south. There, you will be safe."

"Are you coming, Mother?"

"No, son. I will remain here with your sisters. We will find a way to rejoin each other soon."

In just a short time the group had organized, packed heavy bundles, and prepared themselves for the journey ahead. The remainder of their family and friends sat on the floor around the stove. Their sadness at the reality of departure prevented further discussion.

The group of men said sorrowful but restrained good-byes to

their families and then stepped out into the bitter cold together. Go-mang walked with her husband and son along the little road that led south out of their village and in the direction of Hungnam. The surface was covered in several inches of fresh snow. The icy cold north wind swirled the snow around them as they kicked it up with their feet. The snow stung as it slashed at the exposed skin of their faces. Above, a full moon shone brilliantly—yet even it seemed frozen. It was still two hours before sunrise.

After walking the first mile together, Byung-soon spoke to his wife. "This will be far enough, my wife. We will be fine now. We will write you when we get safely into the south." He held her hands gently with his. Go-mang nodded silently and reluctantly agreed.

Husband and wife shared a few final words. Dong-hyuck hugged and kissed his mother.

"I love you, Mother."

"I love you too, son. I am always very proud of you." She leaned close to him now, soaking in his radiance, memorizing every detail of his face. Her hands held his face tenderly. "When you get to the south, you will have freedom. Never squander it. Drink deeply from its fountain and live your life to its very fullest. There is no limit to what you may achieve if you apply yourself."

Dong-hyuck pondered her words. "I will, Mother. But you are coming, right?" he asked, confused.

"Yes, my son. As soon as we are able, we will all come."

Byung-soon exchanged an understanding look with his wife. She smiled and knew the choice was right.

Father and son turned and walked away into the bitter night.

"Good-bye, and take care. I hope we can keep in touch!" Go-mang called out as her husband and son slipped into the night behind a swirl of snow. She watched as the cloudy frost from their heavy breathing, glinting in the brilliant moonlight, slowly faded into the inky darkness. She suppressed a rising tide of sadness from deep within and turned back toward her house. She wiped a tear from her eye.

Without looking back, father and son began their lonely journey to Hungnam.

* * *

By noon on December 11, Jack was stable enough to transport, although heavily sedated with generous amounts of morphine. A young Army nurse spoke to the doctor who was checking on him. "Doctor, can we put Private Stiles on the chopper? I've got another one who needs a lift too."

"No . . . I just talked to the commander, and we're still grounded. Ceiling's way too low. We can't afford to lose any more choppers or men in this kind of weather. Let's get them down to Hungnam by transport instead—they're moving all of us out to Hungnam anyway in short order. He should be okay to transport. I got two others that can go as well, and that'll give us a full load. Who was the medic that brought him in?"

"That was Bobby Monroe, the Negro boy."

"Okay—find him, and we can have him make the run down the MSR to Hungnam. He's experienced, as I remember, and I think they've mostly cleared the route of major fighting. Listen, skip the paperwork on these guys—just get Monroe on the road without delay and get 'em down to Hungnam."

"Yes, sir, Doctor. I'll get it taken care of for you."

In relatively short order, the nurses found Bobby Monroe huddled near a small potbellied stove writing a letter back home and recruited him for the drive to Hungnam. Exiting the mobile surgical hospital, several of the orderlies loaded Jack and three other men into a makeshift ambulance. It was hardly more than a supply truck with a canvas roof and walls and with room for four stretchers—two stacked on each side—but it would suffice. Medics and nurses bundled him and the other injured men with blankets and strapped them tightly to their stretchers. There was just enough of Jack's skin exposed for him to breathe and see, but not much else because of the temperature.

Monroe climbed into the back and gave the men his own personal once-over. He tugged gently on each of the straps, not wanting these men to suffer any more than was necessary. He then looked carefully at each man's tags and spoke gently with his slow, deep Louisiana drawl.

"Stiles? Stiles—remember me? Good to see you again. Can you hear me? You hear me okay? Stiles? Can you hear me?" he asked a bit more loudly this time. Jack stirred and tried to open his eyes.

"Listen, my name's Bobby Monroe, and I'm from Monroe, Louisiana," he offered in a way that emphasized his hometown as if no one had ever heard of it before. "Everybody thinks that's kind of funny, me having the name Bobby Monroe and being from Monroe and all that. Reckon you will too when you wake up." He smiled broadly, exposing perfect white teeth against his jet-black skin.

Jack stirred slightly and tried to focus on the strange dark-skinned face hovering over him. He managed a small, tight smile. In his mind, he seemed to be lying still while the world spun around and around. Jack felt like he was variously huge in size with all his surroundings tiny, and then tiny amidst wildly outsized surroundings. The disorientation was a bit too much for his foggy mind, and he faded slowly and without resistance back into the comfort of the morphine.

"Stiles, do you remember me, boy? I drug you off the front lines. I guess that didn't feel so good, and I'm real sorry about all that."

Jack barely stirred.

"No, don't guess you remember. Well, that's for the best. Anyway, you'll thank me later. As for now, I'm getting you out of here, boy. Well, you and three other men. You're a lucky fella. Most of these poor boys done lost something . . . a foot or a leg or an arm . . . I mean, I ain't saying that a man can't be a man without a leg, but I'm just saying that you are one lucky fella. You lost a lot of blood and everything, but you're going to make it. I'll get you out of here. That's my personal guarantee."

Through a fog, Jack's fragile thoughts drifted to Edgar.

Dead . . . why? Who would tell his parents?

"Anyway, we're going to Hungnam. Commander said something about getting everybody there—got a big evacuation planned. Get everybody out of this sorry place. Long ride ahead of us—just relax—I'll check on you later." With that, the dark-skinned face was gone as quickly as it had appeared.

Jack stared up at the stretcher above and noticed a crimson circle of blood from the man who lay on it. He pushed back hard against the morphine to try to collect his thoughts. *Edgar. Where is he? Is he okay? I need to get back to the squad. Where have they taken Edgar?*

In an instant, and for only an instant, Jack was back at home in Midland. He stood outside, watching his mother hang sheets on the clothesline. He felt the crisp morning air on his face. His mother stood at the line in her bare feet, wearing her pale cotton dress. She hung a few shirts of his and a few of his dad's.

Jack heard a familiar voice. He turned to the front porch and saw Richard and his dad talking, laughing and playing checkers on the old porch table. How long had it been? His dad had only lasted a few months after Richard was killed. Jack walked to the porch in disbelief.

"Richard, I thought you were gone. When did you get home?"

"Hey, little bro. I was always here. You're the one who went away."

"That's how it was, Jack. I tried to stop you from going, but you wouldn't listen," his dad added from the porch.

Jack turned, confused, looking back at Richard and then back at his father. Then they were gone.

With blinding confusion, he turned back toward his mother at the clothesline, but the line and the clothes and the sky and the grass began to melt away and pool at his feet. Fear grabbed him by the neck, and he looked into his mother's eyes and she into his as she slowly melted away too.

In the real world, Monroe climbed into the cab of the transport and cranked the reluctant engine until she belched large clouds of black smoke into the air. Across the way, he saw an officer trotting over to his cab.

"Monroe?" the man called out.

"Yes, sir, what can I do for you?" Monroe replied as he left the engine to roughly idle and belch its way to warmth.

"Second Lieutenant David Barkman. Nice to meet you. The docs mentioned you were heading down to Hungnam. Can I catch a ride? I'm supposed to meet up with one of the planes at Yonpo down there." He grinned happily. "Just got papers to go home."

"Of course, got room up front here. Jump in on the other side. I'm sure not going to stand between a man and his way home." Monroe waited until the lieutenant hurried around to the other side, jerked the door open, and flung his lanky frame onto the big bench seat in the cab.

"Thanks, man—really appreciate it."

"You're welcome. I can't promise much about the ride of this old beast. Can't promise much about the conversation either. But I'm always happy to have a man with a gun. Never know around these parts." Monroe snickered.

"Well, any conversation that is going my direction is a good conversation. But I'm afraid my pistol won't do us much good.

Let's hope we don't even have to think about that."

"Amen to that, sir. Well, let's get to it, Lieutenant." Monroe babied the old engine and revved it higher. He worked hard to persuade the frozen gearbox to find first gear. Finally, the teeth agreed to join their forces.

The revving engine and sharp metallic grating from the worn-out transmission signaled the start of their long journey down the frozen one-lane mountain road that was the direct route to Hungnam.

CHAPTER SIX

Road to Hungnam

The makeshift ambulance groaned halfheartedly along the snow-covered dirt road as it struggled its way up and down the mountains of North Korea. The road to Hungnam was once again proving equal parts tortuous and dangerous. This far south, no major battle lines along the main supply route remained. But rogue pockets of North Korean and Chinese activity in the hills above the road could sometimes muster enough force to pose a credible threat to passing convoys and troops. Sometimes, the crudely painted Red Cross symbol on the side of the faded white canvas sides and roof of a medical transport would grant safe passage for the dead and dying. Sometimes, but not often enough.

Along the MSR down to Hungnam, Monroe counted off their progress with the passage of names. He drove through places on his map that included the aptly described Hell Fire Valley. Farther along, his ambulance climbed the narrow road through Funchilin Pass and rattled across the makeshift Treadway Bridge, which had been parachuted down in pieces, hastily assembled, and now allowed the continued flow of men and materiel toward Hungnam.

Jack was mostly oblivious to the gravelly churning of the old engine, woefully underpowered even before its human cargo was loaded. He and the other injured men lay still, with only the occasional groan of pain. Each hole in the road, each necessary swerve jostled and swung them back and forth. But due either to morphine or dying, they mostly lay still.

In the cab, slumped against the passenger-side door frame, Lieutenant Barkman slumbered, having finally acquiesced to many days without sleep, the gentle rocking of the transport, and the deep growl of the engine. Monroe longed for sleep, but he fought back against its siren call as he wrestled the wheel of the overloaded truck along the narrow road. This was exactly the job Monroe had wanted when he enlisted in the Navy, and it suited him just fine. He supposed that fixing the troops was a good skill. His momma back home told him to do whatever he did to the very best of his ability, and when he got home from this war, he could get a good job. Maybe he'd move closer to New Orleans and work at the hospital. With a good job, Monroe figured he could find himself a good wife.

As he navigated the precarious roads, he smiled in fond recollection of the girl he was sweet on. He'd always had an eye for Florence Condreau. He'd even dared to write to her a time or two from Korea, but hadn't heard anything back. He figured it was only a matter of time. He knew for sure he liked her, and he figured she maybe liked him too. With a job that paid well, maybe she'd like him more. Maybe they had a bit of a chance at a future together.

They had been on the road nearly four hours now. Because of the winding roads and the snow and ice, the progress to Hungnam was slow. Darkness started to overtake the land, and Monroe let more and more thoughts of home take refuge in his mind. It helped him not to feel so alone.

The driving was challenging and not without strategy. Monroe had learned by experience to keep the headlights turned off at night, at least as much as possible. He preferred instead to hide in the shadows and eek out enough vision by the light of the moon. It was his way of trying to regain a slight advantage over his enemy—if they were out there in the shadows tonight. What they might gain by means of surprise, perhaps he could regain by means of the shadows. It was like when he was a kid back home: hide and seek in the dark—it kept things more equal.

At the five-hour mark, the little villages of Chinhung-ni, Sudong, and Majon-dong lay behind him. Up ahead, Monroe saw a couple of US Army vehicles that were stopped on the main road. He slowed his transport and brought it to a sliding stop on the snow-covered road. Monroe kept the engine idling and eased himself out of the warmth of the cab.

"Howdy, fellas," he hollered at the soldiers ahead. "What ya'll got up here?"

"Hey, I'm Sergeant Tompkins," one of the soldiers on the road hollered back.

"Bobby Monroe, Navy medic. I've got four boys that need to get down to Hungnam. What's the story with the road?"

"Well, we're the tail end of a convoy heading the same direction. Couple of our lead vehicles got ambushed. It's going to be several hours at least before we get the road cleared."

The news jarred him. He glanced back at the truck and then at the stalled convoy ahead of him. He had never lost any men en route to Hungnam. He wasn't about to start now. "Several hours? I really need to keep these boys moving. Any way around?"

"Well, if you go back up the MSR about two miles or so, there's a small road that cuts off through a small village—it'll be to your left as you go back that way. It's a little longer, but it'll be faster than waiting on us. It kind of parallels the MSR but eventually rejoins it, and you'll be on your way down to Hungnam."

"Is that the road that goes through Oro-ri?"

"Yeah, I think so, but I can't keep all these little villages straight. Listen, take care—I've got to get back to my guys here. Be careful."

"Hey, thanks, man, appreciate it. Ya'll too."

Monroe climbed back into the warm cab of the transport. Barkman was awake.

"What's up?" he asked as he shook the sleep away.

"Convoy got ambushed. It's going to be a while before they get the road clear. Got another way around, if we can get backed up and turned around."

"Which way are we going?" Barkman asked.

"Well, just a couple of miles back, there's a little road that cuts off through a small village and then rejoins the main road. It should be a pretty good way around this mess."

"Safe?" Barkman mumbled.

"Mostly the ambushes happen along the main roads. I reckon it should be okay. Besides, you still got that pistol, right?"

Barkman sat up straighter and laughed. "Yeah, sure. What you need is my pistol and a company of angry Marines, my friend."

Monroe grinned. "It reminds me of that little joke. What do you bring to a knife fight?"

"What do you bring to a knife fight? I don't know, a bigger knife?"

"No, a gun—and you call all your friends and ask them to bring their guns," Monroe laughed.

Barkman laughed. "Bobby Monroe from Monroe, Louisiana. You are most certainly unique."

Monroe laughed in agreement and turned his attention back to his driving. He backed up to a wider spot in the road, and in a series of little half-turns, eventually turned his vehicle around and began heading for the small cutoff road. Just as the sergeant had described, he spotted the smaller road after about two miles. Monroe made a sharp left turn. The small road was steeper than the main route, and narrower, but Monroe was glad to be moving again.

After another half-hour of cautious driving up and down the

smaller road, Oro-ri lay just ahead. Monroe thought of these villages as pitiful little affairs. Usually, the broken dirt road went right through the middle of them. Scattered on either side of the road were houses—or to be more precise, shacks. They had them in the bayou where his granddaddy's people were, but here the shacks were *all* they seemed to have. The walls were made of mud or dung and scrap metal or wood, and the roof was anything that could support its own weight: grass, leaves, plywood, and anything salvageable.

What always puzzled Monroe most were the children. Even with the bitter temperatures, he would often see them playing outside. He noticed that while they had no toys, they did have rocks and sticks, sometimes an old bicycle tire. With such, it seemed to him, they were content. He wondered how much they knew about this sad war, all this killing and suffering. He figured they knew nothing about the reasons why—just the reality of soldiers and guns and death in their immediate vicinity. He thought it remarkable that in their childhood innocence they played with rocks and sticks while three nations did their best to kill each other's men for these children's little patch of frozen ground.

He entered the village of Oro-ri slowly, mindful of unseen animals or children on the narrow road. Darkness had now fully entered the equation. An acrid smoke hung in the frigid air, trapped within the little valley. Each shack had a fragile little stovepipe which belched putrid smoke as the byproduct of whatever had been found to be burned. The residents were not particular. In a strange way, the sight took him home again. He had seen such places with his grandfather, where some of the old people still lived. Little shacks, smoke hanging thick in the air, children playing. Monroe eased off the accelerator and slowed to a crawl. The village seemed unusually quiet tonight.

* * *

Tae-bok turned back toward her home, only marginally successful from her day's search for food and firewood. She, her two sons, and her father would make do with what little she had found. As the evening's darkness lay heavy across the land, she descended out of the surrounding hills down into the small valley and approached the narrow dirt road that ran through her village. The crisp mountain air revealed a beautiful night sky, marred only by the settling cloud of smoke that collected most evenings. Tae-bok girded her old coat against the advancing cold. With the setting of the sun the temperatures plunged quickly, so she hurriedly pressed on. In her left arm she clutched a small package of rice she had successfully bartered for. In her right, a few more pieces of wood for the life-giving fire.

Tae-bok crossed the narrow road and then descended from the road down through the brush and into her village. Her eye caught movement, and she paused, straining to see. With barely enough moonlight, she eventually resolved the crouching form of two soldiers in the brush. One took note of her and looked over his left shoulder. He stared. Cautiously, she steered away from them. Most soldiers left her alone, but not all. Deftly and with more urgency, Tae-bok moved through the brush, out into a clearing, and weaved her way the final hundred yards to her shack.

* * *

From the warmth of their cab, Monroe and Barkman looked out through the dirty windshield and watched a lone woman walk gingerly across the road and head toward the little village about a hundred yards in front of them. She carried a small package in both hands. She was alone. She moved quickly, with a sense of determined purpose. To Monroe, she looked like any of the other

90

thousands of Korean women he saw on a daily basis: short, slim, and bundled heavily against the brutal elements. He watched as she stepped across the road and into the frozen brush.

"Something wrong?" Barkman asked.

Monroe took a moment to answer. "I don't know what it is . . . something just feels a little off, you know what I mean?"

Barkman peered into the darkness. "Seems quiet. Nothing really going on. The road's pretty sorry, like usual—just full of potholes."

"Yeah, I guess. Just keep your eyes open, okay?"

* * *

Huddled in the dense frozen brush, a Chinese soldier held two flimsy wires in his hands just above a large battery; another soldier secured the wires carefully as they passed through the undergrowth and onto the road to a small package of explosives. They watched the American truck slow to a crawl. A Red Cross symbol painted on the side was just visible through the silver moonlight, but it was a symbol they neither understood nor cared to understand. The truck idled forward slightly. The soldiers strained to see the driver of the vehicle but could not, yet they knew he must be there in the cab.

* * *

Tae-bok shifted her delivery of rice and wood as she stepped quickly toward her small house. She opened the makeshift door, closed it quickly behind her, and sealed it as well as she could in a mostly futile effort to close out the cold. Her slight frame stood scarcely five feet over the dirt floor of her family's shack. The thatched roof ceiling loomed barely two feet above Tae-bok's head. She unwrapped the covering from around her face, exposing her short-cropped jet-black hair and rosy cheeks. She stooped down near the ancient wood-burning stove and added a few fresh pieces of wood to the fire. Her blind father sat near the fire on a straw mat, soaking in what heat the little stove pumped out.

"Trouble tonight?" he asked his daughter in their native Korean tongue.

"It is growing more difficult to find wood, Father. It seems each day I must go farther to find what we need. But I found what we needed for tonight, and I will keep searching for it, do not worry. And in the morning I will search in some different areas."

"My daughter, I listen every day to the noise of trucks passing nearby. Each day, many come. What troubles me most is that they are heading south. In the past, we heard them all heading north, but now they head south. When I sit very still, I feel the vibrations from large weapons. I believe it is the Chinese. They too draw closer. I fear the fighting is coming nearer. You must be more careful than before."

"I will, Father—I will be safe."

Tae-bok's father listened without reaction, concerned more for what he would say next. "You must think about the children. This place is not their future. They must find a future elsewhere. You must move on from this place and find a future for them."

"Father, this is not necessary. I can travel farther each day. I will find what we need," she said.

No matter how right her father was, Tae-bok would not accept the option he had presented. Her father was much too old, too weak and frail. They had moved a short distance a few years ago from the valley they once farmed. Even the short move had nearly been too much for him. He would not endure yet another. Months of recovery had barely brought him back to his currently feeble level of health. They would remain here. They would be together—no matter what.

Determined, Tae-bok held her youngest son tight as he slowed his nursing and drifted back to sleep.

* * *

The Chinese soldiers lay completely motionless and waited as the truck inched closer. It seemed to be looking, waiting. Had the driver seen their explosives on the road? One of the men inched forward on his belly through the brush as much as he dared until he thought he could surely go no further without detection by the driver. His new position improved his ability to see the truck and its relation to their explosives. Painful seconds ticked by. The soldier's pounding heart beat double-time as adrenaline coursed through his body. More time passed. All was silent.

Suddenly the old engine growled and the gears whined as the driver put the truck back into first gear and lurched forward a few fateful yards.

At precisely the right moment, the soldiers closed the circuit with their wires. The bulky lead acid battery they had been assigned for just this purpose sprang into action. The brutal cold had sapped much of the electrical strength from the old battery, but just enough remained to complete its mission. At the speed of light, current flowed through the connection and reached the fuse within the package of explosives. In a partial second, the fuse superheated the surrounding chemicals and set off a complex reaction that immediately spiraled out of control. The result ruptured the quiet of the little village. The visible results were immediate: a blindingly bright flash, a deadly ball of white fire, and a thunderous explosion that pierced the frigid night air.

The explosive force pulverized the cab of the old truck, simultaneously shattering the lives and dreams of Private Bobby Monroe and Second Lieutenant David Barkman. The impact pushed its way backwards through the cab, killing both men instantly. As its shock wave continued through the truck, it flung the injured men in the back of the transport helplessly into the air. They landed with sickening thuds on the dirt road as the fireball flared above them. The Chinese soldiers turned from the brilliant fireball, glanced at each other's faces as they were briefly illuminated by the explosion, and exchanged a brief, grim-lipped nod of approval.

* * *

Setting her son aside for a moment beside her father, Tae-bok knelt to add more wood to the fire, but a vicious explosion startled her and the wood fell from her hands to the dirt floor.

"Father!" she instinctively cried out and brought her son back to the safety of her chest. Simultaneously, Tae-bok's five-year-old son cried out in terror and seized her around the legs so forcefully she nearly lost her balance.

Regaining her balance, she comforted her young son. "Shhhh . . . son, it will be okay," she said to Yong-ho. As the shock from the explosion faded, an idea quickly came to her mind. She ushered the boys back to her father. She lingered for a moment, counting her blessings for their safety, and gently caressed their jet-black hair. Confident of what she must do, she quickly donned her heavy outer coat.

Although blind for many years, blindness did not mean unawareness for her father. Every sound had meaning and painted a visual picture in his mind as sharp as any person with vision. He knew the rustling of the coat and that she was about to go outside into the night again.

"Tae-bok, you should not go—it is only more violence. Please, remain here with your children."

"Father, I must go—there will be something we can use."

With no further discussion, she stepped out of the dim light of her house and into the bitter black coldness. The door slammed behind her. Her father's worn hands tenderly held on to the two boys—the little one at his side and the infant in his arms. Facing the shack's only door, he felt the cold brush his cheeks as his daughter left. He sighed with frustrated concern.

Outside in the cold, Tae-bok stood for a moment as her eyes acclimated to the dark. The bitter shock of the cold froze the moisture in her nose. Her eyes watered, but the tears froze on her exposed skin even as they trickled down her cheeks. Large plumes of moisture billowed from her mouth with each breath and instantly froze into a million tiny crystals. It was at least thirty degrees below zero.

Wincing, she squinted to see through the darkness. She could see no fire, only a massive cloud of smoke drifting slowly away from an explosion on the road. She stumbled through the darkness and cautiously closed the distance. Each step brought a few more details into sight.

She first saw a mangled truck and immediately thought that it must have belonged to the American military. She had seen many like it before, but this one lay on its side, its wheels facing her, so she could not be sure. The front had been shredded in the explosion. She then saw the two Chinese soldiers she had passed in the brush just a short time earlier. They stood and walked among the smoking carnage that once was a truck with great interest.

Tae-bok drew closer, and additional details became clear in the dark and smoke. She saw a total of six bodies on the road, scattered like little twigs someone had dropped haphazardly on the ground. They lay crumpled and motionless. She watched as the soldiers moved between the bodies, kicking them or probing them with the bayonets from their field rifles.

She crouched quietly in the brush as she watched them

searching. Periodically they talked. Occasionally, they laughed. They seemed to find little of value, and apparently satisfied with their mission, they drifted off into the blackness of the night and disappeared from her sight. Tae-bok waited long minutes before daring to approach closer to the road.

* * *

Jack Stiles's crumpled body lay on the frozen ground. Suddenly his body seized fiercely, and he sucked in air as though he had not breathed in a very long time. He sputtered, coughed, and breathed again. He lay still. His mind flickered around the edges of consciousness, toying with it but not embracing it. Minutes passed as years, and he drifted between consciousness and death. Somewhere in the darkness of his mind he clung tenaciously to life as his brain desperately fought back against his injuries.

His mind was clouded in equal parts by the morphine and the concussive force of the explosion. Blinded and deaf, he felt his way along the road. Whether it was two miles or twenty feet he did not know, but eventually his hands landed on a body. He ran his hands across it and felt the torn stump where the man's arm had once been. He felt his way down the man's side and found a holster and a pistol. In his stupor, Jack managed to release the pistol and tried to crawl away with it. But after only a few feet, Jack slowed to a stop, unable to command his muscles to move. A bitter gall rose up within him as he ordered himself to escape, but his body would not respond. He slumped forward onto his face and slipped out of consciousness.

* * *

Tae-bok waited patiently. When the time seemed right, she moved silently from her position and stepped into the wreckage. Most of the bodies were bleeding. None moved. She could see clearly now that they were indeed Americans—and that usually meant food. She quickly began to rummage among the bodies for any meals the soldiers carried. Body by body she pushed them over. They were all dead. Disappointed, Tae-bok soon concluded that perhaps no food would be found this evening.

Just to be sure, she continued methodically searching each body. Finally she stepped to the last man. He lay facedown, legs and arms twisted and contorted from the blast. She roughly pushed him onto his side. She rummaged through his pockets but found nothing. Then he softly groaned.

Tae-bok startled and jumped back. Her pulse raced wildly, and her pupils dilated further. She watched his body closely. He made no further movement. She waited; perhaps it had been her imagination or some final futile gasp for life. Then he moved again. Slowly, his right hand trembled. Then the American grimaced and coughed. His entire arm moved now, and he clawed at the dirt. Tae-bok then saw what the Chinese soldiers had missed: this man had a pistol. She rushed to it, pried it from underneath his body, expertly loaded a round in the chamber, and fiercely pointed it at the man's face.

Crumpled on the road like discarded trash, Jack lay on his side with his face pressed hard into the dirt. He felt pain, and he briefly reasoned that if he felt pain, perhaps he was still somehow alive. He struggled to turn his head out of the dirt. In the dim light, his eyes struggled to focus through a blurry, drug-induced fog, compounded by the brutal force of the blast. It was an unknown world without sound and only a little sight—deafened by the fireball, he heard nothing save the pounding of his heart. In his vision, yet too close to focus, was a shaft of steel pointed directly at his face. His eyes gradually traveled down the black steel barrel and came to focus on the face of a woman—a woman pointing a pistol at his face.

Jack didn't move. He couldn't move. He forced himself to breathe, but it was the only voluntary movement he dared. His right hand trembled, and he tried furiously to restrain it, but it would not cease. For a moment, he saw his father's trembling hand. He struggled to focus on the woman's face.

Tae-bok held the pistol firmly, her right finger on the trigger. Her hands were small and worn, but they felt comfortable on the gun. It was not her first time handling one, nor would it be her first time to kill.

Tae-bok steadied herself to kill another of the brutal invaders of her country who had caused so many broken lives and spilled so much blood belonging to her people. She watched the man as he began to tremble uncontrollably, starting with his right hand. Blood leaked from his mouth, trailed down his chin, and landed in crimson splashes on the frigid dirt road. He was caked in dirt and mud. His face and hair had been singed in the explosion. Only in spots was the grime washed away by the blood of some fresh laceration.

Disgust boiled up within her. Now was the moment for vengeance. Now she could avenge the murder of her husband. She did not know him, but she hated this soldier with a rage that boiled up within her. But before she killed him, she wanted him to know. Tae-bok leaned closer toward the face of the broken soldier. She spat in his face and watched as her spittle rolled down his battered cheek.

Seconds passed. A dog barked in the distance. Somewhere a door slammed on its hinge. She was content to watch him suffer in pain. She told herself to kill him and fingered the trigger of the US-issued model 1911 .45-caliber pistol. Yet she did not pull the trigger.

Jack watched her in agony. His body was wracked with a magnitude of pain unlike anything he had ever felt or imagined before. He pleaded with God for death. He feared death, but feared more that it would not come soon enough. He wanted desperately to be home with his mother. He suddenly felt her soft hands washing his hair in the sink as a little boy, straightening his shirt, and tucking him into bed at night. He could smell the Sunday lunches she was so well-known for back in Midland—the farmhouse table filled to capacity after Sunday morning church. The smell of those dinners flooded back to him. He longed for the wide-open spaces, the hot winds of the high Texas plateau. He remembered the pretty girl who worked at the diner down at the main square in town. What was her name?

Lit only by a few fleeting rays of moonlight, Tae-bok saw a single tear pool in the man's right eye. It held for a brief moment and then trickled down his face, removing a tiny path of dirt before it fell to the icy ground and promptly froze. For a brief second, she saw not the face of a mortal enemy but the face of a mother's son—a mother's son immersed in grief, a wife's husband breathing his last in a strange, distant land. The look of death—it was something she was far too well acquainted with. Thin clouds passed in front of the moon and flickered shadows across the man's face. She stepped back slightly in shock. In the gray monotone of the night, she saw her husband's face looking back at her. The wind, the clouds, and the moonlight took her to a bitter place of memory. She heard a plaintive cry in her mind as it rang out across the distance, a mournful cry for help.

Tae-bok lowered the gun slightly as Jack slipped back into unconsciousness.

* * *

Tae-bok opened the door to her shack. Behind her, she dragged the body of the American soldier. With strength inconsistent with her scarcely five-foot frame, she dragged him by his arms into a small open space by the stove.

"What have you done, Tae-bok?" her father asked, aware by the sounds of her exertion that she had brought back something more than mere scraps of wood.

"He is an American soldier. I could not kill him, and I could not let him die. I believe he was already injured and perhaps was being taken for treatment."

She looked at her astounded father. He stood motionless—disbelieving what she had done.

"I don't know why, Father. I just couldn't do it again."

"My daughter, this is a great risk. It is wise that you did not kill him. This man has not harmed you. But it is not wise that you have brought him here. If the Americans do not look for him, then it is certain our soldiers or the Chinese will be searching. You will bring them to this place."

"I understand, Father. There were other soldiers in the wreckage. When they search, they will find them. They will not know about this one. I know it is not wise, Father, but I believe I had no other choice."

CHAPTER SEVEN

Decisions

Jack's mind fluttered around the corners of consciousness as the morning sun of December 12 streamed through the gaps in the makeshift walls of the little shack. The things he did not know about his situation greatly outnumbered the few things he did know—or thought he knew. Apart from knowing that he must be alive, he did not know where he was, why he was here, or when or how he got here. He scarcely even knew *who* he was. His head ached like it was being pressed in a giant vise, and all the other parts of his body hurt in ways he had never imagined. In truth, Jack Stiles could not identify a single part that did not burn with pain.

Tae-bok kneeled near the foot of the straw mattress on which Jack lay. She watched as he tried to stir to life. His six-foot frame extended well past the end of the primitive mattress. With the sizable knife in her right hand, she cut out part of the side of his military fatigues and exposed the bullet wound in his right thigh. Gently she removed caked dirt and dried blood from the wound, hoping that the American would not yet fully regain awareness.

Earlier in the morning she had risen and retrieved a small collection of medicinal herbs she had dried and stored before winter. Mashing the dried leaves into a sticky white paste, she added other medicinal leaves and crushed them all together. She stirred it all with a small twig. It would burn badly, but it would speed the healing of this man's wound. The sooner this American soldier could leave, the better. Her father was right about that much: while she couldn't kill him and couldn't let him die, the longer he stayed, the greater the risk to her family. Soldiers from both sides would surely be looking for him.

Tae-bok began to pack his wound with the caustic paste. The same qualities that would speed his healing burned his thigh with a searing, acidic pain. Jack lurched out of his stupor and grabbed his leg with his left hand, writhing in agony.

"Ahhhhhhhh!" he cried, angry and agonized as the paste continued to burn. "What are you doing to me?"

His hands flailed on the floor beside the straw mattress and landed on a pistol. He only faintly remembered finding it, but his instincts commanded his next actions. He jerked the Model 1911 sidearm from the floor, drew the slide to put a round in the chamber, and held it point-blank at the Korean woman's head. His finger quivered at the trigger. The fire in his leg continued to burn, and he jerked and trembled from the pain.

Through his hate-filled eyes, he watched fear overtake his enemy as sweat broke out on her brow.

"What are you doing to me, you stupid gook?" Jack demanded with a shout.

She replied as calmly as she could—but her words did not penetrate his still-deaf hearing, and if they had, nothing she said corresponded to the few words of Korean Jack knew.

Jack struggled to hold the pistol, but his hand began to tremble again, and his arm felt heavy. The gun in his hand felt like it weighed five pounds, and then twenty, and then fifty.

"My arm! I can't . . ." and his arm fell limp to the bed. Helpless, Jack watched as the Korean woman picked up his gun.

Will she kill me now like she tried to before? he wondered—not at all sure when "before" was, but remembering looking down the barrel of his own gun sometime before this moment.

Tae-bok held the gun and pondered it briefly. Bitterness rose within her again.

"I was trying to help you. You're a typical American. I try to save your life. You try to kill me. I saved you out there, and what do you care?"

Her peripheral vision caught movement. She glanced up to see her five-year-old son. Yong-ho walked playfully to the bedside, and Tae-bok quickly hid the gun behind her.

"Is he well, Mother?" Yong-ho asked simply as he reached over to brush the strange man's hair from his forehead. For a brief moment, Jack smiled at the little boy. It was perhaps the only kindness Jack had experienced in the past four months.

"Will he be all right, Mother?" he asked again.

"Yes, son. Please go to be with Grandfather."

His hearing coming back, Jack knew nothing of the words, but everything of the tone—it was the warm, familial tone he remembered from his days with his own mother, days that seemed worlds away. Days when his mom made the most splendid pancakes and bacon in the world. He remembered the way the smell drifted through the house. It was such a great way to go off to school in the morning.

His momentary diversion was shattered as the boy left the room. Tae-bok removed the gun from behind her back. She looked intently at him with jet-black eyes. She looked at the gun and then back at Jack. She spoke. He understood nothing. She spoke again—louder this time, but still nothing Jack could comprehend. Slowly, Tae-bok turned the gun around and returned it to Jack's hand. Cradling his limp hand, she moved the barrel directly to her head.

"If you will take my life, then take it and be done. I do not care anymore. I have lost enough for three lifetimes. Do whatever you want to do. We did not invite you to our country. You invited yourself. Kill me if you wish, but I will not kill anymore. My people and yours have killed far too many already. But if you wish, do what you must."

Jack still did not know the words. But yet again, he knew the tone. It was the same tone she used with her child. For the first time in a long time he felt something he scarcely recalled: compassion.

Her hand still cradled his, holding his hand as he held the gun —holding his hand so that he could hold the gun at her head. The absurdity of it all flashed through his mind as she eventually loosened her grip, and his weakened hand again fell to the bed. Jack dragged the gun back toward its place on his jacket on the floor. Tae-bok took his hand one more time and helped him.

She turned her back to him and returned to tending his wound.

Jack watched her closely for a few more minutes before he drifted out of consciousness.

* * *

Jack rolled in and out of consciousness as days and nights blended together. He awoke occasionally as Tae-bok fed him with an old battered spoon and gave him water from a dingy metal cup. She dipped an old wrap into hot water and gently cleaned weeks of dirt, grime, and blood from his face. The little boy returned also, and would sometimes crawl onto the straw-mat bed to check on this strange man until his mother ran him off.

He dreamed in ways he had never experienced before. He was back home in Midland, Texas. In vivid details, he saw the house and its long dirt drive. He saw the porch. Sometimes his dad was there. When he was in the dreams, he was there in a clearness that was more lucid than his waking thoughts. When awake, Jack couldn't draw back all the subtle details of his father's face, but in sleep—in dreams—every wrinkle, every scar, every intonation was all there again, in perfect detail.

Most of all, his mother was there. She was always standing—maybe in the kitchen, maybe on the porch, sometimes at the clothesline—always wearing the simple cotton billowy dresses. Always barefoot and always beautiful.

For reasons unknown to him, Jack would wake and be torn out of the placid beauty of his dreams. It took him a few minutes each time to figure out where he was. After a few minutes of uncomfortable disconnectedness, it would finally come back to him in sequence: boot camp, Korea, Pusan, Chosin, and now some long-lost village. When he was unable to sleep, Jack lay awake in the lonely black hours of the night wondering how he got here, how he would join up with the evacuation, and more important, how he was going to get home. As hard as he tried, he couldn't remember *where* the evacuation was taking place. Eventually, sleep would start to overtake him again, and he did his best to slip back into his preferred reality: thoughts of home.

Eventually, one of the passing mornings brought with it bright sunlight and a small but promising bit of mental clarity. The fog that dulled his thoughts was still there, but it had lifted just enough to hold promise that he might eventually feel whole again. His head still pounded and his leg still burned, but he could sense some improvement. He even heard noise outside the house for the first time in a few days. He surveyed his circumstances and observed that the little house, really just a two-room shack, seemed empty. With significant discomfort, he rolled onto his left side and began the arduous process of trying to lift himself up to a sitting position.

"Are you better?" he heard someone ask.

Am I hallucinating? The voice spoke English with a heavy Korean accent, but still something he could mostly understand.

"Are you better?" he heard again.

"Who are you? Where are you?"

"I am here," Tae-bok's father offered as he shuffled out of the shadows and away from the stove to the entrance of the room where Jack was recuperating.

Jack saw the slight, rail-thin Korean man appear suddenly at the door. His face looked like weathered leather and gave no sense of emotion that Jack could read. It was marked by empty, disfigured sockets. *He has no eyes.*

"I cannot see you, but I can hear you, and I think you can hear me also, yes?" Tae-bok's father said through his thick Korean accent.

"Do you speak English, or am I just hearing things?" Jack asked.

"Yes, I speak a little English. Are you surprised?"

"I am. I didn't think anybody here knew English."

"Well, we are not quite the savages you may think. Before the previous war, the Japanese occupied Korea. During that time, some missionaries came from Canada. So, we learned some English," he replied with a smile.

Jack studied the old Korean man's face and his disfigured eye sockets. "Are you blind?"

"Yes, I am blind," the old man replied.

"What do you want from me? Are you planning to kill me now?"

"Mr. Stiles, we did not rescue you from death only to impose our own death sentence on you. In any case, I believe you are the one with both the eyesight and the gun. It seems to me that the power to kill lies in your hand, not mine. Are you going to kill *me?*"

"No," Jack said, shaking his head. "I really just want to leave and join up with my company. I want to go home." He rubbed his aching head. "What day is it?"

"By your calendar, I believe it is the sixteenth day of

106

December. Where are you going?"

"I remember something about evacuation, somewhere on the coast . . ." Jack said, faltering. "The medic said something about an evacuation from a port city. I just don't remember the name."

The old man seemed to stand up straighter with interest. "An evacuation? What was the name?"

"I just don't remember. I've probably told you too much already."

"Is it Hungnam? Is your military evacuating you from Hungnam?"

Jack recognized the name, and recognition pumped sudden energy through his veins. "How far is it? Can you help me?"

"Please tell me if this is the place for the evacuation. Tell me, and I'll tell you how to get there."

"Yes, that must be the place—at least, that's what I think I remember. Now, how do I get there?"

The old man shuffled to Jack's position and put a slight hand on the Marine's shoulder. "You must not travel yet. Some more days, and then you should be strong enough to go. Please answer more questions for me. Why is your military evacuating?"

Jack painfully lowered himself back down onto the straw mattress, too weak to stay up anymore. "We've been up at Chosin Reservoir. Something like a hundred thousand Chinese troops came across the Yalu River and surrounded us. There's just too many. We had to retreat. Now that you've said the word, I'm sure that's the name of the city. Hungnam. The Chinese won't rest until they push us into the sea."

Tae-bok's father trembled at the revelation. While the Americans were enemies to the North Korean army, the North Korean and Chinese armies were enemies of all the Korean people.

Jack lay helpless on the firm bed as his head spun from his minor exertion.

"Mr. Stiles, I will speak again with you about this. You rest now."

Jack could hardly argue as he slumped back and rested. It seemed the slightest exertion left him drained and empty. Over the next few hours, he slept fitfully. Wild dreams filled his mind: dreams of war and combat, and more dreams of home.

In time, Tae-bok and her children returned to the little shack, and she prepared a meal in the small kitchen. The cooking and preparation filled the tiny house with the typical noises of a home, and Jack stirred from his sleep. His mind shook its way loose from the shadows as she reentered the small room, carrying with her a small bowl of food and the same disfigured spoon she had used previously. She rested softly on the edge of the straw mat and carefully offered Jack a spoonful of the soup. Jack carefully sipped. It had a sour taste that was unfamiliar to him, but his intense hunger prompted him to swallow it down happily.

"The old man speaks English—do you?"

Tae-bok looked inquisitively at the American soldier.

"Do you speak English?" he asked again and a bit slower.

"I speak some English. The old man of whom you speak is my father," she replied with a shy smile as she served Jack another spoonful. He took in her soft, delicate facial features. He realized he hadn't been around a woman in a very long time. It was nice to see her smile, and he couldn't resist a small grimace of a smile in return. It seemed like forever since he had found much of a reason to smile.

"I'm sorry. I didn't mean any disrespect."

"It is okay," she said as she inspected his wounded leg.

"So, what's your name?" Jack asked slowly.

"My name is Tae-bok. I am the one who found you. You seem a little stronger today. Your injury looks better."

"Tae-bok. That's a name I have not heard before. I feel better today. May I ask you something?"

108

"Yes," she replied, serving him another spoonful.

"Did any of the other men on my transport survive?"

"No. By the time I arrived, they were dead. You too were nearly dead."

Jack shook his head. It was all a fog to him. "I barely remember any of that. I do remember you pointing a gun at my face. Why did you do that?"

Tae-bok looked away, embarrassed at her actions. "I was angry."

"Angry with me? Why?"

"I was angry with all the American soldiers. Someone important to me was killed by an American soldier. For a few minutes, I thought I might avenge his death."

"So why didn't you?"

Tae-bok thought for a moment and served him another spoon of the bitter soup. "You were badly hurt. In those few moments I looked at you, I came to understand that even if I killed you, it would not bring back the one I have lost. I am tired of all the killing. I am tired of all the death. I made a decision that it stops now."

"Well, for my sake, I'm glad you made that decision. Thank you for saving me. My mother would be very pleased," Jack said with a smile.

"Mothers are important. You and your mother are welcome," Tae-bok said, smiling as she served Jack yet another spoonful.

"There's one other thing I'm not clear on. Why did you give me my gun back?" Jack asked, motioning to the pistol beside the mattress.

Tae-bok smiled. "I did not, at first. But then my son found it and wanted to play with it. I decided it was safer with you, and I did not believe you truly had the strength or the desire to kill me."

"Thank you, Tae-bok. Thank you for everything. You know, I'm probably strong enough to serve myself now. You don't have to keep serving me." But he quietly hoped she would linger.

She smiled and served him another spoonful.

Jack looked intently at her gentle features—her dark oval eyes, jet-black hair, and soft, olive-colored skin. And he smiled.

CHAPTER EIGHT

Improvement

The *Meredith Victory* arrived safely back at Pusan late in the evening on December 17. The crew busied themselves with necessary housekeeping. Fresh food was loaded and stored away under the direction of Chief Cook Herbert Lynch. Staff Officer Lunney dealt with the necessary matters of cargo documentation and paperwork, wrote the payroll records for the crew, and handled the occasional disciplinary matter. In the engine room, oilers attended to all the moving parts and pieces of the boilers and turbine.

The Japanese stevedores who worked on the *Meredith Victory* scrambled to and fro across the ship like a small army of ants as they wrested the cargo of jet fuel out of the edges of each hold and into the center of the hold directly below the hatches. From there, the ship's cranes plucked the fifty-five-gallon drums out of each hold and delicately swung them to the docks for further distribution. Chief Mate Savastio oversaw the loading and unloading of cargo and ensured it was distributed properly. The offloading of the cargo continued well past midnight. In the early morning hours of December 18, satisfied with the pace and progress of the unloading, Savastio went ashore to get details on their next destination and cargo.

The half-shaven harbor dispatcher looked over his clipboard

at Savastio. "How soon can you guys be ready to go? We need you up there right away."

Savastio did a couple of quick calculations. "Well, we got a fresh load of fuel earlier this evening. All we need to do is get the rest of the jet fuel off the ship. We probably won't be done until sunrise. I'm sure we can be ready to sail by noon if necessary."

"No, forget it. That's too late. Stop your offloading; we'll send you up there just as you are. Can you leave by sunrise? You got all your crew onboard?"

"Yeah—but don't they need the rest of our jet fuel here in Pusan?"

The dispatcher grimaced. "Forget about the jet fuel, Savastio. Just get north as fast as you can. Tell the crew they can sleep later. You've got until sunrise, and then I expect to see the south end of the *Meredith Victory* heading north. Here's your paperwork. All the signatures are there. Get that ship moving!"

Savastio took the packet from the dispatcher. "All right, all right. I'll tell the captain. Just give us a little time and we'll be on our way." Without delay, Savastio jogged down the length of the dock, dodging men, cargo, and equipment that was still being moved about in the early morning hours. Reaching the *Meredith Victory,* he scrambled back onto the deck and headed straight for the bridge to find the captain.

He burst onto the bridge half out of breath from his rapid climb up several of the ship's ladders.

"Captain. I need to talk with you, please."

"Sure. What's got you all worked up?" LaRue asked.

"We just got emergency orders," Savastio explained between huffing and puffing.

"Emergency orders where?" LaRue asked cautiously—as though not really sure he wanted to hear.

Savastio took a couple more breaths. "You won't believe it. Back to Hungnam, sir! We've been ordered to stop offloading the jet fuel. They want us out of here no later than sunrise."

"Sunrise? So much for the crew getting a little rest! And they want us to stop the offloading? How much jet fuel do we have left?" LaRue paced the small bridge, trying to make sense of the change of orders.

"I'm guessing we're down to about three hundred tons. They said just forget the jet fuel and get up to Hungnam fast."

LaRue nodded silently as he walked a few steps to the brass speaking tube. "Engine crew, get the boilers ready—we need to be underway by sunrise."

LaRue waited for the question he knew would work its way back up from the engine room.

"Uhh, Captain—you said sunrise?"

"Yes. Emergency orders."

"Okay, sir. We'll get the turbine warmed up. We'll get moving by sunup."

"Thank you, fellas. I always appreciate your work." LaRue turned away from the speaking tube and back to Savastio. "Obviously they're in a huge hurry. Did they say what the fuss was about?"

"Well, you remember the reason they said we couldn't offload the jet fuel in Hungnam. It was because MacArthur had ordered the retreat, right?"

"Yeah . . . go ahead."

"So the UN forces are fighting their way out of Chosin—the Communists have got them surrounded. Assuming our boys can break out, they're all heading down to Hungnam where the Navy is going to get them and everything of value out of there. But they're certain the Communists will also make a move south toward Hungnam. In the meantime, the civilians are already on the move. They're starting to move toward Hungnam as well."

LaRue grimaced and glanced at Staff Officer Lunney. Neither one liked the direction this was going. "Anyway, they want us to help take equipment and supplies out. They're determined not to leave so much as a can opener for the Communists."

Lunney thought for a moment. "Well, if there's anything I'm happy to do, it's depriving the Communists of everything of value. Let's get to it then. This ought to be interesting."

* * *

After two more days of being gently nursed back to health, while still slipping back and forth between waking and sleep, December 18 was finally a better day for Jack. Tae-bok thought a change of scenery might be useful, so she roamed around the village a bit, weaving her way between houses as nonchalantly as possible, until she was satisfied there were no North Korean or Chinese troops lingering about. Deciding it was safe, Tae-bok ushered Jack outside for some fresh air and a bit of morning sunlight.

"Mr. Stiles," she urged, "you should go outside. It is not as cold today, and the sunlight is good for you."

"Okay, let's see if this leg is up to the task."

He hobbled severely on his wounded leg—each step sending a wave of pain up his leg. Despite Tae-bok's assurances, it still felt quite cold outside, and he immediately missed the warmth of the little shack. But the sunlight on his face was rejuvenating, and it felt good to walk on his two feet again, albeit with a painful limp. The bullet wound in his right leg wasn't gone, but it looked far better than he had expected. Content that he was reasonably stable on his feet, Tae-bok returned inside.

In a few minutes, five-year-old Yong-ho joined him in the sun and dutifully brought Jack a stick and a few rocks. Jack looked down at the little boy holding a handful of rocks and a scrawny stick.

"Are these your toys, little man?" Jack asked. He couldn't help a fleeting thought that it had not been many years since he had lived in such innocence. Yong-ho cocked his head a bit. *Of course, he doesn't understand,* Jack thought.

"Let me show you," Jack said as he took the little stick and the rocks from Yong-ho. Yong-ho looked a bit puzzled, as though concerned that this man was taking his toys.

Jack held the stick like the finest bat in the hands of Hank Aaron. "Okay, now watch this. You see, the goal is to throw this rock in the air and smack it with this stick. Now, if you hit it right over there—between second and third base—you can easily make a single out of it. Okay? You got it, kid? Of course you do. Okay, let's try it."

He tossed a little rock into the air and swung mightily, hitting the little rock solidly and sending it flying twenty yards away. Jack let out a peal of laughter as he surprised even himself.

Yong-ho cackled with glee and toddled off on his little five-year-old legs in search of the rock. Finding it quickly, he returned it to Jack. Jack couldn't help but laugh.

"You like that, huh? Only problem is you're supposed to run the bases, kid."

"More!" Yong-ho said in Korean.

"I think you want me to do it again . . . okay, here goes," Jack said as he tossed another rock and swung. This time Jack missed wildly with an empty whoosh of the air. The rock dropped to the ground, and Yong-ho tilted his head with a puzzled look. Then he figured out the strange man's antics and laughed hilariously again.

"You missed!" the little boy said in Korean.

"I don't know what you said, but I'm thinking you like it more when I miss than when I hit," Jack laughed as he ruffled up the boy's hair. "Let's try again."

Another toss and swing, and Jack missed again. Yong-ho doubled his laughter and nearly fell to the frigid ground.

"You think that's funny, little man? Well, I don't remember you being recruited in high school for the minors!" Jack laughed, but the comment stirred back to memory something he had long since buried: thoughts of old dreams.

That seems like a lifetime ago, Jack thought. He had been a solid—not great—but a solid pitcher in high school. Scouts from a couple of the minor league teams were courting him for their farm teams. But that was when he loved Jessie, and at the time, he couldn't bear to move away and leave her behind. So he turned his back on the offers, and soon enough the war started and the military took care of the moving-away business for him. Jessie had declared her undying love for Jack and how she would wait for him no matter how long he was gone. Jack clenched his jaw as he reflected on her empty theatrics. In just a few months she had turned her back on him, and now little Jessie Nelson would become Mrs. Jason Baumgartner.

Baumgartner, Jack thought. *What a ridiculous name.* Jason had been two grades ahead of Jack in high school and about four levels of society above him in the real world. His daddy was a big oil man, and Jack figured Jason knew it. He certainly took every advantage of the situation. Jack seethed when he thought of that deferment for flat feet.

"Man! Man!" Yong-ho shouted as he tugged on Stiles's coat.

"Oh, sorry, buddy, drifted off for a second. Got any girls around here that you're sweet on?"

Yong-ho just looked inquisitively impatient.

"No, I didn't think so. Well, don't wait for 'em. Live your life, do your thing. Don't be a fool and wait around for something that will never happen."

Yong-ho smirked as though he was growing tired of all the strange language.

"Hit rock!" Yong-ho demanded.

"Okay, boy—let's try again." Jack threw the rock in the air, and this time he connected squarely and sent the little stone careening across the frozen field. Yong-ho erupted again in

116

shouts of glee, and Jack couldn't help but join in.

Inside the little shack, Tae-bok heard shrieks from her son, and her heart jumped. She peered through a seam in the wall where the sheet metal gapped and watched the American with her son. She saw him take Yong-ho by the hand and gently lead him around the field, limping as he went but moving slowly so the little boy could keep up. As they approached the place where they had been hitting the stones, she watched Jack pick up Yong-ho and carry him the final few steps before erupting in cheers. The American said something to her boy and then tossed another rock in the air and swung a stick. Tae-bok watched long enough to see the two of them collapse in hilarity at their mutual foolishness.

Tae-bok's curiosity piqued, and at least momentarily comfortable with Stiles's behavior, she kept watching. The man and her boy had made a game of hitting rocks, and her son was happier than she had seen him in a long time.

How long has it been since he has played? How long has it been since he has laughed?

She watched as Jack and Yong-ho spoke to each other, knowing neither understood a word of the other's tongue. Tae-bok smiled at her boy and his love of the moment. From a distance, she did not understand all the words the American spoke, but it really wasn't necessary—his laughter was universal.

"My daughter," her father said as he interrupted her quiet observation.

"Yes, Father," she said as she jumped slightly and turned to face him.

"The American is leaving soon. Maybe in a couple of days. He told me that his military is evacuating all of their men at Hungnam."

Tae-bok spun around to face her father. "Leaving? The US military is leaving?"

"He told me the Chinese forces at Chosin are too many for

the Americans. They must retreat. The Chinese will follow them to the sea. And that means the Chinese will be here soon."

Tae-bok's blood ran cold as she pondered what that meant. She turned back to Jack and Yong-ho as they played outside.

"My daughter, I have heard many American trucks passing near our village. You have seen them as well. You and I know the American speaks the truth. And you and I know the Chinese will not spare any of us. They believe we have aided the Americans."

Tae-bok did not reply.

"Indeed, my daughter, we have. We will surely face their punishment," he said. "You must leave with your children. This American will take you to Hungnam. He is grateful for what we have done for him, and I believe he will take you and the children also. You can leave and create a future."

Tae-bok stared out at Jack and her son. "You must come too, Father."

"That is not possible, my daughter. You know very well that I am much too old to travel, and I will only serve to keep you from reaching safety. You must leave me here."

"I will not, Father!" Tae-bok replied angrily as she spun around and cut her father off. Her disrespect was without precedent.

Her father gasped at her insolence. "Will you so disrespect your aged father?"

"I will not so disrespect my father as to leave him to certain death at the hands of the Chinese!" Tae-bok replied sharply.

Her father shuffled a bit closer to her. By the sound of her voice, he knew exactly how to place his weathered hand on her shoulder.

"My daughter, I am the past. You and your children are the future. I have lived my life. It has been a good life. Look around you. I lack for nothing. I know we do not have much, but I have the things that cannot be measured, and of those things, I have all and more than I need. Please listen now to this truth. We all must die. I will die some way and for some reason, surely not many months or years from now. Whether it is by the forces of the Chinese or by the forces of time, I will die regardless. But you do not have to die. Your children do not have to die. You and your children are the future."

Tae-bok abruptly turned away from her father. "I cannot do what you ask, Father. I will not disrespect you by leaving you to die at their hands."

"Then you will disrespect our family name by making certain your children—my grandchildren—will die in this place? Is that what you will do? Will their blood be on your hands so that you can have the privilege of accompanying me in my death?"

Her father's tone was stronger now. "Listen, my daughter. I believe this American soldier is a decent man. I do not have to see him to know this to be true. I have lived enough days to know that even good men can be swept up in the horror of war. This man can get you to safety. You can live. The children can live."

Tae-bok looked again through the crack in the wall and watched the man and her son playing and laughing. Tears welled in her eyes and began to stream down her face.

"I do not disagree with you, Father. I can see that he is indeed a good man. Last week, I wanted to kill him and almost did. But I could not. But no matter how good a man he is, I will not forsake you to certain death. Surely you remember what Mother always said?"

"I remember much of what she said," the old man said with a faint smile. "But what is it you have in mind, daughter?"

"She talked to us about hope. She said there is *always* hope, and that we must never abandon it. She said that when we lose hope, we have lost the *only* thing there is. I've lived on those words, Father, ever since the day the Japanese took her and my sister from us. You can't ask me to give up hope now. Those words have permitted me to survive this far. If I have no hope, then there truly is nothing more I can live for. Do you understand, Father?"

"I understand, Tae-bok, but hope is not gone. You must realize that hope is alive for you and these children. I am a very old man. I have no further need of hope. My life has been good. It has been full. Would I deny you and the children hope of escape so that you can hope foolishly for the salvation of an old man? To extinguish hope in that manner would be a true tragedy. Do not crush the hope of a new generation for the sake of one old man."

"Father, I can speak of this no further," Tae-bok cried. Tears welled in her eyes and threatened to pour down her cheeks. "You are not simply 'one old man.' You are my father; you are my only father and my only family. Please, no more of this discussion. I lost my mother and sister; I've lost my husband. How much more must I lose, Father? Will this war take the last bit of family that I have left? Must I pay this price again and again? Is there no end to my loss?"

Her father stood mutely for a moment, unable to suggest anything that might change her thinking. Then, with a soft whisper, he said, "Remember, daughter, it has been my loss too."

Tae-bok turned slowly away from her father and looked through a gap in the wall. She saw Jack kneeling on the ground next to her son.

She watched closely as the American gently helped her son write something with the stick in the frozen dirt. She heard them laugh and watched as Jack placed his other arm on the boy's shoulder and drew him close with a father's tenderness.

She swallowed hard. Her father's words rang in her ears. *"Do not crush the hope of a new generation for the sake of one old man."*

* * *

Captain LaRue stood confidently on the bridge as they hurriedly departed the harbor of Pusan. He possessed a calmness of demeanor that was infectious to his crew. It was a relaxed, yet certain confidence that stated clearly that he was the master of his ship.

As the *Meredith Victory* cleared the Pusan harbor, she began pushing against rough seas en route to Hungnam. Several hours outside of Pusan, her pace had significantly slowed as she plowed through the angry water. She rolled left to right in the turbulent waves, but always righted herself within a few seconds. Her bow was constantly bashed by rolling waves that splashed up over her forecastle, raced across her steel deck plating, and then drained off the port and starboard sides and back into the sea.

Her turbine engine produced its eighty-five hundred horsepower without fail and turned the shaft at a steady one hundred rpm, but she still struggled to make scarcely seven knots against the contrary seas.

LaRue found a certain peaceful calm in the command of his ship. He could have remained in his quarters, but instead he enjoyed quiet moments when he could stand on the bridge. He enjoyed watching his men work. He took it as a special responsibility to teach them and counsel them in the skills he had perfected over many years at sea. He viewed himself as more than the master of the *Meredith Victory*. He thought of himself as a servant to all.

Even more than his men, LaRue knew this ship. She was his, and he knew her through the subtle vibrations that spoke to him. She spoke to him. He guided her. Together they communicated. He took care of her, and she took care of him and his crew. He reckoned such thoughts would be absurd to those who had not lived on the sea, but he cared not for the false sensibilities of those who lived and died on land. He lived the sea, and his life depended upon this unique partnership with his ship: *her*.

The moment of quiet reflection was broken by a young officer with a message from the radio officer.

"Captain, message from the Navy, sir!" The young crew member handed the transcribed message to LaRue.

LaRue unfolded the small slip of paper and read it briefly. Without verbal reaction, he stroked his chin and disappeared in thought. He glanced away from the note, out across the ocean, and then around the bridge of his ship. *Was she up to it?*

"Son?"

"Yes, sir?"

"Have the radio operator tell them yes."

"What did they want? If I might ask, sir . . ."

LaRue's calm remained. "We knew that General MacArthur was retreating from a battle up at Chosin Reservoir—the Chinese have entered the fight. Twenty thousand Marines are surrounded and fighting their way out. They're going to try to make it down to Hungnam. From there they need to be evacuated . . . and . . ." LaRue faded off, looking far away, focused beyond the bow of his ship where the ocean's deep blue met the unending horizon of sky.

"Yes, sir?"

"The Chinese have made it clear that they will behead any of the Koreans left behind. They think the Koreans have sympathized with the American forces. The Koreans know it, and they're all fleeing to Hungnam. Thousands of them. They sent us up to Hungnam for cargo and equipment, but now they've asked if we can help with a humanitarian evacuation."

The young man balked. "Yes, sir, Captain, but they want *our* help? We've only got space for another fifteen or twenty men . . ."

"I'm well aware of the capabilities of my ship, son. Have the message sent at once."

"Yes, sir!" the young man said as he smartly turned and

walked back down the passageway to the radio shack.

LaRue looked over his ship's bow as it pushed through the angry waves. Each rolling wave crested over the rail and sent a shower of spray across the steel deck.

With both hands firmly clasped behind his back, contemplating the wisdom of what he had just agreed to, LaRue prayed silently.

May God Almighty be with us.

CHAPTER NINE

Honor

Jack felt quite sure the boy had never learned to play tic-tac-toe. He was right. Unfortunately, Jack lost three games out of five to Yong-ho—the humor of which seemed to slice through all the cultural barriers between them as Jack and the boy laughed at his trouncing defeat.

Their carefree frolicking having mostly run its course, Jack saw Tae-bok exit the house carrying a large water pot. Knowing the boy wouldn't understand, he nonetheless politely excused himself.

"I'll be back, kid—I need to help your mother."

Jack approached Tae-bok as she let the door close behind her. In the soft morning light, he found himself paying more attention to her delicate features. Her jet-black hair hung close around her face and rested lightly on her shoulders. She reached just barely to his shoulder and looked up at him with her large oval eyes, smiling. Her eyes seemed damp, almost as though she had been crying.

"May I?" he asked as he took the pot from her hands. Tae-bok smiled, agreed, and glanced away.

"Thank you. We need some water, please." She gestured to the pump house.

He glanced at her face again and noticed how young she looked. He judged her to be in her early twenties. Her slim features might have caused her to seem even younger back home. He smiled; her eyes met his and then retreated in shyness. *Funny,* Jack thought, *she didn't look nearly so pretty when she had a gun in my face.*

Jack hobbled along next to her as she pointed the way toward the pump house. The uneven path and frozen ground made the way slippery, and his arm bumped hers slightly as they walked side by side to the pump.

"Nice day, huh? What is it—maybe twenty degrees or so? Positively balmy, wouldn't you say?" Jack asked. Tae-bok smiled at Jack and nodded, not at all certain of her reply.

"Balmy? What does this mean?"

"I'm sorry—it means, uh, it's a nice day?"

"Yes, it is a nice day," she replied.

"How often must you get water?"

"Please watch your foot here," Tae-bok cautioned as they stepped down from a rocky ledge in the path. She stepped down deftly, but Jack moved much more slowly as he tried to navigate the small height difference with his injured leg.

"Are you okay?" Tae-bok asked, pausing for him.

"Yeah, I just can't bend it like I used to. Okay, so how often must you retrieve water?"

"Usually I go to the well twice a day. We take a small amount in the morning for drinking and cooking, if I can get rice. In the afternoon I sometimes get more for bathing."

He paused. "You said, 'if I can get rice.' Do you not always have rice?"

"No," Tae-bok said with a tight smile. "Rice is difficult to buy now, especially in the wintertime. The war destroyed much of the crop at the end of this past season. The fighting even destroyed some of the rice in storage. Now that winter is here, our supplies are very small. Sometimes we cannot find rice to buy."

"So what if you can buy no rice?"

"If we have no rice, I try to find something for the children to eat. Sometimes it is very little."

"What about you?" Jack asked, stopping in the pathway.

Tae-bok sensed he had stopped walking behind her. She paused as well and turned to answer. "If there is nothing to eat, I don't eat. I make sure the children eat first."

"How long does that go on?"

Tae-bok smiled again. "One time, it was six days before I could buy more rice."

"Six days?" Jack asked incredulously.

"Yes, six days. Up ahead, there is the well house. Shall we continue?"

"Yeah. Six days, and you had nothing to eat? What did you do?"

"Well, it is better not to ask," she smiled.

"Why? I don't understand," Jack said.

Tae-bok paused again. She spoke more softly. "My father has sometimes said that anyone who goes hungry for three days will be inclined to steal. My father speaks the truth. I do not say that what I have done is right. I do say that sometimes it seemed at the moment to be necessary. This is our life right now. Do you understand?"

Jack paused for a moment. "I do." He thought a bit more as they walked. "Can I ask you another question?"

"Yes."

"When you fed me, these past few days—where did you get the extra food?"

Tae-bok smiled as she thought about her reply. "I do not believe I mentioned anything about having extra food."

"Then how did you have enough food to feed me, the children, and you and your father?"

"I fed the children and you," she replied.

"What about you and your father?"

"Better not to ask," she said with a smile. "Here, we have arrived. This is where we get water."

Jack contemplated her answer for a moment and then felt tightness in his throat as the reality of her choices hit him squarely between the eyes.

The last few feet to the pump house were well-worn, and ice had collected along the dirt path. It made walking a bit tricky, and Jack maneuvered his injured leg carefully to avoid falling. Nearer to the pump house, water had frozen into a clean sheet of ice. Jack set the water pot down to open the door as Tae-bok stepped up to the small building. Without warning her foot slipped on the icy surface, and Jack quickly caught her in his arms to prevent her fall. He held her slim arm with his hand and wrapped his other arm around her back. She smiled appreciatively at him, and he looked at her closely.

"You okay?"

Tae-bok felt the warmness of his accidental embrace and the strength of his arms. She smiled. "I am fine. Thank you. Shall we get water now?"

"Sorry, I just thought you were going to fall," Jack explained as he released his hold and removed his arm from around her back. Tae-bok just smiled again. She opened the primitive door, and they stepped into the small well house.

Inside the small shack, the temperature was pleasingly warm. Jack had wondered how it was that they could keep the well from freezing over in such conditions, but like Tae-bok's house, the pump house had a small stove which provided some essential heat. Tae-bok and Jack warmed themselves from the heat of the little stove for a few minutes. As the cold left his fingers, Jack placed the pot under the mouth of the pump and began working the long red handle up and down. Each push begrudgingly exhumed a trickle of ice-cold water from deep within the earth. Operating the pump was far more difficult than he had imagined.

"Do you need help?" Tae-bok laughed.

"I suppose I probably do—I don't seem to have the strength I once had."

"Let me," Tae-bok said as she joined her hands to the red pump handle, nearly touching his.

"Ah, yes, much better," Jack noted as he much more easily operated the handle now, and the trickles of water turned into gushes.

"You are very tired from your long recovery. Now a woman is stronger than you!" Tae-bok laughed.

"Hey, hey, hey—I was nearly killed twice in the past week; I think the situation is understandable," Jack replied as he flashed her a quick smile. Tae-bok smiled back as they continued to persuade the water out of its dark lair far below the surface of the earth and into the pot. As the water nearly filled the pot, the pump gurgled, gasped, and hissed like some belching creature from the world below their feet.

Jack began to laugh uncontrollably.

"What is it? What is funny?"

"This pump," Jack answered between fits of laughter. "The thing must be a hundred and fifty years old. Sounds like it has some serious intestinal problems."

"It makes these noises sometimes," Tae-bok innocently replied. "I have never thought of it as funny. What is instest . . ."

Jack tried to compose himself. "It's, uh . . . never mind." Jack quaked with uncontrollable laughter again. His eyes watered as he tried to restrain himself. "What did you ask me?"

"What is instest . . . that problem you said it had? Why are you still laughing? What is funny?"

The silliness of it all was too much for Jack, and he broke down again. Now Tae-bok began laughing, but she didn't let it go.

"What did I say? What is funny?" she asked more urgently now.

"It's just the way you said it." Jack searched for a suitable explanation. "What I said about the pump, it means the pump ate some bad food."

"Oooh . . ." Tae-bok said as she pondered the illustration. "But the pump does not eat food. What do you mean?"

Jack wiped more tears from his eyes. "Don't worry; it's okay. I'm just being silly. I do feel better now," Jack said. "I don't think I've laughed the whole time I've been in your country. That actually felt pretty good."

"Are you okay now?" she asked cautiously.

Jack breathed deeply, filling his lungs with the damp air. "Yes. I'm okay now. Hey, what is that in the water?"

Tae-bok crouched close to the pot of water, nearly full to the brim, to get a good look. "What do you see?"

"It's right there—don't you see it? What is it?"

"I do not see anything. Where?"

"Right here," Jack pointed with his fingers just as he slapped a dash of frigid water into Tae-bok's face. Tae-bok sputtered, wiped her face, and scowled at him.

Jack feared he had overstepped some unrealized social bounds. He suddenly felt very stupid. "Hey, I'm sorry, Tae-bok, I was just messing around. I shouldn't have done that . . ."

Tae-bok erupted into laughter. "You are a very strange man, Mr. Stiles. First you laugh at our water pump. Then you tell me the pump is sick and has eaten bad food. Now you splash me with water in my face. I will not trust you, Mr. Stiles. I must warn my father about you." She laughed again.

Jack joined her in laughter, deeply relieved that his feeble attempt at humor had somehow successfully crossed cultural divides. "Okay, I suppose I deserved that. Let's go, I'll carry it back to the house."

Jack estimated the pot held about five gallons of water. Filled, its forty-plus pounds added to the struggle he was having with his injured leg. Tae-bok noticed and helped hold the edge of the pot as they hobbled back together.

Their fingers touched slightly as they worked together, something Jack was not at all unhappy about.

* * *

Since leaving their home in Unchon-ri a week earlier, Dong-hyuck and his father had walked all day, every day. They rested briefly at night, finding some small shelter from the elements, huddling together to preserve their precious heat. They rationed their small amount of food so they would hopefully arrive with a small amount to spare. Through bitter snow and driving wind, they slowly trod their way toward Hungnam. The unrelenting wind, bitter cold, and icy snow wore away at their exposed skin.

Finally arriving on the periphery of Hungnam, Dong-hyuck and his father said good-bye to their friends and travel companions and began their own search for safe passage out of the harbor city. They all thought it best to split up in their search for transportation out of North Korea. They believed they could move through the city more nimbly as a small group, and more effectively find safe passage out of the city.

They now spent their time meandering around the streets of Hungnam. They searched for information and options. They talked to an endless stream of refugees just like themselves. They spoke of escape and food and rumors. They added together little threads of information, stitched together rumors and suppositions, and wove them all into the fabric of belief and hope. They clung to their bundles of possessions even though they were repeatedly told there was no room on the ships for their things.

Byung-soon eventually had heard that claim enough. It was, he grudgingly decided, a painful but small price to pay to increase their odds of escape. And so they made a short walk through Hungnam and stood on the edge of a trash pit used by the city's residents.

"Son, put as much rice into your pockets as you can. When you've filled your pockets, we must discard our bundles and throw them into the pit."

"Everything, Father? We have all of our linens and blankets here, things we need for our trip."

"I know, but we hear the same thing from many. They will not let us on the ships with all of these things. We must discard them here. Remember, these are only material possessions. These things can be replaced."

Dong-hyuck did not look convinced. He looked at the mounds of trash filling the pit. Several pigs braved the cold and rummaged among the piles, looking for something remotely edible. He could scarcely see the wisdom of throwing their remaining possessions into this trash pit.

His father sensed his reluctance. "Son, these things are just our material possessions. When we've thrown them all away, we will still have each other. And at the moment, that is what counts the most." He smiled at his boy.

"I know, Father. I understand," he said reluctantly.

"What is it Dong-hyuck? What is wrong?"

"I only wish Mother and the rest of the family could have come with us. When will we see them again?"

"It should not be too long. I believe the Americans will return to the north after they reorganize in the south. When that happens, and as soon as we get settled, we'll arrange for the family to travel to us in the south. Let us not be occupied with these matters now. Finish taking some rice for yourself, and then help me get rid of our bundles."

When his coat pockets could hold no more rice, Dong-hyuck helped his father take their bundles and hurl them into the trash pit. They watched as their last few possessions bounced across heaps of refuse and careened to a stop in the middle of the pit. Father and son reluctantly turned and walked away.

* * *

The morning of December 19 brought a light snowfall to the village of Oro-ri. It also brought the monotonous noise of military transport trucks coming out of the mountains, passing down the main supply route not far from Oro-ri, and heading south toward Hungnam. The noise woke Jack from his light sleep. He recognized the sound and knew the Army and Marines were on the move.

Jack dragged his aching leg out of the bed and rested it painfully on the floor. He winced. It was worse in the mornings. He tried to calculate how far and how fast he might be able to walk. A solid knock on the rickety door interrupted his calculations.

"Mr. Stiles, may I speak to you?"

"Yes, please come in."

It was Tae-bok's father. "Are you leaving soon?"

"Yes—I think I must be on my way tomorrow. I'm sorry; perhaps I've stayed too long. I am very grateful for all that you and your daughter have done. I really can't think of any way to thank you enough." Jack studied the man's slight, almost frail frame. He seemed in poor health and perhaps malnourished.

"I can think of a way you might thank me, Mr. Stiles."

"How so?" Jack asked warily.

"My daughter and her children *must* go with you," Tae-bok's father said abruptly, in an authoritarian but strangely emotionless way.

Jack considered the father's declaration. He could not deny that he felt something for Tae-bok and her children. It occurred to him that perhaps his role in this war was not so grandiose as bringing about the collapse of Communism, but perhaps something much more personal.

"I wish she would. I probably can get her to safety. But all of you need to leave. You also should leave. I think you understand what the Chinese will do to you—to all of you."

"I am very aware of this. But I am far too weak to travel. I will slow down the others and put them all in danger. The real problem, Mr. Stiles, is that my daughter refuses to leave without me." Tae-bok's father paused. "I wish for you to speak to her."

"I'm happy to do that, but I really doubt she will listen to me."

"You talk. It will do some good," the old man quickly offered, as though that was the sum total of the matter.

Without warning, the thin door opened, and Tae-bok entered the room. She looked at her father and then at Jack. She sensed this was no casual conversation.

"Am I interrupting something, Father?" she asked in Korean.

"Tae-bok," her father started, "I have asked Mr. Stiles to take you and the children south to Hungnam with him."

She scowled, continuing to speak in Korean. "I was very clear with you, Father. I will not leave you behind. If you are trying to arrange something, you are wasting your time. We can head farther south on our own. Or we will simply stay here. We will be fine."

Jack discerned from the tone that her answer was intensely negative. *Why so stubborn? Has she got some sort of a death wish?*

"Tae-bok, will you listen to me, perhaps?" Jack asked.

"Mr. Stiles, please do not speak. This involves only me and my father."

Jack ignored her and took a step closer. "Tae-bok, please, listen to me. You *will* die here. If you come with me, I think I can get you to safety. I don't know where exactly, but I think we can get you and your children someplace safe. You will live. This is

133

what your father wants."

Tae-bok listened to him, but her face grew rigid and stern.

"Mr. Stiles, I ask you again, please do not speak. This is not your concern."

"It is my concern, Tae-bok. I care about what happens to you and your children."

She moved close to Jack and looked him in the eye. It made Jack a bit uneasy, but he wasn't sure why—this little five-foot-tall Asian woman looking up at his muscular frame.

"Mr. Stiles. The answer is no, I will not leave this place and leave my father. Do not speak any further of this. I do not know why you are concerned for me and my children. Please do not mistake a few moments of laughter for something more than it was." Tae-bok turned away from Jack.

"Tae-bok, look, you *need* to leave. There's nothing left here for you. There's no future here, there's no hope. There's no reason to stay." Jack watched her closely for signs that she was softening. She didn't respond. "Look, don't be stupid. Do it for your children if for no one else. Don't condemn them to live like this the rest of their lives—their short lives—in this worthless, forsaken little village. All there is here is death. I've seen firsthand what they will do to you. I've seen what they do to villages when they think they've helped the Americans. I've seen the mutilated bodies of men and women when the Chinese and the North Korean People's Army think they're dealing with traitors. Get out of this pit while you still can. There's so much more of the world out there."

Tae-bok spun around and glared at Jack. She closed the few feet of distance to him and without warning shot her right arm forward and across and laid a harsh slap across Jack's face.

"Please translate this, Father," she said in Korean, and she turned angry eyes on Jack again. "Perhaps I should have killed you when I had the chance. I brought you into this house and fixed your wounds. I restored your strength. Now you insult my people and my land. You insult my father. You insult my children. This matter of which you speak is *none* of your concern. Leave tomorrow morning and no later."

A dead-still silence slowly filled the house.

Her father spoke softly. "She wants me to tell you that you need to leave by tomorrow," he said. "I'm sorry, Mr. Stiles. I was wrong to involve you in this discussion."

Tae-bok still stared directly at Jack. He massaged his reddened cheek to rub out the pain and looked deep into her jet-black eyes. He nodded his head and replied simply, "You want me gone? You can consider it done."

Satisfied with his answer, Tae-bok turned and exited the door of her house.

Jack's emotions churned a bitter mixture of regret, anger, and grief. He convinced himself that she had obviously not seen the realities of war and was clinging naively to some simplistic notion of honor. He turned toward her father. The old man seemed resigned to failure.

"It's fine, we did what we could. It's her choice now," Jack said.

* * *

LaRue stood on the bridge of the *Meredith Victory* as the morning's sun warmed away the chill on the ocean breeze. She was just a day and a half or so from Hungnam, and he pondered what might lay in store for them with the planned evacuation. His calendar on the bridge said December 19, and he hoped they could conduct their business quickly and be on their way. His duties prevented giving much notice to the reality that Christmas was less than a week away.

"Captain—we've got another message from the Navy, sir!" the

young man reported.

"All right, let's see what you've got."

LaRue opened the folded message and read it carefully.

He gave a little half-snicker, intended really only for himself, and then exhaled deeply.

"Gentlemen," he announced to his bridge crew, "when we arrive in Hungnam, we'll need to anchor a couple of miles from the harbor entrance."

"Two miles out from the harbor?" the senior officer on deck asked with a puzzled look.

"Yes, sir, two miles out—we'll need to wait for further instructions before continuing in."

"Yes, sir, Captain. Two miles off the entrance to the port. Plot a course, gentlemen."

* * *

Intensely frustrated by the morning's events, Jack roamed the village and the surrounding hills for several hours in a feeble effort to walk out his anger. The whole landscape before him was strangely monochromatic: gray clouds in the sky, gray snow on the ground, gray, flat, and without contrast. After the sun had reached its peak for the day and started its slow decline, he turned toward Tae-bok's house and walked along the main road leading into the village. For the first time in his walks, he stopped and stared at the burned-out wreckage of a US military transport truck. The front half had been pulverized by an explosive, the steel bent and grotesquely deformed. A light dusting of snow covered most of it, camouflaging it with the rest of the nondescript landscape. It took a few moments, but he slowly recognized it as the truck he had been transported on.

"Great," Jack muttered to himself. "Didn't take 'em long to strip it bare." The tires were long gone. What was still salvageable of the heavy canvas covering the back of the truck had been stripped and no doubt quickly repurposed. Pieces of sheet metal had been pried away and were certainly now serving as parts of a wall or roof for some nearby shack. Jack walked the length of the old truck, kicking little pieces of fractured metal too small to be of any use to the Koreans. He kicked one fist-sized piece twenty or thirty feet and watched it skittering across the snow-covered road and into the ditch. He walked in the direction of its resting place.

As he got closer, he caught sight of a small bit of debris sticking out from a snowbank alongside the road. He looked at it intently, not sure at all what it was. But as he closed the distance, he made out the shape of a small book. Drawing closer still, he realized it was no ordinary small book.

"My journal?" he asked himself out loud. "I can't believe I found it." Jack bent and retrieved it from the snow. He thumbed through the frozen pages. The leather cover was singed in spots and stiff from the cold temperatures, but otherwise it seemed intact. Jack looked for the most recent entry. He processed his own writing and placed the narrative as having occurred just a day before Edgar was killed.

"Well, I've got a little catching up to do." Jack tucked the book into his jacket and headed back to the warmth of Tae-bok's house. When he reached the primitive door, he opened it gently and stepped inside. The heat, albeit little, was a welcome contrast to the bitterness of the outside air.

His eyes adjusted slowly to the darkness of the house, chased away only by the flickering of two small candles. He noticed the two children snuggled together, napping on a small blanket—not even a pillow for their heads. The old man sat in a small chair, upright yet asleep, his head tilted forward.

Jack watched Tae-bok working in the small kitchen. She glanced at him briefly, their eyes meeting for scarcely a second before she abruptly turned away in a universally understood expression of disgust.

* * *

For the remainder of the day, Jack sat quietly on the small bed. He wrote in the small diary and recorded all the events since he had left Chosin. He paused occasionally as he struggled against his faded memory, wrestled with the tragedy of Edgar's death, and debated why he had arrived at this village.

As day gave way to the rise of evening, Jack sat quietly on the floor and played a few more games of tic-tac-toe with Yong-ho. The primitive candles cast long and wavering shadows across the floor and over their games. The boy had found a few small rocks that could leave a mark on the stone floor. With each round's conclusion, Jack and the boy scrubbed the floor with their hands and wiped the slate clean. Besides the value of the simple entertainment, the warmth of the stone floor felt good on his leg.

Tae-bok worked in the adjoining kitchen. Through the unsteady light, she caught his eye more than once—but Jack reminded himself it was time to move on. Still, his curiosity was too great, and he watched as Tae-bok dug into a small bag and emptied the last of the bag's rice into a small pot sitting over a pale yellow flame.

Outside, the wind howled especially hard around the small house, finding spots where it could blow its bitter temperatures into the living area. The candles gyrated wildly in the bitter draft, threatened to surrender to the breeze, and righted themselves finally. Jack looked up from his game and spotted a hole between two pieces of wood where the old rags used to seal the gap had been pulled away by the wind. Jack awkwardly hoisted himself back to his feet.

"Excuse me, boy, I need to take care of something real quick.

You stay here."

Yong-ho looked confused, but he had grown accustomed to Jack patting him on the head affectionately while uttering strange words. "Okay," the small boy answered back in the one word of English he knew.

Jack felt the bitter cold air pouring in through the gap between the rickety wall panels of the house. He spent a few minutes attempting to plug the gap from the inside. Eventually, the old rags seemed to find a place where they could at least temporarily lodge and resist the subfreezing outside air.

Jack turned back toward the kitchen and noticed Tae-bok watching him, but she did not speak.

"I'll be back." Jack grabbed his heavy jacket and bundled himself against the cold. He picked up the pitcher of water Tae-bok had earlier emptied and stepped out into the night. The frigid air burned his nose, and he inhaled deeply, waiting for his eyes to adjust to the dark.

When his eyes grew accustomed to the limited light, Jack eased his way back down the worn trail to the pump house. He stepped gingerly inside, avoiding the frozen patch on which Tae-bok had slipped. Jack pumped the long red handle for a few minutes until the pot was about half-full. He thought wistfully about the pleasant moments they had shared, on one hand cursing the weakness of his emotions, on the other hand longing for a few more minutes with her. And yet he hated her unyielding stubbornness, her refusal to consider reasonable options. It would be a lot easier to simply not care.

He continued to work the handle of the old pump as he debated his conflicting emotions. If Edgar had been here, he would have had some words of wisdom to share. *If only Edgar were here.*

A creak of the old door interrupted his thoughts. Jack backed away, unsure of who or what was entering. The door sliced open just slightly before a small face peered into the gap.

"Hi," Yong-ho said in English with a huge smile.

Jack smiled. "I see you're learning fast. Hi to you too."

"Hi," the boy repeated, showing his full set of white teeth, and then disappeared back into the night.

Jack's mind wandered back to far more innocent, simple, days in Texas.

* * *

Jack carried the pot cautiously back to the house and found the corner of the house with the rags just barely holding steady against the wind. He gently raised the heavy pitcher and poured the water along the gap, soaking the rags and causing them to swell. By his estimate, it would only take a few minutes for them to freeze. He watched in the dark, using the glimmer from the waning moon to illuminate his subject as he huddled against the howling wind.

As he suspected, the rags froze in just minutes, forming a nearly impenetrable barrier against the drafts. Feeling rather satisfied with his own creativity, he found a few more spots that could benefit and gave them the same treatment. *This ought to last them until May,* he laughed to himself.

Having exhausted the water, Jack rounded the corner and reentered the house.

Tae-bok turned to him from the stove. "What did you do outside, Mr. Stiles?"

"I soaked the rags that you're using to seal the cracks. The water makes them get bigger. They'll freeze. They'll seal better that way and keep more of the cold out. I think it will help."

"Thank you. We are grateful for your help. Will you take some rice?" she asked as she handed him a small bowl of white rice.

"No, that's not necessary."

"You'll need it for strength for your travels. Please take some rice, Mr. Stiles."

Jack couldn't argue. He looked at the rice and realized he had not eaten all day. "Okay, fine. Thank you."

* * *

In the distance, hiding around the corner of an adjacent house and immersed in its shadow, a young Chinese soldier took special interest in the sight of an American soldier disappearing into the little shack. His superiors would be pleased.

He scampered off into the night.

CHAPTER TEN
Blood

Jack woke the morning of December 20 feeling even stronger and almost back to a semi-normal measure of life: he felt stronger, his mind was clearer, he felt confident in his recovery. The past few mornings had brought successive improvement. He dressed quickly and tucked his pistol under the small pillow and out of sight of the children. As he entered the main living area, Tae-bok was bundling herself up.

"Where's she going?" Jack asked of her father.

"She is going to the next village. She is hoping to buy some food there. We have no more rice."

"Hey, Tae-bok. May I come?" Jack asked.

"You are leaving today. Do you remember?" she replied stiffly.

"Of course I remember. I think you made that very clear yesterday. How long does it take to get to this village?"

"It is a walk of about two hours."

"Well, I'm not scheduled to leave for about four hours—so I guess I'll go with you," Jack laughed.

"What is the purpose of you coming?"

Jack thought quickly. "I need some fresh air. I need to exercise this leg before I head for Hungnam." Jack fished in his pocket for a moment, remembering that US dollars were highly prized by the Koreans. "Here—maybe you can use a few dollars to buy rice, huh?"

Tae-bok looked a bit skeptically at Jack, and then she snatched the tattered dollars out of his hand.

"Thank you," she curtly replied.

Tae-bok finished bundling the coat around her while Jack quickly threw his coat on. Her father sat near the fire holding the infant while Yong-ho drew scribbles on the floor.

Tae-bok stepped out into the cold as Jack followed closely behind.

* * *

Their walk was mostly silent for the first thirty minutes or so. Tae-bok walked amazingly fast for a small woman, and Jack struggled to keep up on his bad leg. Tae-bok didn't want to talk, and Jack wasn't quite sure what to say or where to begin. He was quite sure there was little changing her mind. Her decision had been made abundantly clear.

"Tae-bok, slow down for just a moment, okay?"

Tae-bok slowed a bit as Jack caught up. She looked annoyed by the delay.

"Listen, I want to apologize for what I said yesterday. I'm sorry," Jack emphasized as he touched her slightly on her arm. "I didn't mean to insult you, or your people, or your country. I didn't mean to do any of that, but I obviously did. I'm sorry. Do you understand?"

Tae-bok looked cautiously at him.

"Please, I'm sorry."

Tae-bok sighed deeply. "You know nothing about us. You think that because we are poor and because we don't live like you, that this makes us animals. You think because our nation is divided by war, that we have no value. I have heard only a little bit of the history of your nation, but I believe that even your nation has been divided by war. Is this true?"

143

He winced inwardly, remembering the long conversations with Edgar and his vivid characterizations of the North Koreans as mere animals. She didn't know how right she was. "Yes, that is true. Again, I'm sorry for what I said. It's just that I think you really should consider leaving. The Chinese have made it very clear: it's death, or at best a prison camp, for you and your children. However you live now and however you feel about how you live now, this life is over. You will be captured. A prison camp is not what you want."

She considered his comment and replied in a calm, predetermined fashion, as if the matter had been decided a very long time ago. "You are right, Mr. Stiles. But sometimes, there is no suitable choice. You would have me leave my father? He cannot travel. That is not possible. It will kill him to travel, and thus we will not leave him. If you agree that a prison camp is no way for us to live, do you suppose it is suitable for my father?" Tae-bok stopped and turned to face Jack.

"Well, no, it's not suitable for him either, it's just that . . ."

"What you do not understand about us is that we believe in unconditional honor. We believe in respect for our elders. Perhaps you do not believe in such a thing. What you suggest I do is unthinkable. I cannot leave him behind. It may be that I do not know what will happen to us. But I have learned that when I have doubts about which choice is the right choice, I must always choose that which is honorable and respectful. The rest will take care of itself."

"Look, Tae-bok, I don't quarrel with that. What you propose, staying here, is honorable. I can't deny that. Doing what is honorable and right is always right. My point is just that there are two right choices. There are two honorable things that you must choose between. One is securing the future for you and your children. The other is respecting and honoring your father. Both are proper choices. *Both* must be considered. But right now, you

144

are rejecting the one choice without consideration."

Jack paused for a moment to catch his breath a bit as they crested the top of a small hill. "Listen, I don't have the answers. Obviously I can't make the choice for you. And there is a lot I don't understand, and there is a lot I don't know. But I do understand this, and I do know this: your father, the man you respect and honor, believes you should leave."

Tae-bok paused in her walk for a moment. She turned to her left as Jack caught up.

"Mr. Stiles . . ." She paused thoughtfully.

"Isn't it time you call me Jack?" he asked with a smile.

"Fine. Jack. Do you have a father?"

"I did. He died a few years back."

"I am sorry. Did you always do everything he suggested you do?"

Tae-bok's question made Jack pause. He replayed in his mind a few encounters with his father he wished he could do over.

"No, I don't suppose I did."

Tae-bok smiled. "Then it seems we have something in common, Jack," and she resumed her walk toward the distant village.

A few minutes passed without further conversation. Jack tried to think of some way to resume the headway he hoped he was making.

"Tae-bok, can we stop for a few minutes? I just need to rest my leg."

"The big American soldier, Jack Stiles, needs to rest?" Tae-bok asked with a touch of sarcasm.

"I'm a Marine, not just a 'soldier,' and yes, if you will recall, I've got a bullet hole in my leg, and I was nearly killed by a bomb. I need just a short rest."

"Fine, we will sit here," she said, motioning to a rocky outcropping along the walking trail. Jack brushed a light coating of snow off the rocks and gladly sat, stretching out his leg and gently massaging his cramping muscles. Tae-bok sat next to him, not close, but not distant either. He looked over the small valley into which they were now descending. He examined the undulating hills that ringed the valley. Although it was mostly snow-covered, he imagined the scene in more peaceful times. The morning sun was breaking through the clouds and casting long shadows across the valley. In the distance, the low, rolling thunder of back-and-forth artillery battles echoed—a firm reminder that the country was still at war.

"Your country is very beautiful. I'd like to see it in the spring —when everything is green."

"So now you like our country, is that it?"

"It's just that I have not really had a chance to sit still and think about it without having someone try to shoot me. But yes, truthfully, it seems very nice. I wish I could see it separate from war."

"I wish that I could see it separate from war as well," she replied softly. "It has already been a long time. The flat section over there. Do you see it?" Tae-bok gestured to the far end of the valley floor. Jack nodded.

"In the summer, we grow rice there. I have fond memories of working those rice fields as a little girl. Then the Japanese came to our area more and more. Then everything changed."

"How so?" Jack asked.

Tae-bok grimaced a bit and shook her head as she turned away. "It is better not to ask."

Jack tried a different topic. "Okay. Do you have family?"

"Do I have family? You know my family. Why do you ask?" she asked curtly.

"No, I mean, besides your father and your children. Where is your husband?"

"My husband? You want to know where my husband is, Jack

Stiles? I suspect you do not really want to know where my husband is."

"Yes, actually I do. I'm interested—believe me, I'd really like to . . ."

"Why do you want to know?"

"Well, it's what people do when they try to communicate. They try to learn something about each other. That's normal, don't you think?"

Tae-bok cinched her jacket tighter against the morning cold. "Fine. My husband is there." She pointed to a place on an adjacent hill.

"He's there? What do you mean? He doesn't live with you?"

"No, he doesn't live with me. My husband is dead. That is where I buried his body—on that hill."

"Oh . . . I had no idea. I'm very sorry." Jack sat silently.

"Now you can ask the next question."

"Okay. *How* did he die?" Jack asked softly.

Tae-bok's eyes narrowed as she looked across the valley. "He was a simple farmer. A gentle man. He had a certain way with animals. Of course, he planted rice and worked the fields as we all did, but he really loved taking care of the animals. The other villagers said he could talk to them. He could not, of course, but it was like he could. They trusted him."

"What happened?"

Tae-bok delayed answering, as if first replaying painful memories in her mind.

"The North Korean People's Army came for him earlier this year. They came for him and any other man, or even boy, who could hold a gun." Tae-bok gritted her jaw tightly as the pain of it all came flooding back. She turned and looked Jack squarely in the eye. "I am told he fought bravely in many battles. But then he was shot by an American soldier."

She looked away and stared at the ground. "A few of his

friends, men from the village here, brought me his body. I took him up there," she said, looking back at the adjacent hill. "It was a favorite place of his. I dug a hole and put his body in it."

Jack's gut wrenched as she poured forth her details. He could not help but think of Edgar's lifeless body. He shook his head gently, not knowing what to say. "I'm really sorry, Tae-bok . . . I had no idea."

"One of your American soldiers, or 'Marines' or whatever you want to call them—men trained to kill other men, men skilled in all the arts of fighting. They killed my peasant farmer husband."

"I really don't know what to say. I'm just so very . . ."

"How do I know it wasn't you that killed him?" She looked up at Jack, her eyes wet with tears.

Jack froze, unable to breathe. Through his mind flickered the faces of all the men he had killed. *Brutal beasts,* he had thought at the time. Jack hung his head, unable to bring himself to look her in the eye. At the time, his finger had itched to pull the trigger. *Such a simple pull of the finger to snuff out a life.*

His answer came slowly. "I will admit, I have killed many such men. There was a time when that did not concern me. But I will tell you that it bothers me much more now. I wish it had not been necessary. They surely would have killed me without thinking if I had not acted decisively. But whether right or wrong, I know I will live with my actions for the rest of my life. I hope you understand that in war, sometimes we have no choice. Just as I believe your husband did not have a choice."

Long, painful minutes crept by. Tae-bok spoke first.

"I do understand the difficulty of war. I know this firsthand. I too have taken life. And I too believed, perhaps correctly, that I had no other choice. And as you have said, I will also live with my choices." She paused and then changed the topic. "You told me of your father. Do you have any other family?"

Jack pondered the question for a few seconds.

"Yes. Some are still living, some are dead. Most are dead, I suppose. My brother, he was my older brother, he died in World War II. He was killed fighting the Japanese. My father was badly wounded in the first war, and he never could deal with the loss of my brother. He died just a few months later." Jack fought back the rising lump in his throat. "And I had this good friend, Edgar. He was like a brother to me. My brother died when I was about fifteen. Edgar . . ." Jack trailed off.

"Yes?" Tae-bok asked.

"He died just before you found me. A Chinese soldier killed him in a firefight. At the same time I was injured, he was killed. Should have been me. He was gone before I ever realized anything was wrong. Somehow I thought he and I would go back to Texas, and life would resume just like it was before the war. Obviously, that will never happen now." Jack's mind flickered to a haunting image of immaculately dressed Marines arriving at Edgar's house to notify his unsuspecting parents that their only child was dead—images he was sure had already played out halfway around the world.

Her voice had softened. "Perhaps we have a little more in common than we realized, Jack. Your brother died fighting the Japanese. Is this what you said?"

"Yes, on an island called Iwo Jima."

"I have never heard of it. I am sure the death of your brother was very sad. You never asked me about my mother. Do you have a mother, Jack?"

"Yes, don't we all?" Jack managed a slight smile. "She's the most wonderful person on the face of the earth. I look at my watch sometimes and think about what she's doing right now. See, right now she's sleeping. She's all alone in our farmhouse back in Texas. In a few hours, she'll wake up and start her day. I see her all the time. She wore these cotton dresses; she'll be standing outside hanging laundry on the line, gentle breezes blowing the laundry to and fro. I'd give a lot to be back home right now."

"I can tell she means a lot to you. I hope you get to see her very soon."

"Me too. I can't wait to get home."

Tae-bok paused, contemplating her words.

"Jack, home is important to you, is it not?"

"Very. That's where I feel I'm supposed to be."

"You really do not know much about my home, do you? You know very little about Korea."

"No, I really don't. I'm sorry. All I know is that they put me on a ship, sent me over here, put a rifle in my hand, and told me to fight."

"That is unfortunate, Jack. The things you could learn about us might prove to have value. Do you remember your President Wilson? Is that his name?"

"Sure . . . I mean, he died before I was born, but my father used to talk about him."

"Well, your President Wilson gave a speech in 1918 that was called, 'The Fourteen Points.' He later spoke at what you call the Paris Peace Conference in 1919. Part of what your president argued for was the right of a people to determine their own form of government and rule."

The story sounded familiar—something he had learned in school. "Yeah, I remember hearing about some of his speeches in one of my history classes back home. For me it wasn't very interesting, I suppose."

"Well, in Korea we heard about your President Wilson's speech. We had been under the control of the Japanese since 1910 and hated what they were doing to our people and to our culture. They even prohibited Koreans from using Korean names —we were required to give our children Japanese names. On March 1 of 1919, millions of Koreans assembled in thousands of protests all around the country to try to get the Japanese to change so that we might have the self-determination of which your President Wilson spoke. We even wrote our own Declaration of Independence, and many men signed it."

Jack pondered what he previously had judged impossible. *A Declaration of Independence? In Korea?* "Did it have an effect?" Jack asked.

"It did have an effect, but not the effect we were hoping for. The Japanese massacred our people. More than seven thousand were killed in one day. Perhaps more than fifteen thousand were wounded, and more than forty-five thousand were arrested. Many of them we never saw again. To this day, we still speak of the March 1st Movement."

"The Japanese just slaughtered that many Koreans? Just civilians?" Jack asked in disbelief.

"Yes. In one case they even locked our people in a church, set it on fire, and shot at them inside the church as they burned inside."

Something inside his stomach twisted. "I'm so very sorry. The Japanese are filthy butchers. I wished we had killed every last one of them."

"No, Jack," she said forcefully. "You do not yet understand. In any place there are good and bad people. All people sometimes get caught up in war and hatred. They were soldiers swept up in a national hatred that was created by their leaders. They did great wrong. They were very cruel to us. We cannot deny this. But the people as a whole are not bad."

"I'm not so sure about that. If they're Japanese, I think they're trouble."

Tae-bok pondered his statement quietly for a moment.

"Jack, do you think me trouble because I am your enemy?"

Jack looked at her skeptically and managed a smile. "You're not my enemy," he said.

"But I am North Korean, am I not?"

"Yes, but . . ."

"And your nation is at war against North Korea, is it not?"

"Yes, but you're not a part of this."

"And do you not think there are many such men and women in Japan who were not filled with hate for my people or your people? Do you not think there were such women in Japan just like your mother? Women who went to bed at night fearful for their sons who fought in a war far away? Women who lost their sons in a war they hated?"

"Well, yes, I suppose you're right."

"Do you not suppose there are many in Japan like me?" she asked, laying her hand on his forearm.

Jack looked at her delicate hand resting on his arm. He almost thought he could feel its heat through his jacket. He smiled at her. "I get your point, Tae-bok. You are very persuasive. Maybe it's not so simple."

Tae-bok smiled. "Jack, you still never asked me about my mother."

"Oh, I'm sorry . . . yes, please tell me about your mother."

Tae-bok paused as if mentally digging through archives in her mind, trying to determine where to start.

"In all of our history as a people, no one has been more brutal to us than the Japanese soldiers. As I have said, there must be good people in Japan, as there are in all places. But I do know with my own eyes what their soldiers did to us." She looked away as if looking into a distant land of faded memories.

"Your mother?" Jack asked—afraid of the answer.

"They came for her. My father tried to intervene, but the Japanese soldiers cut out his eyes as a message to our village. When the Japanese found my mother, they murdered her, but not before they made her suffer. I will not describe what the Japanese did to my sister."

Jack sat mute, unable to form a reply.

"The problem, Jack, is that I was afraid, and I hid. I was a coward. When my mother and sister needed my help, I abandoned them."

"What?" Jack asked.

"I hid," she repeated. "My older sister. My mother. They suffered while I hid. I should have saved them. I should have helped. They cried for help. I heard them. I should have done something. But instead I was a coward and ran away."

Jack's heart broke for her as pieces of the puzzle fell into place in his mind. Scales of ignorance fell from his eyes as understanding replaced blindness. "Tae-bok—I don't know what to say. There's no way you could have saved them. You certainly cannot blame yourself for this. If you had tried to help, you would have been killed, too."

Tae-bok sat for moment before replying. "You may be right. But honor does what is right, not what is easy. I had a moment to make the right choice, and I failed. I chose a path of shame and dishonor. And now I live with my choice, and I shall live with it the rest of my life. I still hear their cries late at night, when all is quiet. There are times when the clouds, the wind, the moon, are all just exactly as they were that night. It takes me back. I hear their cries for help. I drink the bitter cup of my shame over and over again."

Jack sat in silence, considering her words. Tae-bok spoke after a long few minutes.

"So you have said I should leave this place and escape with my children. Perhaps now you understand what you ask of me. For hundreds of years my ancestors have lived here in peace. We have farmed this land, built our lives here, and died here. It is true that for the past forty years we have suffered. It is true that the future is uncertain. But perhaps you understand now that I have no fear of death—neither for myself nor for my father. What I do fear is to leave my father to die alone, with not even a fitting burial.

Death will certainly be his fate if I leave. Perhaps you understand that I must do what is honorable."

Both Jack and Tae-bok sat in silence for a few minutes.

"I understand. Thank you for telling me about everything. I'm very sorry for all you and your family have suffered."

"And I am also sorry for what you have lost, Jack." She stood. "It is time for us to be going."

* * *

The visit to the small village went well. Several men and women gathered near a water well to trade and exchange a few things of value. The two American dollars were received with much excitement among those who came to trade, and Tae-bok was happy with her purchase of rice. To Jack it did not seem nearly enough.

"Is it really enough?" Jack asked.

"It is nearly a kilo. If we are careful, this will last a week and perhaps longer." Jack was reminded of the burden his presence had placed on her limited food supply, and he stayed silent.

The walk back was mostly quiet. Jack inquired a bit more of the history of Korea, and Tae-bok delved into the place where Jack had lived, called "Texas," a place she had heard of only distantly. Otherwise, there wasn't much left to say. He saw the world, at least partially, from her vantage point. He knew her mind was fully convinced of her course of action. Jack's mind was now resolved that he had done all that could be done. He began to mull over the logistics of getting back to Hungnam. He recalled what her father had explained, that the small road through Oro-ri would lead him back onto the main route down into Hungnam.

Just a mile or so from her village, Tae-bok saw a woman she knew. "Jack, please continue on, and I will follow in a few minutes."

Jack nodded his consent. The two women greeted each other in a flurry of animated Korean words. As their voices faded behind him, Jack turned and noticed that Tae-bok was pouring some of her small stash of rice into the woman's open hands. Tae-bok's eyes met his as he paused to watch. Tae-bok smiled just a bit, almost apologetically. Jack nodded and considered that perhaps generosity was one of those universal qualities that did not belong to any one culture.

He continued on the path to Oro-ri.

$$* * *$$

As Jack approached the outskirts of Oro-ri, he saw the outline of a disturbance outside of Tae-bok's house. It took only a moment or two, and a corresponding thirty or forty yards, for him to recognize two Chinese soldiers in uniform. He immediately hated his decision to leave his sidearm in the house.

Jack modified his path a bit to blend in among the shacks on the outskirts of the village. He was still about sixty yards from Tae-bok's house, but he started to make out the scene before him. As it came into view, he felt the old familiar boiling in his stomach. Tae-bok's father's hands were handcuffed behind his back, and he was kneeling before the younger of the two soldiers.

The older soldier had his hand wrapped around Yong-ho's small neck and was jerking him to and fro as Yong-ho cried pitifully. Rage erupted within Jack as he watched the soldier's treatment of the child. Without delay, Jack decided what must be done: strike suddenly and viciously while the element of surprise remained. He glanced over his shoulder at Tae-bok about three hundred yards behind. She had not yet seen her family's jeopardy.

Quickly, before she reacts, Jack thought.

Jack slipped into the shadows between one shack and another, jumped over a pile of trash, and moved quickly past a scrawny stray dog. A quick jaunt across a small dirt path between the rows of shacks put him back into the shadows and out the other side. Now he turned to his left and walked along the row of houses, changing his angle of approach on the two men. *I'll approach them from behind, and the fight will be mine.*

Between two houses now, Jack caught sight of the men again. The old man was pleading while Yong-ho cried desperately. Jack watched the older soldier reach for his sidearm. He drew it out and pressed it against Yong-ho's forehead. Yong-ho closed his eyes and started sobbing all the more.

The younger man bent over in an apparent effort to jerk the old man to his feet.

This is the moment, Jack thought. With his heart pounding and a bitter metallic taste on his tongue, Jack raced at full speed from the shadows and cleared the thirty feet to the soldiers.

Just as Jack approached, Yong-ho opened his eyes and caught sight of him. The boy's quick glance was enough to tip off the older soldier, who squeezed off a single round from his pistol in the air. An instant later, Jack caught the man's chin with his burly fist and put the other hand on the back of the soldier's head. A fierce twist with every ounce of Jack's strength marked the man's instant death.

The younger soldier, although caught off guard, responded immediately by dropping the old man on the ground and drawing his sidearm. Jack braced for the inevitable and twisted away as he pulled the older soldier's body into the line of fire. He felt two rounds penetrate the dead soldier's body.

Somewhere in the minuscule space between the second and third rounds, Jack thrust himself forward into the younger soldier and wrapped his right hand around the firearm. His left hand joined the struggle for the gun, and the Chinese man's spare hand did the same.

For a split second they stood eye to eye, faces just two inches apart, muscles locked in mortal struggle. The Chinese man screamed with rage, but Jack held the gun firm. Seconds passed as they stood in a deadly stalemate. Jack had not met a man of this strength in a long time. He normally found himself significantly stronger in hand-to-hand combat than his Asian counterparts, but not with this man—and his own weakened condition didn't help, adrenaline notwithstanding.

With muscles twitching and arms on fire with pain, Jack summoned up some primitive animal rage and returned a bloodcurdling scream at his mortal enemy.

* * *

Tae-bok had drifted away into her own thoughts as she walked the final distance to her house. Despite her intentions, her mind kept returning to Jack. Barely over a week ago, she had been ready to kill him. Now her feelings were considerably harder to explain. On one hand she disdained his ignorance of her culture and people. Yet she also sensed a goodness and decency within him that was hard to quantify. And she could not deny that she had enjoyed his presence in the house. Nevertheless, she chided herself, it was simply impossible for her to leave her father behind. Her father and the children were all she had.

Her conflicted thoughts were pierced by an animalistic shriek. Her eyes darted up, and she witnessed a horrific fight between two men. One man, she quickly discerned, was Jack.

She dropped her purchase of rice and raced the final fifty yards to the melee. Yong-ho spotted his mother and ran crying to her as fast as his short legs would carry him. They crashed together as she swept him into her arms. Holding him tighter than she ever had, she looked over Yong-ho's shoulder and saw her father on the ground, hands cuffed behind his back. Her eyes quickly refocused on the two men. They were brutalizing each other like enraged wild animals, almost indiscernible as two separate humans now. Arms, legs, and fists wrapped around each other as they bludgeoned each other without mercy. Grunts and shrieks filled the air as the men fought for their lives.

Tae-bok rushed Yong-ho to the safety of her house. She checked that the infant was sleeping on the floor and then rushed outside, back to the fight. She saw another Chinese soldier lying nearby, bleeding and dead.

Tae-bok stood helpless, terrified by the struggle. Long seconds crept by as the vicious struggle continued. Suddenly a gun was flung out from their midst and spun its way across the dirt toward Tae-bok. She rushed for it, seized it, and pointed it toward the men. But identifying a target was impossible. The men's bodies were so twisted together that their faces were not even identifiable. Blood pooled around the men and flung in her direction. One of them gasped and choked. Someone grunted and groaned pitifully.

Arms, knees, and legs flailed about wildly, boiling the dirt beneath them into a factious frenzy. Tae-bok furiously tried to decide which man to kill, which life to end.

Suddenly, all movement stopped.

No motion at all. No sound. Had they both killed each other?

Now she began to discern the bodies. The Chinese soldier lay on top of Jack. She saw the Chinese man's uniform rising.

"Jack?" she whispered under her breath, fearing the worst.

The Chinese man's body moved away from Jack but then slumped limply onto the ground as Jack finished pulling himself free. Tae-bok looked at the frozen scowl of terror on the now-lifeless face and noticed the knife Jack had embedded deep within the soldier's chest. Her eyes darted back to the other dead soldier on the ground. She recognized them. They were the soldiers with the explosives the night she had found Jack.

"Jack!" Tae-bok cried as she ran toward him. She grabbed him quickly without thinking and tried to pull him to his feet.

"Ahhhhh!" Jack cried as he recoiled from her grasp and collapsed back into the dirt.

Tae-bok retreated and looked at his battered face. One eye was in the process of swelling itself shut, and several large cuts oozed blood down his cheeks.

"I am very sorry," she breathed as she wiped blood from his forehead and mouth with the sleeve of her white cotton blouse. "Come inside, and we will fix this."

Jack painfully brought his legs underneath him and stumbled his way to his feet. A fiery pain erupted in his ribs as he tried to stand. He faltered, and Tae-bok helped him to his feet. Bracing against the shooting pain in his ribs, Jack paused to lean over the younger of the two soldiers and rummage around in his pockets for a moment until he found the key to the handcuffs. He passed the key to Tae-bok, and she quickly unlocked the handcuffs binding her father.

"Let's go, old man," Jack half-laughingly muttered as he reached to help the old man to his feet. It was then that Jack saw the pool of blood under his head.

"No!" Jack gasped.

Tae-bok knew at once what Jack's cry meant. She had lost him. As deep sorrow began to submerge her in grief, she sat gently on the ground next to her father's lifeless body, cradled him in her arms, and wept bitterly.

CHAPTER ELEVEN
Survival

They sat for the better part of an hour. Tae-bok held her father's body until the last of its heat had drained away. Jack sat next to her and tried to find words of comfort. Yong-ho stayed close to his mother's side and gently patted his grandfather's shoulder. Jack considered that in this place, children learned about the brutalities of life at an early age.

Tae-bok eventually lifted herself from the ground and wiped her eyes.

"Jack," she said softly. "Please help me move his body into the house. I will bury him tomorrow morning."

"Let me stay and help you, Tae-bok. You don't need to do this alone."

"Please, for the moment, just help me bring his body inside the house."

Jack bent down and reached his left arm under her father's neck and his right arm under his legs. Searing pain pierced his ribs again, but Jack stood up firmly, gently cradling the old man's broken body in his arms. Tae-bok quickly opened the door to the house, and Jack stepped inside. She motioned to a place along the wall, and Jack gingerly laid the body on the dirt floor. Together, they covered him with an old, tattered blanket.

"Tae-bok, I will stay one more evening. I'll help you bury him in the morning, and then I'll go."

160

"No, Jack. It is not possible. You need to go now. We will be fine. The most important thing you can do now is leave. You know that the soldiers will be reported as missing. I have seen them before—they are regulars. Others will come soon. If you are found, you will be killed or captured. You must leave now, Jack."

"Tae-bok, I'm sorry to mention it again now, like this, in these circumstances—but I need to know whether you're coming or not. Will you come to Hungnam?"

She shook her head, her face marked with grief and confusion. "I don't know, Jack. Too many things have happened too fast. In the morning I will bury my father, and then I will make my decision."

"You would stay even now?"

"Jack, as I told you, this is the place of my ancestors. The thirst this land has for our blood seems endless. But this land has sustained us and kept us. I do not know how I can leave this place when so much of our blood has been shed here."

Jack knew it would be foolish to argue anymore with her about it. He had already alienated her once, and winning back her trust had been a battle. And she was right: he could not stay.

"Listen, whatever you decide, don't wait too long. Those soldiers that you said will come looking for me—they'll find you too. They'll find the bodies of their soldiers. You don't want to be here when that happens."

"I understand. We will be fine, Jack. We know how to survive in this place."

"I know you do. I'm just trying to persuade you to . . ."

"I know what you are trying to do. We will be fine. It will all work out fine. Please, you need to leave now. You should have just enough sunlight to make it out to the main road. We heard many trucks each day, but the trucks mostly stop at night. Perhaps you can find a truck before the sun goes down and get a ride into

Hungnam. It is not very far."

Jack deeply regretted the choice, but she was right. He gathered up his few belongings and made his final preparations for departure. He heard her voice from behind.

"Jack, I do wish to say one more thing to you."

Jack slowly stood and turned to face her. She stood alone near the fire, her father's body nearby. Her jet-black hair graced her olive skin. She smiled reluctantly, as though battling regret.

"Yes?"

"My father used to say that blood that is shed for a noble cause is received by the earth and returns an increase ten times for those who have given it. Perhaps it is just an old saying, or perhaps it is more than that. But for the kindness you have displayed to my family, I wish that all of your days be blessed. I wish that your way in life, wherever it may take you, will be smooth. Whatever the road of life brings before you, may you go into it knowing that you made a real difference in this world. If nothing else, you have made a difference to us."

Tae-bok smiled gently and abruptly turned away and walked toward the door.

"Tae-bok . . ." Jack said. She had reached the door, but she turned back slowly to face him. Her eyes were unmistakably moist.

"I wish very much that you will decide to come, for the sake of your future and that of your children. I care about what happens to you—all of you. But if you will not come, you must know something as well."

Jack walked slowly over to her. "You could have killed me. You did not. You could have simply left me to die. That would have been easier. You did not. And yet our people are at war. As I have admitted, I have killed many of your men. But for some reason I do not understand, you didn't kill me, and you wouldn't leave me to die. More than that, you nursed me to strength. You healed me and fed me and showed me great kindness. Even more than all of that, I found some things I had lost a long time ago. My humanity. Hope. Maybe I even found a little bit of happiness again."

Jack paused and stared away for a moment. "Mere words will never properly tell you how I feel, but words are all I have. For some strange reason, our lives intersected for just a moment in the middle of this brutal war. I didn't get enough time with you. But I am grateful for what I did get . . . and I will always remember it."

Jack paused, waiting for Tae-bok to look at him again. Slowly, she did. Her eyes were glistening.

"Please listen to me. You *must* escape from this place soon. It may yet be possible, if you can move quickly, to escape farther south with your children—just far enough for you to be clear of the worst of the fighting. Forget Hungnam—anywhere south of here should permit you some safety. But wherever you go, I want you to understand this. Wherever you are, and for however long I live, I will always think of you and remember you. Not a day will go by that I will not remember what you did for me."

Jack moved closer to Tae-bok, gently brushed aside a strand of her hair, and traced his finger down her soft cheek. He looked into her damp eyes.

"Thank you," he said softly.

Jack slowly turned from Tae-bok, knelt on the floor, and took Yong-ho by the shoulders. He smiled and kissed him gently on the head.

"Remember, don't wait for those girls, and keep your eye on the ball."

Yong-ho peered up at Jack with a puzzled look, and Jack reassured him with a simple smile as he rubbed his head. Yong-ho smiled back.

Jack eyed Tae-bok's youngest son, sleeping quietly on a small mat. A white makeshift strap hung from the wall above him. He had seen Tae-bok frequently carry the boy by using the strap as a sort of sling. Jack quickly tore a page from his diary and wrote neatly on it with a pencil. He then pinned the note to the sling in such a way that it would be readable by those who saw it.

"What are you writing, Jack?"

Jack smiled in realization. "You never learned to read English, did you?"

"No, we were happy just to speak a little."

Jack smiled again. "If you decide to come, make sure any American soldier you meet sees this. They should protect you, okay?"

"I understand."

"Good-bye, Tae-bok."

"Good-bye, Jack Stiles. And thank you."

Jack reluctantly moved away. He took one more glance at Tae-bok and her son Yong-ho, and then he turned and walked out of the house.

The walk to the village road was a mere hundred yards, but it felt to Jack like it was miles in duration. His eye had completely swollen shut, and the cuts on his face continued to ooze blood. The ache in his leg and pain from what he figured were broken ribs was meaningless compared to the pain in his heart. He knew the family he had just left would face almost certain death in a matter of days. He felt separated from them, not so much by miles or distance, but by language and culture—and it was a separation he did not want. He knew this was a place he did not and could not ever belong.

As Jack reached the dirt road, he turned one last time to look at the little village and the house where he had stayed for the past nine or ten days—how many exactly he could not recall. Tae-bok stood in the doorway, looking much more beautiful than he had ever realized. He choked back a rising tide of sorrow and regret.

Tae-bok studied Jack's tall frame as he stood motionless on the road. She pondered what America must be like if this was one of her sons. With a faint smile, she decided it must be a special kind of place.

* * *

Jack knew that in a matter of hours he would stumble upon a military transport and ride the rest of the way to Hungnam. Before he got completely out of sight, he took one more look over his shoulder at the little shack. Tae-bok was now absent from the doorway. Full of regret, he shuffled down the road brokenhearted.

The distance from Oro-ri to Hungnam was just sixteen miles. The major battles were over, and most of the UN forces had arrived safely at the harbor. But a few skirmishes continued, and troops continued to trickle out of the combat zones and down the main supply route to Hungnam.

After a steady walk of about two hours, Jack began to approach the tattered remnants of a Marine company heading down to Hungnam. By Jack's estimate, they had about eighty Marines left. Their progress had come to a stop as they tried to clean up some Chinese snipers in the hills above the road. Jack joined up with the company, thrilled to finally be among US troops again. But his heart quickly sank as he saw what was left of the men.

It was the arms he saw first. Strapped to the hoods of the trucks, tied to the turrets of the artillery pieces, and piled in the backs of the trucks were the bodies of the men who had perished. Their arms were extended in grotesquely frozen rigor mortis, raised outward as though making their final defense. Their faces were locked in fear, their final emotions captured in death. Jack forced himself to look at their faces, pondering whether he knew any of them.

Among the surviving, no one spoke. They focused on quickly dispatching the snipers in the hills and then returned to their sullen march toward Hungnam. No one greeted him. They walked as a funeral train of living dead, as though in permanent shock. Their eyes were devoid of focus or life, their faces sullen and smeared with grime, dirt, and blood. Each man seemed injured in some fashion: broken bones, bullet wounds, bloodied cloths wrapped around their heads or limbs. Jack knew they had lived with the very face of death every hour of the days and every minute of the brutal nights.

Jack joined them silently in their march. A disheveled sergeant finally spoke.

"Bad limp you got. Face looks like you've been beaten half to death. Jump up in the truck—there's a little room left." He gestured to the nearby transport truck.

Jack didn't feel worthy. Over the last couple weeks he had lived in some measure of small comfort while these men suffered and died. "Nah, I think I can make it."

"Private, take my advice and get in the truck. There's no heroes left here, son."

Jack grimaced and hoisted his body into the back of the truck.

* * *

Fifteen other injured Marines sat in the back of the small transport with Jack. The transport moved slowly, keeping pace with the men who walked, always alert for snipers and ambushes. Their slow pace continued into the early morning hours of December 21. More men joined as they progressed toward Hungnam and crowded into the transport. Larry Jackson, an older Marine vet, sat across from Jack and talked as incessantly as he smoked. He talked of his battles in World War II. He seemed to especially delight in showing Jack the ebony black fingers of his hands. He took his time explaining in detail that they had been so badly frozen up at Chosin Reservoir that the docs figured they would either fall off soon or have to be amputated.

Jack studied his face. It was roughened by equal parts weather and combat. Deeply grooved wrinkles on his forehead and around his eyes spoke of the pain of war. His hair was greasy, matted, and splayed wildly around his blocky head. His lips were swollen and split from constant exposure to the howling wind, yet they clung tenaciously to a cigarette. The Marine had death in his eyes.

Jackson spoke in a raspy southern growl as he sucked on the rest of the cigarette held crudely in his black and purple fingers. Jack thought they looked so swollen with blood they might burst if touched.

"So, Stiles, What's got you so dazed? Look like you got shell shock or something. Who beat the living daylights out of you?"

Jack sighed deeply. He wished the trip was over already. Conversation was not on his agenda. "Nothing, man. Just tired."

"Right," Jackson replied with sarcasm as thick as his south Georgia drawl. "Don't give me that nonsense." He leaned forward. "Look, boy, I was in three of the major battles in the Pacific back in the big one, and I can tell you that I didn't face over there the kind of fighting we faced up at Chosin. So don't give me that 'nothing, man, just tired' kind of garbage. What's going on, Marine? Come on now, Marine to Marine."

Jack decided there was no escaping this conversation. "I was up at Chosin as well. Buddy from back home, childhood friend of mine, got killed. I was with him when it happened. I got shot as well. Transport taking me down to Hungnam for a medical evac got ambushed. Best I remember, I was left for dead in the middle of a road—wishing I was dead, praying I would die. Some Korean woman found me and patched me up, got me better. I think I was with her and her family maybe ten days, maybe two weeks, I don't know. When ya'll picked me up, I had just left them, her and her two kids. She wouldn't come."

Jackson grunted, threw the last of his cigarette on the floor, ground it out with his boot, and exhaled a blue cloud of smoke into the compartment. "Sorry about your friend, boy. Happens a lot. Lot more than folks back home realize. All the good boys we've lost over here, pitiful shame. I'm gonna tell you what you need to do."

He leaned forward with stone-faced seriousness. "You get home, you go tell his parents and everybody that will listen what a brave man he was, okay? You tell 'em how he served his country and how he paid the price of liberty with his own blood. Won't bring him back, but it'll give his folks something to hold on to."

Jack nodded agreement.

"I'll do that."

"So tell me about this woman."

Jack rolled his eyes. "What's there to say?"

"She got a husband?"

"Used to. He got killed up at Chosin too."

"Yeah, him and about thirty thousand other Chinese and North Koreans. This girl nice-looking?"

He shifted his position uneasily. "What?"

"The girl, the Korean woman that fixed you up. She nice-looking?"

"Yeah, I guess you could say that."

"You like her, I reckon?"

Jack bobbed his head back and forth, not really wanting to answer.

"Come on," Jackson said. "One Marine to another. You sweet on her? Nothing to be ashamed of. Happens a lot. She saved your life, fixed you up, tended your wounds. That's some sort of syndrome thing they call it . . . Nightingale or something. I don't know. Common in any case."

"Yeah, she's nice. She, uh . . . she did save my life. I can't forget that. She's got these two kids, really cute. One's about five or so, the other's just a baby. Anyway, I tried to encourage her to get out, get down to Hungnam and join the evacuation. I don't think she'll do it. But if she does, I figured maybe I could find her."

Jackson just stared and fished for another cigarette, found it, and started to light up again.

"You ever stop smoking?" Jack asked.

"Nope, just when I sleep or when I run out. You probably don't want to be 'round me when I run out," he said with a tight grin. "Anyway, forget about her. She won't come. If by some chance she does, it ain't because she's interested in you, boy. She's just trying to save her own neck. Get her out of your mind as soon as you can, get back home to the States, and move on." He whispered with a half-wheeze of his lungs as he jabbed at his own head, "She'll mess up your brain, boy."

* * *

Dong-hyuck and his father huddled in a small house in central Hungnam, cold and weary and desperate for sleep. They had tried several times to get passage out of Hungnam, but to no avail. Each ship seemed to take only a small number. After some would board, a man in uniform would come to the line and motion for everyone else to go away. Even more painfully, they watched as many other Koreans boarded ships for departure, with their full supplies bundled about them. They realized tossing away all their possessions had been a serious mistake. Perhaps they had been deceived. In vain they had returned to the garbage pit, but they found nothing left of their supplies. All they owned was gone, and perhaps it was all for naught.

As they searched for escape, the situation deteriorated in Hungnam. Just one entry point into the city was being held open by remaining US forces. Now father and son crowded together in a house packed with other men, each desperately waiting for escape from the city as Chinese forces slowly tightened their noose around Hungnam.

* * *

The small transport vibrated to a halt as its brakes squealed for mercy. Jackson got up and looked out the back of the transport, parting the canvas cover. "Looks like we're here. Welcome to Hungnam. By the way, there's about ten thousand of them women out here," he laughed. "Pick ya out one of 'em—they all look the same anyway. See ya around, boy. Don't forget what I told you about your friend's parents. See to it, Marine."

Larry Jackson jumped out the back of the transport, leaving a swirling trail of smoke as he went.

"Yeah. Sure, thanks for the encouragement, Smokey," Jack replied sarcastically as he started to stand.

A young black Marine sitting next to Jack spoke up for the first time.

"Ignore him."

"Huh?" Jack asked.

"Ignore him. The old vets get a little crazy. Sometimes they've seen so much they don't believe in anything anymore. You love her, you find her. Don't let anybody tell you otherwise. Look, if you're in a firefight and trying to get home in one piece, you want that old boy covering your back. I've seen him walk through fire for his men, without a second thought for his own skin. But don't listen to him about matters of the heart. All he knows is war. He don't know anything about love."

Jack let the words settle for a moment. He reckoned he didn't know much about love either. Maybe he could learn. Maybe if he could somehow find her again, there might be the possibility. "Yeah, you're probably right. Good advice." Jack extended his hand and smiled. "By the way, Jack Stiles is my name."

"I'm Joshua Jackson. Same last name as him, but no relation, obviously," the young Marine said with a wry smile.

"Thanks, buddy. Take care, and maybe see you around."

Jack slowly took to his feet and stretched his wounded leg, which had grown stiff on the rough ride. He eased his way out of the transport and let himself down awkwardly to the ground.

As he settled to the ground and adjusted to the dimness of the early morning light, he stood in motionless shock at the sight before him: a sea of humanity filled all available space in the harbor. He turned slowly, three hundred and sixty degrees, surveying the unreal scene before him. Everywhere, Koreans thronged the beach and the harbor. A sole military ship remained at the docks, loading a few remaining soldiers and military vehicles. A few cargo ships were loading refugees as well. Humanity was everywhere, each person carrying children, babies, and all of his remaining worldly possessions in a desperate attempt to escape the surging Communist forces.

Jack pushed his way through the throngs of North Korean civilians until he reached the military ship. He spoke to the first MP he could find.

"Hey, buddy, where are they taking the civilians?"

"All the civilians are going to Pusan. That's where most of the military has gone as well. But we're probably the last military transport ship out. We've got orders to get the last of the military personnel out, except for the guys holding the perimeter."

"You going to Pusan as well?"

"No, we've actually got orders to go to Koje-do—they need some help down there."

"Koje-do? But they're taking the civilians to Pusan, right?"

"You got it, buddy. You catch on quick, for a Marine."

Jack smirked off the comment. "Listen, I need a ship to Pusan —I've got to find someone there. It's important. You got any suggestions?"

"Look—it's like I already explained: civilians to Pusan, the military to Koje-do. That's it. There's no other choice. I got no suggestions for you. Just be glad we're getting out when we are. We're down to the last perimeter, and our guys are taking heavy casualties. When they drop the line, there's nothing left to stop the Chinese from flooding in here. Just get on the ship, and you can sort everything out later. Maybe you can get a ship or a flight over to Pusan later if it's that important."

Jack turned and looked back at the countless civilians trying to find escape. He pondered if she would come. If she did, would she come in time? And if she did come in time, she would be taken to Pusan. How would he ever find her?

"Are there going to be any more military ships leaving Hungnam?" Jack asked.

"Look, buddy, just like I told you—we're supposed to be the last, but I don't know. Maybe. I wouldn't wait around if I were you unless you want a close-up experience with tens of thousands of angry Chinese soldiers. Get on the ship, okay?"

Jack took one more look at the crowds. He spotted a mother with two young children, but it was not her. He hated the decision, but there was nothing else he could do. He reluctantly boarded the ship to Koje-do.

* * *

Tae-bok sat quietly on the bed where she had tended Jack back to health. The sun had begun its slow climb. She had not slept during the lonely night hours. She stared solemnly across the small room as she processed the events of the past twenty-four hours. A few candles flickered across the interior of her little shack, their flames dancing in the drafts which intruded from the howling winds outside. Both her father and Jack had been gone less than a day, and yet her tears seemed to know no limits, and she knew they would never suffice to reach the depth of her grief. She clutched the worn sheets to her face.

Yong-ho saw his mother on the bed. Within the limits of his five-year-old perspective, he sensed her sadness. He walked to the bed carrying the small stick that had served as his toy and then sat as close to her as possible. For a long while, he said nothing. Finally, he broke the silence.

"Are you sad, Mother, because Grandfather died yesterday?"

Tae-bok managed a slim smile and wrapped her arm around her son. "Yes, son, I am very sad."

"Are you sad because the soldier left?"

"Yes. No, well . . . yes, son—I suppose I am. I'm sad for many reasons."

"I'm sad too, Mother. Will Grandfather come back?" Yong-ho asked innocently.

Tae-bok choked back her grief. She spoke in a whisper. "No, my child, he will not be back."

"Then we should go to him, Mother. Can we go to him?"

She leaned closer and kissed her son on the head. "No, son. We cannot go to him."

"Will the soldier be back? The nice man?"

She paused. "No, my son, he will not be coming back."

Yong-ho looked perplexed. "Can we go to him?"

Tae-bok pondered the question. There was something in it—a glimmer of hope in her son's innocent wondering. "Yes, it might be possible, but it would be difficult. Why do you want to go to him? We have what we need here. All of our family for many hundreds of years is from this place. Should we not stay here?"

"But Mother," Yong-ho asked with a look of puzzlement,

"where is our family now?"

"Well, son, they are our ancestors. They are the ones who went before us. They have all died. Only you and me and little brother are left."

Yong-ho puzzled over her answer. "If they are dead, we cannot go to them, right?"

"Yes, that is right."

"And they cannot come back, right, Mother?"

"Yes, that is right."

"So we are all alone here. We should go find the soldier, Mother. We should go to him because I liked him, and he liked me, Mother. Nobody really liked me before, well, except for you and Grandfather, and now Grandfather is gone too." Yong-ho looked up at his mother, his face lined with a childlike concern.

The little boy paused for a moment and played with his stick.

"I think he liked you too, Mother," he said with a wry grin. "Oh, and he was fun. I liked having fun. Do you think we can have fun again sometime, Mother? It was really nice to have fun. Do you think we can have fun tomorrow, Mother?"

Tae-bok's eyes filled with tears. She laid the side of her face on her son's head and cried bitterly but silently. Her tears moistened her son's short black hair.

She knew the decision was made and that she had been a fool not to make it earlier.

* * *

In the harbor, Jack hobbled his way to the deck of the troop transport ship and watched sadly from the railing as they slowly pulled out of their berth and began the trip to Koje-do. He saw the thousands of refugees still left and the only two small civilian ships remaining—one had already begun to make final preparations to sail. He scanned the masses for any sign that she had decided to come, but it was fruitless. The faces blended together as the sun rose in the east and began to throw its long morning shadows around the Hungnam port.

* * *

The SS *Meredith Victory* slowed and dropped anchor at a point exactly two miles out from the port of Hungnam, as LaRue had ordered. Staff Officer Lunney made the entry in the logbooks as 1731 local time on December 21. A fading orange glow illuminated the western sky over the Korean Peninsula as the sun quickly retreated to the night.

LaRue was in his captain's quarters, reviewing the charts for the harbor. Despite the previous passage a few weeks earlier, he still considered this the most risky port this side of Inchon. The same four thousand mines were still in the Hungnam harbor, and it was his job to inch his way through unscathed yet again. The channel was still being swept clear of any stray mines and was still being maintained by the Navy's minesweepers, but it was scarcely a hundred yards wide and marked only with small floating white markers.

LaRue went over the routine in his head again. It was much the same as their earlier entrance into Hungnam. Every move through the harbor, every turn, every speed command had to be perfectly right, and it had to be perfectly right every time. It would only take one mine, and his beloved *Meredith Victory* would be ripped asunder. The three hundred tons of jet fuel would explode, and he and his crew would go to the bottom with her.

The call over the ship's intercom confirmed what LaRue already knew from the slowing speed, the hush of the engines, and the noise of the anchor chain being released. He stood and put his hand on the door of his cabin—and then paused. He glanced back at the charts on his small table and the Bible beside his bed. Which one he needed more right now was a question he hadn't yet answered. He retrieved his slightly worn but exceedingly warm wool captain's jacket, carefully buttoned every button, put his hat on his head, fitted his wool gloves, and grabbed the binoculars that sat on his shelf.

LaRue made his way to the bridge of his ship and looked intently toward the harbor. He saw flashes in the mountains outside Hungnam from Chinese artillery shells that were being lobbed in his direction. Most landed short of the city. A few overflew the port area and splashed harmlessly—so far—into the northern edge of the harbor. He realized the Chinese were trying to work out the distances necessary to bring the docks within their range. If the winds remained steady, it wouldn't take much more before they had it. Behind him, ships from the Seventh Fleet launched massive artillery shells into the surrounding hills. In particular, the USS *Rochester* ripped the skies apart with her five- and eight-inch guns. The USS *Saint Paul* supported the effort, and the USS *Missouri* rained fire and brimstone onto the Communist Forces with her massive sixteen-inch guns.

LaRue raised the binoculars to his eyes and began to survey the docks of Hungnam. He saw that every available dock space was taken by civilian ships like his, along with a few remaining Navy ships. With just a bit of refocusing, he trained his eyes on the docks themselves and at once convinced himself that what he thought he was seeing could not possibly be real. He pulled the binoculars away as if to impugn their honesty and then raised them to his eyes again.

"What a pitiable scene!" LaRue breathed.

Jamming the docks, seated and standing and moving everywhere, were Korean refugees. They had with them everything they could carry, wheel, or cart. Their most precious possessions of all were crowded with almost every family: little children huddled around their parents like frightened chicks. They were everywhere LaRue looked—an unimaginable throng of people, huddled and cold, scared and tired. Men carried bundles of their possessions. Women carried similar bundles on their heads, perched delicately as they milled among the crowds. They appeared to him to be caught in a horrible vise. On the one side, the horrific Chinese army that would kill or enslave them. On the other side, the icy waters of the Pacific. Between the refugees and the Chinese stood a thin line of US troops providing just enough time to load the remaining refugees into their only possible escape: every floating vessel that could be imagined. Between the refugees and freedom stood the unforgiving and icy Sea of Japan. Everything that could float had been enlisted.

LaRue recoiled as the *Missouri* launched another volley of massive rounds into the hills—they screamed overhead en route to an explosive landing among the Chinese troops. The volley would do its small part, LaRue thought, of holding the Chinese back just a little bit longer.

LaRue lingered longer in the bitter cold. The orange glow of the fading sun had completely faded into the icy night. Even in the dark, he marveled at the sea of humanity before him. He caught sight of a mother carrying a bundle on her head and a baby on her back. She stood amidst a surging sea of refugees, all desperate for escape. As soon as he noticed the one, it seemed like he spotted hundreds more just like her. Yet he noticed how stoically they all stood—no pushing, no fighting, just a certain calm, patient resignation as they waited for a salvation they could only hope would come. Finally, with light fading and temperatures rapidly falling, he forced himself to return to the relative warmth of the ship. A few final responsibilities completed, he retired for the evening.

Sleep for LaRue and most of the crew was nearly impossible. The constant and competing bombardments by the Chinese and American forces wore on through the night. Each explosion rumbled across Hungnam, spread out across the harbor, and echoed deeply against the steel hull of the *Meredith Victory,* rattling her welded-steel plates. The initial chorus was made up of the distant sound of incoming shells echoing from the hills around Hungnam as they were fired by the Communist forces. The return fire from the US warships offshore was different and much closer: it fractured the frigid air with the sharp, brutal shock of impact, and it felt as if his ship was shoved aside with every blast. By day, the US military ruled the skies. F4U Corsair World-War-II-era planes saw continual duty as long as there was daylight as they dropped a steady stream of bombs and napalm in an effort to slow down the surging Communist forces. Even the new F-80 jet aircraft entered the fray in a ground attack role. By night, the flying machines and their brave pilots rested.

As the nighttime combat droned on nosily, and the giant guns lobbed shells into the hills, Navy demolition teams silently went about their work of wiring hundreds of tons of explosives that would destroy everything in the Hungnam harbor of any possible value to the Chinese.

And all the while, the refugees waited.

The idea of sleep seemed rather fanciful to LaRue.

CHAPTER TWELVE

Escape

With the first light of dawn on December 22, and with dark sorrow too deep for words nestled in her breast, Tae-bok spent a few final moments at the makeshift grave of her beloved father. Using a small cart borrowed from a nearby family, she had brought his body to a quiet spot in the surrounding hills and carved a shallow grave from the frozen ground. The location had an abundance of rocks, which she used to cover his final resting place.

She sat in solitude. The place she had chosen granted a picturesque view from the hills above Oro-ri, the quiet valley, and the small road through the village. In her eyes, the village and surrounding hills seemed so very small, so isolated. She imagined a world far larger, somewhere just beyond the boundary of her sight and imagination.

"I hope I am making the right decision, Father. I hope I am preserving the honor of our family. You often told me that it is not the length of days that is the measure of our life. Rather, it is the measure of our life that is the length of our days."

Tae-bok smiled as she remembered his words. She had heard him say it many times when she was just a child, but it had never resonated quite so richly as now.

Tae-bok returned to her house and gathered the sling she used to carry the infant. As she strapped it to her chest, she followed

Jack's instructions and positioned it so that any American soldiers she might meet would see what he had written.

With the infant strapped to her chest, Tae-bok kneeled in front of her older son. "Listen, son, let's take a little walk. Let's see if we can find the soldier, Mr. Stiles. Yes?"

"Yes, Mother," Yong-ho said, clearly cheerful at the suggestion. "Let's see if we can find the man."

Tae-bok bundled herself and her children against the bitter cold. She cinched closed their coats and checked the straps holding the infant to her chest again.

Tae-bok stood by the door and looked again at the interior of the house. Her mind instantly relived a flurry of images she had accumulated in her time in this place. She knew now that she would never see it again. She imagined her father sitting by the stove. She heard his voice again. She wished in that moment that she had even a very small photo of him that she might always remember him by, but there had never been an opportunity.

She heard his voice in her mind: "Go, my daughter, before the time is gone."

"I will always love you, Father. I will always remember," she said to the empty house.

Tae-bok opened the rickety door and stepped outside. With a last glance back at the interior of the house, she permitted a lone tear to stream down her cheek. She turned toward the road, toward Hungnam, and toward an uncertain future.

The old door slammed behind her one last time.

* * *

On the deck of the *Meredith Victory,* the morning of December 22 carried more of the same violent monotony. LaRue stood and watched as small arms fire drew closer to the city limits. Small explosions ricocheted around the perimeter lines as US forces did their best to hold the tenuous lines of defense. LaRue noticed more fires burning through the frail wooden houses of Hungnam as incoming Chinese rounds now fell more commonly into the city. The Chinese continued firing their mortars into and around Hungnam, but they reserved their heavy artillery shells for the harbor area. Their accuracy was intermittent; the shells only occasionally reached the harbor. When they did, they exploded harmlessly away from the *Meredith Victory*—so far at least. LaRue was grateful for their inaccuracy thus far, and equally grateful for the continuing heavy fire from the US Navy ships, deafening as it was.

Still uncertain of their exact role, LaRue checked and rechecked all aspects of his ship, reviewing paperwork again with Staff Officer Lunney. Perhaps it was purely nervous energy, but he had to do something productive. This waiting, while shells occasionally splashed into the harbor, was unbearable. *Give me the open sea,* he thought. *Don't park my ship out here as a sitting duck just waiting to be hit.*

LaRue returned to his binoculars time and again, and the trend he witnessed concerned him all the more. The throngs on the docks of Hungnam grew blacker and blacker as more people crowded together, hoping for escape. There seemed scarcely any room between individuals. They had merged in his vision, not as separate people but as one mass of frightened, bitter cold, and suffering humanity.

Finally, while under strict orders of radio silence from the US Navy, a blinker signal light reached the *Meredith Victory* with a message. LaRue watched as Chief Mate Dino Savastio deciphered the pattern of light flashes and relayed the command he wanted very much to hear. It was time to dock.

"Captain," Savastio said, "we've got our clearance into the inner harbor now. The minesweeper off the starboard side is going to approach and will shoot over a chart for us."

"Excellent—let's do our job, gentlemen."

The Navy minesweeper slowly drew alongside the *Meredith Victory,* preparing a package in their Lyle gun. LaRue and a couple of his officers went down to the deck to wait the arrival. In a moment, they saw the flash of the gun and heard the distinctive thud of the small explosive. They watched the package arc between the two ships, trailing a thin steel wire behind it. The bundle reached the height of its arc and then descended perfectly on target to the *Meredith Victory.* The small bundle landed squarely on her deck, and LaRue's crew scrambled to retrieve it. The men disconnected the trailing cable, gave a hand signal to the minesweeper crew, threw the cable over the side, and watched for a moment as the minesweeper quickly wound the trailing cable back.

LaRue and his crew opened the canvas package and found a small white sheet of paper inside. LaRue carefully unfolded it with a slight smile. On it, scrawled in pencil, was a hastily drawn chart of the Hungnam harbor. A small X marked the current position of the *Meredith Victory.* Leading into the harbor, the chart depicted the same swept channel they had traversed before. The swept channel led all the way into the inner harbor and the docks. A different route, more to the northeast, would lead them out of the harbor through a second swept channel.

"Well, Chief, there's your chart. Let's make the most of it," LaRue encouraged his assembled officers. "All right, fellas, finally we get to do something today. Let's take her in, and gentlemen," he grinned wryly, "let's try to avoid hitting any of those mines, okay? It would really make the day downright unpleasant."

"Yes, sir, Captain," Savastio replied as they all turned, climbed several ladders, and made their way quickly back to the bridge, clutching the hastily drawn chart.

Under LaRue's oversight, the SS *Meredith Victory* inched her way through the Hungnam harbor, following the Navy minesweeper. Her steam-powered turbine turned her single screw and maintained a steady five knots. LaRue stood and calculated a mental course through the harbor, based on the scribbled chart and intelligence from the Navy and other Merchant Marine ships. Without any mine detection equipment, she still had to weave her way safely through those four thousand mines in the harbor. Now that they were in the thick of it, LaRue did not permit himself to consciously think of the risk.

Occasionally, a fleeting image of the result of a stray mine would slip into his mind: the initial fireball, the wrenching of steel, and then the secondary fireball from the ignited jet fuel. He knew that the flames would simply engulf her too quickly for the crew to even attempt escape. What LaRue feared most were the "counter" mines. The North Koreans chained this form of mine to the bottom of the harbor. By means of magnetic detection, the mine incremented a counter each time a ship passed overhead. At a predetermined number of clicks, arbitrarily defined for each mine, it would release from its cable and quickly rise upward until it impacted and detonated the unsuspecting ship. The mere one-inch steel walls of the *Meredith Victory* would be torn open like a tin can.

LaRue and his crew again performed with exactness the delicate balancing act required to navigate the minefield. To stay in the narrow one-hundred-yard-wide swept channel, he needed just enough speed to keep a good flow of water across the rudder. Too slow, and the ship would be unresponsive. Too fast, and he had no margin of error if he spotted some new danger. With his experienced crew at the helm, LaRue stood deep in thought in front of the bridge portals—making countless mental calculations, feeling the ship, feeling the waters, adjusting for all the unseen variables, and issuing new orders as they went. Occasionally he stepped onto the bridge wings on both the port and starboard sides, monitoring their distance to the edges of the swept channel. LaRue zealously watched their distance from the floating white markers—the distance between life and death.

After an hour or so of navigating the treacherous harbor, LaRue ordered the engines to idle and then directed his crew through their docking procedures for the day.

"Pull her up next to that Liberty ship, boys—the *Norcuba,* I believe it is. I'm afraid there's no room at the docks for us. We'll just tie up next to her, and that will work just fine."

"Sir," one of the bridge crew members asked, "next to the *Norcuba?*"

"Sure. No room at the inn, right?" LaRue quipped with a smile. "Oh, and keep her bow directed seaward, and let's keep the engines hot. Keep men at the lines in case of an immediate departure. Have them standing at the ready with axes to cut the lines if we have to get out quick. When it's time to go, we'll need to leave with absolutely zero delay."

The men down in the engine room at once began the tedious procedure designed to ensure their ability to depart immediately should the perimeter lines protecting Hungnam suddenly fall to the Communists. LaRue's command to keep the engines hot meant keeping the boilers hot and maintaining sufficient steam for an immediate departure. The turbine had to stay hot as well. The ongoing process that would continue until departure time began with the crew slowly opening the forward valves ever so slightly. Before the *Meredith Victory* could begin to creep forward noticeably, they immediately closed the forward valves and opened the reverse valves. In so doing, they kept the turbine moving and equally warmed by the superheated steam. If they didn't balance this just right, the ship would begin to move prematurely with disastrous results.

Without this process, too much steam applied to the turbine too quickly in support of an immediate departure could warp the turbine and limit their ability to sail at full speed. LaRue knew they would likely load until the last moment and would then need to make an immediate departure. Worse, if the lines protecting Hungnam from the Chinese should fall prematurely, the city would be flooded with Communist troops, and the *Meredith Victory*'s departure would be even more urgent.

As his men attended to the details of the tying up next to the *Norcuba,* LaRue had a few minutes to notice that the harbor was still packed with ships of all varieties: both military ships and cargo ships of the Merchant Marine. Most of them, he noticed, appeared to be making preparations to sail.

When the *Meredith Victory* was fully secured, LaRue excused himself from the bridge, descended the ship's ladders, and stepped outside onto the deck of his ship. He walked across the steel deck plating, past the cargo booms, and toward the stern. He commended a few men for their good service on this part of the trip and thanked them for all they did. LaRue reached the rail at the stern and finally allowed his tired eyes to look closely at the docks of Hungnam. What he saw involuntarily sucked the breath out of him. He stood, holding the rail tightly, as a bitter chill raced up his spine. He tried to process the scene that filled his eyes, but for a moment, he simply was not capable.

The refugee situation had grown much worse. What his binoculars had only partially resolved from afar, now his own eyes saw in full clarity. His eyes darted from the thronging crowds to the tenuously held fringes of the city. He saw the fear and desperation on the faces of the thronging refugees. In the hills around the city he saw the flash of artillery and heard the dull report of mortar shells. He looked back at the crowd and saw the fear in the eyes of the children, clutching tightly to their mothers or fathers. Men huddled their wives close; he knew they feared the Chinese as much or more than he did. His eyes cut back to the broken city, smoke billowing through its streets, fire dancing among the rooftops. It seemed to him to be a scene out of

Dante's *Inferno*. Crowded into every available space on the docks at Hungnam was a sea of pitiful, tired, cold refugees beyond number. It dawned on LaRue that he was one of their last hopes of escape. He marveled at the volume of humanity. Was it five or ten thousand?

Maybe more.

* * *

Tae-bok walked quickly as Yong-ho sprinted along beside her. Her infant hung from her chest and jabbered during the long walk. The freezing air bit at her face and stung her cheeks. She checked periodically on the baby, but he seemed pleasantly comfortable. Yong-ho, for his part, enjoyed the quick walk as though it were a game.

Several hours passed as Tae-bok moved quickly down the road toward Hungnam. The ceaseless cold penetrated her thin shoes and numbed her feet. Without feeling in her feet, she stumbled occasionally over rough spots in the road but still maintained her brisk pace. To the side of the road, especially in the hillsides, was the near-constant rattling of combat. Small arms fire and mortar rounds echoed among the frozen hills. Above, she heard the noise of combat aircraft maintaining control of the skies.

In the distance, from the direction of Hungnam, Tae-bok heard the sound of a vehicle. She paused for a moment and listened carefully. The noise of the engine grew louder, and she knew it was approaching. Ushering Yong-ho off the road, she crouched behind some frozen brush in a small ditch mostly full of snow until she could determine better if these were Chinese forces or Americans.

The rumble of the engine grew louder in pitch as it rounded a corner and started to come into sight. Tae-bok knew at once it was Chinese. She crouched even more into the brush and held her breath as the vehicle slowly rolled by. It seemed they were looking for something or someone. Crouching deeper, she pressed her face against the cold snow. She held Yong-ho close and kept one hand over his mouth and one hand over her infant's.

Slowly the Chinese vehicle passed. Tae-bok remained hidden until she could hear the pitch of the engine fading away into the bitter winter air. Only when she was sure it was completely gone did she rejoin the road and resume her walk, ever so cautiously listening for more Chinese.

About an hour-and-a-half later, the sound of a vehicle again approached. This one traveled in the direction of Hungnam. She found shelter behind a frozen snowbank and waited in absolute silence. She motioned to Yong-ho to keep quiet while covering the mouth of the baby.

This time she noticed the distinction immediately. It was a tattered US military transport vehicle. As it approached, Tae-bok quickly left her hiding place, dragging a confused Yong-ho along, and scurried to the road.

The Marine driving the vehicle barely caught sight of the small Korean woman bundled in dirty white clothing, with two small children, standing in the middle of the narrow road. He slammed on the brakes and wrestled the transport truck to a skidding, faltering halt on the snow-covered road.

"Hey! What's going on? Get out of the road!" the young Marine shouted from inside the cab. The woman neither heard him nor moved from her place in the road. "What do you think this is, a bus service? We're not taking any passengers!" he hollered again.

Tae-bok stood perfectly still in the middle of the road, just ten feet from the grill of the transport truck.

"Come on, you gook—get out of the road. This ain't the bus, woman." He reluctantly rolled his window down, leaned out into the frigid air, and tried to wave her on. Tae-bok did not move.

The Marine snorted in frustration. "Hey, Waters. Wake up! Check this out."

Sergeant Waters stirred from his slumped position in the corner of the cab.

"What's up, Martinez? What's going on?"

"This stupid gook is blocking the road. What do you want me to do about her?"

Waters frowned as he sat up straighter. "First of all, don't call her a 'gook,' okay? Last time I checked, they're human beings, unlike you, I might add. They want the same thing you and I want —just to get out of this sorry place."

"All right, all right—just take it easy. I didn't mean anything by it. But what am I supposed to—" He stopped, staring more intently at the woman in the road. "Hey, is that some sort of note pinned to that little kid? Let's check it out—come on."

Both the men opened their doors and clambered out into the bitter cold for a closer inspection.

Walking carefully along the hard snow-packed road, they approached the Korean woman slowly. A little boy clutched the woman's leg tightly—frightened of the large American soldiers.

"What's it say, Waters?"

Waters walked up slowly until he could read the careful writing on the piece of paper pinned to the small child's clothes. "What's wrong, you don't read English anymore, Martinez? It says, 'Please give safe passage to Hungnam,' and it's got the name of some Marine private—some Jack Stiles guy. You know a Jack Stiles?"

"Never heard of him. So what do we do about her?"

Waters thought for a second. If it weren't for the two little kids, he probably would have just left her alone on the road. "I don't know why anybody would do this—but it must be important. Put her in the back. Let's make it quick—we need to hurry if we're going to make Hungnam by dark. I don't want to be outside the perimeter when the sun goes down."

"All right, all right—I'll take care of it. Come on, lady. Come this way. We'll give you a ride."

Tae-bok listened carefully but didn't move.

"Look, lady, we'll take care of you. We're not going to bother you. We're going to Hungnam. *Hungnam,*" he repeated slowly. "Do you understand?" He repeated it again with slow emphasis. "We'll take you there, and I think they're trying to get all of you people that want to leave out, so let's just go around back and we'll take you there. But we need to move quickly, okay? Hubba hubba, okay?"

Tae-bok determined she could probably trust these men. She wasn't sure she had a choice anyway. She slowly followed the American to the rear of the transport. He pulled open the canvas door and reached down to the young boy, hoisting him into the transport. Then, with an extended hand, he helped the Korean woman and her baby into the back of the transport, sealed up the canvas door, and threw himself back into the warmth of the cab behind the steering wheel.

"All right, no more stops now. Let's get to Hungnam. They're not going to hold that entry point open for long after dark." Martinez threw the truck into gear. "Whoever this Jack guy is, he owes us big time."

* * *

Captain LaRue returned to the rail at the stern of his ship periodically as if to verify that what he thought he was seeing was still real. He pondered how inhuman humanity could be. The scene before him burned into his memory, and he despised all the more the scourge of Communism that enslaved and destroyed as much of mankind as possible. He gripped the rail tightly in frustration and bowed to breathe a silent prayer.

"Captain?" one of the junior offices called out. "I'm sorry to

189

disturb you, but there are three Army officers here who have requested permission to meet with you."

"No problem. See them to my quarters. I'll be up in a minute." LaRue replied.

LaRue stood somberly, not yet ready to leave, his heavy wool gloves still resting on the rail. He looked out at the desperate sea of refugees. High overhead, he heard the unmistakable whine of a deadly artillery shell. A second or two later, he heard the thunderous roar from the *Missouri*'s sixteen-inch guns as the sound tried to catch up to the outgoing projectile. As the noise abated, the sound of automatic gunfire echoed from the edges of the trapped city. In the distance, more noises reverberated around the city. LaRue heard the throaty growl from the two-thousand-horsepower engine of an incoming F4U Corsair. He watched as it approached low from the far edges of the harbor and swooped down over the stricken city. Aiming for an apparent assemblage of enemy soldiers on the outskirts of Hungnam, it suddenly discharged its load of napalm onto the enemy lines, resulting in a horrendous eruption of a wall of fire.

LaRue knew such tactics were necessary, but he hated them. He often likened napalm to an insidious gel made out of gasoline. The flaming jelly landed on enemy troops and would burn its way into a man's skin. There was no way to remove it. He had heard the stories of US troops accidentally hit with the insidious weapon begging to be shot by their friends to escape the agony of burning alive. Those who somehow managed to escape death from the horrific burns often suffocated as the mass eruption of fire temporarily deprived the entire area of oxygen. Others who might somehow survive even this brutality would often die from the napalm-induced firestorms with their nearly hurricane-force winds swirling viciously, as if they were the very fires of hell being stoked by the devil himself.

LaRue watched the F4U, lightened of its load of napalm, bank hard to the left, circle back around, and mercilessly unleash a fiery torrent of .50-caliber rounds from its six-wing mounted M2 Browning machine guns at any who had survived the napalm's multipronged onslaught.

A bit further in the distance, he heard the unique whine from the sole turbojet engine of the F-80. Easily outmaneuvered in aerial combat by the Communist forces' MIG-15, the F-80 nonetheless continued to play a key role in close ground support and this final defense of Hungnam. LaRue watched as the F-80 screamed its way across the hilltops. It too unloaded two wing tanks full of napalm. The release and ground impact of the flammable gel engulfed the hillside, and all upon whom it fell, in a wall of unforgiving fire.

In the distance, yet another F-80 streaked over the harbor en route to yet another target.

LaRue marveled at the efforts to hold back the Chinese and North Koreans so these people could flee. But would it be enough?

LaRue pulled himself away from the rail and worked his way back up to his quarters. When he entered, he saw three of the most haggard-looking, half-shaven Army officers he had ever encountered sitting at his private dining table.

"Welcome, gentlemen. I'm Leonard LaRue, master of the *Meredith Victory*. What can I do for you? I can rightly assume you're not here for a social visit."

A man LaRue figured for the ranking officer spoke first. "Thanks for seeing us, Captain. We're deeply appreciative. We'll get right to the point. There have been a total of probably one hundred thousand civilian refugees here in Hungnam. The Chinese will be here in maybe twelve hours. Maybe less. It depends on how long the perimeter lines will hold them back."

"One hundred thousand, did you say? A hundred thousand?" LaRue was stunned, despite the numbers he had seen with his own eyes.

"Yeah, easily that many. Most of them have been evacuated out. But those that are left—they've got nowhere to go. Our ships have been shelling the hills over Hungnam to hold the Chinese back, but ultimately it's a battle we won't win. We're asking every ship to take as many of these Korean refugees as they can. I'll cut to the chase. Will you help us?"

LaRue took a moment to absorb what he was being told. No one spoke. Another explosion rumbled across the city and through his ship.

"I'll do what I can, gentlemen. As you know, the *Meredith Victory* is a *cargo* ship. We don't have any suitable space for refugees. I can only berth forty-seven men, and that's already taken by my crew. I'm not sure what we can realistically do. Beyond all that, I'm a bit concerned about the possibility of saboteurs among the refugees. You may not know it, but I've still got three hundred tons of jet fuel onboard. It would only take one Communist spy to send my ship to the bottom in minutes."

Another officer, a young Army officer named Johnson, spoke as though he had given the speech a hundred times before. "Captain, the choice is, of course, ultimately yours. We certainly can't order you to do anything. And we recognize this is exceedingly dangerous. It's your ship, your crew, and your safety, and no one will blame you for whatever you decide."

Johnson turned from the conversation and looked out the portal at the masses on the docks. "I will tell you," he continued, "that they will die if we we don't get them out of here. At present, the *Meredith Victory* . . ." he paused. "She'll be the last merchant ship to leave Hungnam. When you pull out, the Navy will detonate the surrounding harbor and destroy everything before the Chinese arrive."

The silence among the men was only interrupted by the chatter of machine-gun fire in the distance.

"How many can you take, Captain?" Johnson asked, almost pleadingly.

As LaRue pondered the impossible situation, another powerful rumble of thunder from the *Missouri* rumbled through his ship.

"We're the *last* ship, did you say? How many did the other merchant ships take?"

"The vast majority of the hundred thousand have made it out, but there will still be many thousands left. Some ships took a few hundred. The *Mormacmoon* was able to take twenty-four hundred. Just do whatever you can. Just take them south to Pusan where we can offload them there. Talk to your officers and make a decision. Just say the word, give your crew their orders, and we can start the loading of refugees almost immediately."

"I understand, gentlemen." LaRue paused. "I don't need to talk to my officers. We'll take as many as we can. We ought to be able to start the loading in just a few hours." His voice softened, and he repeated, "We'll take all we can."

"Thank you so much, Captain. We're grateful for your help." And with that, the Army officers hurriedly excused themselves and returned to the docks.

CHAPTER THIRTEEN
Precious Cargo

"Gentlemen," LaRue began as he addressed his crew in a hastily assembled meeting on the main deck. "We have set before us an urgent humanitarian mission. Thousands of Korean refugees down in the city, on the beaches, and on the docks need evacuation. You've seen them out there all day. We are the last ship that can take them to safety. If they remain, they die."

LaRue paused and considered how young his crew really was. "They look different from you and me, but I want you to see in their faces the faces of your mother, grandmother, sister, daughter, brother, and your friends back home. They are humanity as surely as you are." LaRue paused, still sizing up his crew. They were so young, their faces so eager to serve. They would do anything he asked of them, and they would do it with every ounce of their ability. In turn, they trusted him to do what was right. They willingly placed their lives in *his* hands. A burden of the weight of the responsibility of their lives surged up from within him.

He broke the silence with the determined calm of a mind unencumbered by the distractions of what might or could be. Instead, LaRue spoke with the determination of what *would* be. "They are desperate for survival, and by the grace of God, we *will* get them to safety. There is no question about our mission—we have a job to do, and we will do it as we always have."

LaRue paused as if deep in thought. "Men, when I thought about what would be possible for us to do, I remembered the solemn instructions of our Lord: 'Do unto others as you would have them do unto you.' Most of all, when you see their faces, you must see *your* faces. Do to them as you would want someone to do for you." His men stood raptly at attention. He surveyed the faces. They nodded slightly. This was different. It was desperate. It had never been done before. Maybe it was crazy. But they smiled as the mission was laid out before them. They *understood.*

"Now let's get busy, men. Get these people aboard. Put them in every nook and cranny and fill every cargo hold. Don't let any space go unused. Put them below deck and on deck. Stand them on top of each other if you have to. Find room, make room—do whatever it takes. Just get them aboard. Start with the lower decks. When the lower deck is completely full, put the deck hatches back on and load the next deck. Offset the hatches a bit to leave space for fresh air. Any questions?"

A young crew member spoke falteringly. "Captain . . . how *many* do we take?"

LaRue looked at the young man—just barely nineteen years old. He thought seriously about the question for a moment as his crew stood silent, expectantly waiting his answer.

LaRue took a few steps to the rail and again surveyed the helpless masses congregated on the beaches and docks. "How many do we take?" he repeated, looking back at the young crewman. He gestured with his arm, sweeping it slowly in an arc as if to take in the entirety of the thousands crowded below. "Son, we take every last one of them. Load them on until she can't take any more." He turned back to his young crewman and smiled. "When those docks are empty, our job will be done."

* * *

Night fell heavy in Hungnam, and with the ebony shroud, the giant guns of the US 7th Fleet increased their bombardment of the hills around the city. Launched in a fury of fire, their shells shrieked over the *Meredith Victory* and the *Norcuba,* over the huddled masses of humanity on the docks, and exploded into the hills with deep rolling blasts of enraged thunder. Closer in to the city, another weapon held the enemy back. Fires burned out of control on the outskirts of the city as falling napalm ignited everything and anything that was even marginally combustible. The smell of sulfur and dense, acrid smoke hung thick in the cold night air.

A couple dozen or so straggling military trucks arrived in the Hungnam port well after dark and pulled up close to a small freighter that had docked to take out a few more remaining troops. LaRue watched from the deck as the trucks unloaded a few hundred soldiers and Marines, many of them injured and being carried on stretchers. A few Korean civilians also scrambled out of the backs of the trucks and quickly joined the backlog of thousands of refugees hoping to board the *Meredith Victory.*

"Lunney, these soldiers—where are they coming from? Can you tell?" LaRue asked.

Lunney took his turn with the binoculars and scanned the troops. They were haggard and disheveled. Those who appeared uninjured carried guns, grenades, and ammunition. Many lay on stretchers. Others, their bodies frozen by death and winter's ravages, were hauled from the trucks by two men at a time. A sacred vow—man to man, brother to brother—could not permit leaving them behind.

"These have got to be some of the men holding the perimeter. I went down earlier and talked to some of the Army and Marine guys who are still on the beach. They've still got one main line around the city. For the past few days, each time the

196

Chinese get closer, they drop the outermost perimeter and let more of the soldiers retreat to the transport ships. I'm sure there are only a few troops holding that last line. It's mostly the planes and naval bombardment that are keeping the Chinese out of the city at this point. I suspect that by morning, things will deteriorate very quickly."

"Those men holding the final line, they're risking and losing their own lives so that all these people—people they don't even know—can flee the Communists." LaRue's words were framed by a massive blast from the *Missouri* and a thunderous reply from the *St. Paul.* "Where do we find such men, Lunney?"

"I think they're just doing what Americans do, Captain. They came over here for a fight for freedom that was not their own, for a people they don't know—and here they bleed and die so others can live in liberty."

Both men stood silently for a moment.

"They're America's sons, Captain."

* * *

As the night of December 22 wore on, the crew of the *Meredith Victory* turned on all the lights on the ship. It was a necessity for the purposes of speeding the boarding; but LaRue realized they were making themselves a well-lit target for the Chinese as they attempted to fire back at the US forces. For their spotters in the mountains, hitting the *Meredith Victory* would surely be very tempting.

As a pure cargo ship, LaRue's crew had no suitable means for quickly loading the nearly countless refugees. Troubled by the delays and knowing how urgent it was that they speed the boarding process, Chief Mate Savastio came up with a way to more quickly load people into the holds. He and several of the other men, with some help from the Corps of Engineers, fashioned together planks of scrap wood from old crates and made a makeshift ramp. The small bridge carried people across the *Norcuba* and onto the deck of the *Meredith Victory*.

At about 9:30 p.m., slowly at first and then with increasing speed, the cold and desperate refugees streamed onboard: on and across the Liberty ship, up the ramp, over the railing, and finally onto the deck of the *Meredith Victory*.

One of the first refugees across was an old man, carrying his only worldly possession, a broken violin. LaRue's crew at first attempted to persuade the old man into giving up the violin, but LaRue spoke up as he oversaw the process.

"Let him be. That's the last thing on earth he has. I think we owe it to him."

Others carried everything. All carried something. Women carried sewing machines, baskets, blankets, and babies, and always something perched on their heads. Children accompanied adults —some old enough to walk, others just infants. One woman had triplets. Some families had eight or ten children gathered around them. Some babies slept innocently in a makeshift pack on the front of the mother or father. Some older ones clung to their fathers' backs. All shared the same basic look of fear and anxiety, moderated slightly by the power of hope. Each step closer to the *Meredith Victory* seemed to ease their tensions more.

LaRue and his crew spoke in one of the few words of Korean they knew, "Bali, bali, bali!" as they urged the crowds to hurry, ever mindful of the potential of an incoming Chinese round bringing all their efforts to fiery failure.

The process of getting the refugees onto the deck of the *Meredith Victory* had been improved with the makeshift ramp. But the challenge still remained to get the refugees down into the cargo holds as fast as possible. Seeing the developing problem, Savastio and the men fashioned large platforms that could be lifted by the ship's cranes and lowered down into the cargo hold.

With this arrangement, they lowered thirty or so refugees at a time into the lowest levels of each hold. Parents clung tightly to their children, drawing them close as the platforms were lifted from the deck and then swung expertly down into the dark chambers of the ship. LaRue watched the process with fear that some might fall off and plunge to his or her death, but the proceedings continued without incident.

As the captain stood by, humanity flooded aboard the *Meredith Victory*.

* * *

A mile away, Dong-hyuck and his father waited anxiously for news that they could board a ship and escape. They wandered the deathly cold streets together, looking for information on possible evacuation. Dong-hyuck's father grew concerned when he caught a glimpse of the harbor. Yesterday, he had seen maybe ten or twelve ships. Tonight, he saw just three or four. A flurry of activity surrounded them. Their lights glared in the night, reflecting from the inky black water of the harbor. Occasionally, the harbor area was illuminated by the flare of massive artillery fire from Navy ships further out in the harbor. The massive bursts of fire from their guns cast wildly flashing light against the city, illuminating the Navy ships briefly like ghost ships on the horizon.

When they grew weary of their search for answers, they retreated into another small house where men had gathered for sleep. They slept on the floor, surrounded by many others wanting the same thing: escape.

"Will we get on a ship, Father?" Dong-hyuck asked as he and his father settled down.

"Yes, son, I believe we will. Not much longer now. Get a little rest and we'll try again in the morning."

"Yes, Father." Dong-hyuck smiled. "Thank you for what you have done."

"Why do you thank me, son?"

"Because you have done everything in your power to take us to safety. I am grateful to you, Father."

Byung-soon smiled and rubbed Dong-hyuck on the head. "You're a fine boy, Dong-hyuck. Your mother and I are very proud of you. I know that when we get to where we are going, you'll make a new life for yourself. I know you'll accomplish great things." He closed his eyes. "Good night, son."

"Good night, Father."

* * *

Very early in the morning hours of December 23, the South Korean military police roamed the streets looking for more people wishing to evacuate from the city. The loud knock on the door instantly awakened the men crowded into a small house in central Hungnam.

"Out in the street—out in the street, everyone!"

Other refugees streamed out of the adjacent houses, stumbling into the street as they shook the sleep from their eyes.

"Everybody line up," the MPs barked. "A single-file line! Everyone line up!" The repeated shouts were urgent and excited.

Dong-hyuck, his father, and the other men flooded out of the house and lined up in the streets, shivering against the brutal cold. Dong-hyuck placed his hands into his coat pockets to stay warm. He stood directly behind his father in the long line. Temperatures had fallen overnight to nearly twenty degrees below zero.

The MPs blared loudly with a large bullhorn, "Grab the man in front of you—place your hands on his shoulders. Follow the man in front of you. We are going through the streets to the docks to the ships which will take you south. Hold on to the man in front of you!"

Dong-hyuck reluctantly removed his hands from the warmth of his pockets and latched on to his father's shoulders. At the same moment, he felt a man behind him lay hold of his shoulders in the same manner. Dong-hyuck turned and smiled at him and was surprised to see that he was an old man. He flashed a toothless smile back. Perhaps freedom was finally near.

The South Korean MPs began running through the narrow streets of Hungnam, followed by the long column of refugees, three or four hundred in all, each holding on to the man in front. Dong-hyuck marveled as they passed houses and buildings that were burning uncontrollably. The sound of artillery whined above their heads. Acrid smoke snaked through the streets and burned his nose as they all continued to run.

After a half-mile, the distinctive *tap-tap-tap* of repetitive automatic fire grew louder as it volleyed back and forth between defenders and attackers. The occasional grenade explosion drowned out the gunfire for a few seconds. And then the massive pounding of the *Missouri* and the 7th Fleet rolled like thunder through the streets. Still Dong-hyuck and the men ran.

The frigid cold bit at their faces, and yet the men ran. Their breath coursed heavily through them, but still, young and old ran. Dong-hyuck glanced back at the old man behind him. He was panting hard from the exertion and seemed to be falling behind.

"Come on, you can make it! Don't give up—it's just a little bit further," Dong-hyuck cried out. The old man struggled along and smiled at the boy.

They continued to run.

The Korean MPs hustled them along and urged them to maintain their pace as they steered the long column toward the harbor. As the long line snaked its way through the burning city and approached the harbor, US MPs soon joined the cacophony of voices and urged them to hurry by calling out, "Hubba, hubba,

hubba . . . Pusan!"

And so the men ran.

The long column of men covered the final quarter mile. Dong-hyuck saw before him the largest ship he had ever seen. Most of the men marveled as well. As they drew closer, Dong-hyuck saw through the smoke and haze of the night air that only two ships remained in the Hungnam harbor. The MPs directed the men down one of the docks, up and onto the *Norcuba*, and across the makeshift ramps onto the *Meredith Victory*.

* * *

Tae-bok felt the shudder of the old brakes as the truck came to a faltering stop. They had arrived. She parted the canvas and stumbled from the back of the transport, clutching her two children close. Stepping out into the darkness, she was immediately reminded of the unrelenting wind which carried the bitter cold from further north. She drew the children closer and surveyed the port area. The night sky was inky with darkness, and yet bright lights on a few remaining ships illuminated the small port. She pondered where to go next. How to board a ship? Which ship?

Violent explosions from the USS *Missouri* shattered her concentration and scared both the children. As the concussive noises faded, the lesser noises of constant small arms fire on the outskirts of Hungnam returned.

Sergeant Waters rounded the corner to check on the Korean woman.

"Which ship?" she asked him simply.

"I don't know, lady. Just try some of them and see if they've got room."

"That ship?" Tae-bok asked, pointing to a large military transport.

"No, that's military. They won't let you on there. Maybe try one of those," Waters offered, pointing to two remaining ships nestled against each other in the port.

Tae-bok focused her eyes on the two ships tied up alongside each other. One was mostly dark. The other was lit up as though every light possible had been turned on. That's when she noticed it: a long, snakelike line of men streamed its way to the darker ship, its tail still flowing in from the city. The men wound their way up to the dark ship, across its deck, and onto the ship with all the lights, where a bustle of activity was underway.

Tae-bok grabbed both the children in her arms and ran until she joined the long line of men. She trusted they were going to safety and that she could go where they were going. As she joined the end of the line, she looked up and saw a portion of the ship's name, letters she recognized, but could not read.

* * *

The *Meredith Victory* had five separate cargo holds: three forward of the ship's house and two aft of the ship's house. Those holds forward had three levels below the main deck, and those aft of the ship's house had two levels. Refugees were put first in the very lowest level of each of the five cargo holds. Dong-hyuck and his father held each other's hands tightly as they pressed on to the *Meredith Victory*. They huddled together as they stood on a large platform and were lowered into the bottom hold.

Dong-hyuck looked up as the lights of the ship slowly receded, and he and his father descended into the inky bowels of the ship. They stood together, and as more and more people were loaded into the hold, Dong-hyuck and his father pressed closer and closer together.

Soon, the hold was full of humanity. Dong-hyuck stood skin-to-skin with people all around him. He felt their breath on his neck. They silently pressed together in equal parts fear and cold. When it seemed no more could possibly be squeezed into the cargo hold, wooden deck hatches began to be placed over the opening above, and then the light was gone.

As the crew put the wooden deck hatches in place, they offset them slightly to leave a small gap for fresh air from the deck above. Dino Savastio and the men working with him gazed down into the hold and into the eyes of the faces staring up at them. They felt as if they were burying these people in the dark belly of the ship. They marveled that somehow the Koreans seemed to understand what was taking place and demonstrated such great courage. LaRue watched the loading process from the ship's house. *What remarkable faith these refugees have in me, my crew, and this little ship,* he thought.

Deep in the lowest hold, Dong-hyuck pushed his hand into his pocket, felt the little bit of rice he had brought with him, and counted his blessings.

* * *

All through the early morning hours of December 23, the *Meredith Victory*'s crew worked to load the refugees while still more came. Some injured civilians arrived on stretchers. Other refugees were very old and needed help climbing the ramps. And there was the endless stream of babies. Even as the *Meredith Victory*'s crew seemed to make good progress clearing the throngs from the docks, still more arrived. The throngs seemed resistant to decreasing. Although the ship lacked provisions and water, sleeping and toilet facilities, still the refugees came. The crew tried to keep track. They piled the refugees into every corner of every hold. Side by side they stood, next to each other and next to and on top of more than a thousand drums of jet fuel. All through the night, they poured onto the ship.

"Lunney," Captain LaRue said as he peered down on the deck from the starboard bridge wing, "it's just incredible. This is like some giant-sized carnival show where they put all those clowns into one tiny little car."

"Indeed, Captain—just without all the frivolity, eh?"

And still the refugees arrived. Through the night, under a constant crisscrossing of artillery fire, humanity streamed aboard the *Meredith Victory* seemingly without end. Finally, the crew had no more space in the holds. All levels of all the cargo holds below were filled to capacity with precious human cargo.

"How many in the holds?" LaRue asked.

"The men have counted ten thousand down below," Savastio reported.

Ten thousand! LaRue marveled as a lump set into his throat. It seemed impossibly absurd. He glanced at Lunney and then turned back toward the docks, surveying them with a heavy heart. While good headway had been made, thousands yet remained. He had no idea how many his ship would ultimately hold, but he knew his departure would be a death sentence for all left behind. Before him remained men with families and women with babies. He saw old people and young people—all desperate for escape. *How can I possibly refuse them?* LaRue thought. Yet imminent danger pressed in on them all. It was early in the morning hours, it was freezing cold, the sky was still dark, and the artillery shells were still being lobbed back and forth over the *Meredith Victory*. For LaRue, the risk grew higher by the minute. Just one stray shell or one lucky shot by the Chinese would incinerate the ten thousand people loaded so far. In addition, he was sure the final perimeter had completely pulled out. Now, only the naval artillery and airpower kept the Chinese out of Hungnam.

Captain LaRue passed a young man working diligently to load the Koreans. "Keep them coming, son," he said as he put a friendly hand on the young mariner's shoulder. "Put them on the deck. Fill it up. Don't leave any of them behind. You'll know we're done when the docks and the beaches are clear."

"Yes, sir!" the young man answered, but privately he wondered if the captain's idea was truly possible.

In the hours before dawn, the refugees continued to come and to bring with them all their worldly possessions, all that they held dear. With all the cargo holds full, the main deck was filling rapidly. One family came with a piano and tried to roll it up the ramps and onboard. While LaRue permitted almost everything else, he drew the line at that; there simply wasn't room.

Tragedy eventually struck. LaRue supposed it was not possible that so many thousands could move in such difficult circumstances without injury or loss at some point. Somewhere in the throng, an infant slipped from her mother's arms, fell to the docks, and died in the crush of people.

LaRue summoned a couple of Army officers to his quarters for a quick consultation. They urged LaRue to speed his departure and simply bury the child at sea.

"Gentlemen," LaRue explained, "these people are scared. They are fleeing for their lives. Half of them may wonder if we're simply going to take them offshore and dump them in the ocean. If we do that with this precious child, we'll have a panic and we'll never recover."

LaRue prevailed and arranged for a short service on land on behalf of the parents. A couple of MPs dug a shallow grave on the beach and hurriedly tried to console the grieving parents.

* * *

The first light of December 23 peeked over the eastern horizon, and to LaRue's amazement, the docks and the beach finally stood desolate. Not only in the holds below but now on the deck, thousands of huddled masses shuddered against unspeakable cold, trying to stay warm in the frigid temperatures—so much so that there was barely room to walk anywhere on the ship. LaRue feared that by the next morning the deck would be littered with corpses.

Working his way back to the bridge, LaRue replayed the scene that had played out over the past twenty-four hours. As he reached the bridge deck, he turned and paused to consider the masses crowded onto the deck of his ship. He knew that below, ten thousand more were huddled together—anxiously awaiting salvation to the south.

"Lunney, what's the count of those on the top deck?"

"The men reported four thousand more outside."

LaRue staggered at the news. His ship now held fourteen thousand souls.

The ongoing sounds of aerial bombardment raised his eyes back to Hungnam. It lay nearly empty now—barren, stripped of all who could leave and everything that could be taken. He pondered how it must have seen happier times—families living and making their way through life. He wondered where all of that had gone. For now, LaRue realized, whatever was left of all that life was now resting, at least partly, in his hands.

It was time to go. LaRue stepped with authority onto the bridge. He steeled himself for the mission that lay ahead.

"Gentlemen," he said confidently, "now we leave—without delay. Cast off and take us out of here. Once clear of the docks, I want a max of five knots through the swept channel."

With his command, the crew sprang into action. LaRue's confidence, conviction, and clarity of thought bound the men together under his leadership. They worked as one, with one purpose, one goal, with the efficiency of men well trained. Yet each of them also felt the weight of the uniqueness of their cargo on this particular run. While most often they carried the instruments of death, today they carried life itself.

The deck crew quickly released the mooring lines which had held the *Meredith Victory* to the *Norcuba*. The crew immediately began raising the anchor. LaRue watched over the activities from the bridge, listening to the heavy rattle of the ship's chain. No further commands were necessary.

Elsewhere, the administrative crew attended to the necessary details required to keep the ship operational. The mess crew had already begun to prepare meals for their compatriots. Members of the administrative crew attended to paperwork that needed to be filled out and filed away. Basic supplies in the medical cabinet were checked and rechecked. Deep in the engine room—scattered around the engine, turbine, and boilers, perched on catwalks and ladders—the crew stood ready for action. Oilers had been carefully lubricating and maintaining every moving part in the great symphony of gears and mechanics that was the ship's very life. But now the men stood silent. They waited for the command to get underway to reverberate down the brass speaking tubes. As they waited, they listened to the distinct rattle of the noise of the anchor being raised. When the anchor chain fell silent, they knew their job would come next.

The rattle ceased. They waited in eerie silence for the command. LaRue's voice came down the speaking tube crystal clear. "Engine room, ahead one quarter."

"Ahead one quarter," the engine room promptly replied back up the tube. It was merely a matter of turning a few valves. Having worked the tedious procedure to keep boilers and turbine hot all night, their departure was immediate. Superheated steam poured into the turbine and began to slowly turn the shaft which drove their sole screw. The heavy brass screw churned the water and slowly began to push its load forward.

Standing on the deck, LaRue felt his ship shudder and come to life, almost a living, breathing entity, attended to by the delicate coordination of her crew. Under her own power again, the

Meredith Victory crawled away from the dock area as LaRue guided his ship and its cargo toward and through the four thousand mines.

The ship and crew were scarcely a quarter mile offshore when LaRue heard the increased pitch of rapid gunfire and the renewed noise of combat. He stepped outside to see the docks that had been so peacefully empty just a bit earlier erupt in combat as Chinese troops finally poured into the broken city.

* * *

In the cargo holds, Dong-hyuck and his father remained standing in silence. They heard only the whine of the ship's engine, but they surmised enough to conclude definitively: they were underway.

"How much longer now, Father? How long will we travel?"

"I'm really not sure, son. It should not be long. I am sure everything will be fine. Freedom is just a short distance away."

"Then when we are in the south, can we arrange for Mother and the family to come?"

"Yes, son, we'll write to her and arrange to get her and the family down south as soon as possible. We will make that our first priority." Byung-soon embraced his son and held him tight, hiding the uncertainty that swelled in his heart.

* * *

LaRue now focused his attention on ensuring their safe passage. With the tattered hand-drawn chart on the bridge, he guided his crew so that they followed the port-side swept channel as they again traversed the deadly minefield. Beyond the minefield, he knew he would have another concern—Russian submarines. In their present location, LaRue, his crew, and its precious cargo were just a few hundred miles from Vladivostok, home of a large Soviet submarine base. Soviet subs were known to patrol these waters along the eastern coast of Korea and seemed to enjoy nothing more than to sink US cargo ships. But for now, the minefield remained LaRue's first priority.

It was the afternoon of December 23, 1950.

CHAPTER FOURTEEN

Voyage

As he had done on the inbound passage through the swept channel, so LaRue did on departure. He guided his ship through the delicate balance to navigate the narrow and poorly marked channel. But the stakes were higher now. The price for hitting a mine was not merely the ship and crew, but rather the certain death of fourteen thousand innocent civilians.

Slowly, but with reassuring certainty, the *Meredith Victory* responded to her captain's commands as he skirted each mine. Each second put more mines behind them and reduced the number ahead. She sat light in the water and executed each command faithfully. Although loaded to capacity and beyond, the load of fourteen thousand civilians they had taken onboard was of inconsequential weight—perhaps just a thousand tons or so. That, plus the existing three hundred tons of jet fuel, hardly impacted her ten-thousand-ton carrying capacity. Each hundred yards brought more relief to LaRue. Against all odds, a sense of normalcy overtook the crew as they resumed their regular duties.

A few miles away from the inner harbor, the *Meredith Victory* was rocked by an enormous explosion. LaRue anxiously stepped outside the bridge just in time to see the detonation of the entire remaining ordnance that had been left behind, along with the explosives that had been set by the Navy demolition teams. The massive guns of the remaining US battleships also turned their sights on the docks and destroyed them in just a few moments.

After a tense hour, they cleared the final mine obstacles in the harbor. As the mood relaxed a bit, Chief Mate Savastio spoke up.

"Why'd you do it Captain?"

"Excuse me?" LaRue replied.

"Why'd you decide to take all these people? I don't think anything like this has ever been done before."

LaRue paused for a moment before he gave an answer.

"It was already decided, my friend. It is nearly Christmas Eve, is it not? I thought of the Bible story of Mary and Joseph, with no room in the inn for them to lodge, desperately in search of a place for safety." LaRue smiled gently. "Besides that, I believe God's own hand is at the helm of our ship today."

"Maybe so, Captain, maybe so. I do hope you're right," Savastio said.

* * *

With the low rumble of the ship's engines and the gentle response of the ship to the ocean waves, Dong-hyuck huddled with his father in the hold. It did not take long before they learned the location of the toilets: the corners of the cargo hold. Each person slowly shifted his or her way through the mass of humanity when the moment required. In fairly short order, a vile stench began to fill each cargo hold.

As the hours crawled forward in the blackness of the ship's holds, Dong-hyuck grew increasingly thirsty. He realized his last drink of water had been sometime the previous day.

"Father, I am so very thirsty. I have had nothing to drink since before we boarded."

"I know, son, I am thirsty too. We are all thirsty."

"Father, I will see if I can make it above—there must be water above. Just a little bit is all I need. I will bring you some too."

Dong-hyuck made his way to the edge of the hold and tried to ascend the vertical ladder to the next level. But at the top the entrance was blocked, and he could find no way out. He reluctantly returned to his father and resolved to manage his thirst as best he could. But how much longer?

* * *

The journey wore into its first day, and Chief Mate Savastio grew increasingly concerned about the welfare of the passengers. Those on deck especially suffered, as they had nothing to shield them from the bitter wind and frigid ocean spray. The crew handed out the few tarps they had and helped the refugees fashion them as shelter against the elements. Sadly, they had no food and no drinking water for the refugees. All that was available to eat was the sum total of what each family had brought aboard.

As night began to fall, the temperature fell quickly as well. The ship's instruments recorded readings just shy of zero degrees Fahrenheit. The intense cold concerned Savastio greatly for those who were topside. He weaved his way through the throngs on the top deck, trying to reassure himself that they were okay and would be fine until they arrived at Pusan in another twenty-four hours or so. He stepped gingerly between women and children, stepping over the sleeping men and huddled hordes sheltering themselves from the cold as the *Meredith Victory* cut her way through the waves. Men, women, children, all crouching closely against each other, sheltering each other from the salty spray of the ocean and sharing what little precious heat they had among themselves.

As Savastio worked his way toward the bow of the ship, his pulse quickened and then froze as he caught sight of a wisp of smoke ascending out of the number-three cargo hatch. Savastio watched in fear as another deadly stream of white smoke wove its way between the offset hatch covers and blew across the deck. Fire!

Savastio rushed to the hatch and quickly unlocked the ladder that descended into the hold. Hand over hand and foot over foot as fast as he could possibly move, he descended into the blackness and the sea of refugees below. The refugees crowded away from the ladder as Savastio approached. With a few steps to go, he jumped from the ladder and landed firmly on the deck below. He spun to survey the thousands of dimly lit faces before him. They curiously investigated why this ship's officer had descended into their crowded hordes.

In the flickering light and bouncing shadows of a small fire, Savastio saw the cause of the smoke, and his blood ran dry with fear. On top of several of the drums of jet fuel, the refugees had built small fires—apparently to prepare food. On top of the jet fuel!

"No, no, no!" Savastio shouted as he raced for the fires, roughly pushing his way through the wall-to-wall people. There was barely enough room for them to shift to allow him through.

"No fire, no fire down here!" he shouted, hoping they would understand. He reached the site of the fires and looked incredulously as a couple of men prepared a small meal over the flames. They looked dismayed at Savastio's excited pleas.

Desperate to communicate, he improvised. Savastio rapped hard on the side of the metal drums of jet fuel, repeating "No fire!" over and over again. One of the men cooking smiled politely at Savastio, put a spoon into his concoction, and kindly offered a taste to Savastio. He grew more desperate to communicate the mortal danger.

"Fire!" he said, pointing at the flames. "Jet fuel!" he said, banging hard on the drum. Then, with the maximum amount of drama he could muster, he made his best imitation of a deadly explosion and the resulting fireball. Gesturing his hands wildly to their full extension, Savastio screamed as loudly as he could, "BOOOOOM!"

The men cooking stood in stunned silence. They looked at Savastio, still wild-eyed with fear and desperation, his stocky arms stretched to their fullest reach. The Korean men glanced at the drums, inspecting them more closely, then at the fire, and then back at Savastio. Then, finally, they understood.

The men rattled off an urgent string of Korean, and their fellow refugees jumped into action, quickly removing coats and outer garments and swatting at the flames until they were extinguished.

Exhausted from fear but exhilarated with relief, Savastio slowly retreated back into the crowd of humanity, made his way back to the ladder, and ascended to the top deck.

CHAPTER FIFTEEN
Arrival

While Savastio was literally putting out fires, Captain LaRue also made rounds in the evening hours of December 23. As he worked his way around the top deck, he came upon a scene that made him pause. He watched from a distance as his young sailors aided some young Korean women with babies. His sailors took their woolen gloves from their hands and gave them to the refugees. They even took their heavy jackets off and wrapped them around the mothers with young infants to keep them warm.

Until this moment, LaRue had scarcely had time to ponder the tradition of sharing gifts on Christmas Day. It seemed to him there was no finer sense of the Christmas spirit than what his crew was engaged in at this moment. Such *young* men, he thought to himself again—scarcely boys. And yet acting with a compassion and maturity beyond their years.

As the night toiled on, LaRue and his crew did all they could to provide a little nourishment and water for the thousands onboard. The crew found and cooked some limited amounts of rice and distributed it the best they could. But there simply was not enough for all. Below deck, the reality of ten thousand persons without basic toilet facilities was becoming clear. Refugees suffered with the reality of raw sewage on each deck.

As dawn broke early in the morning of December 24, the *Meredith Victory* and her cargo were about halfway down the coast of Korea, heading toward Pusan. LaRue remained concerned about the possibility of Russian submarines or even a simple aerial attack from a lone enemy aircraft. But much to his relief, such threats never materialized. Instead, a certain monotony set in among the refugees. On the top deck, they huddled together tightly as they had through the freezing cold, wet night. LaRue looked at their faces and saw their fatigue, their hunger, their unquenchable thirst. He pitied them and wished he could do more for them.

What he could do, he set about doing with all his ability. LaRue maintained maximum speed around the clock in order to get their precious cargo to Pusan as fast as possible. The *Meredith Victory* maintained her top speed of seventeen knots. At times, the engine room was even able to push it up to eighteen knots as she raced toward Pusan, toward safety and freedom. The rapid pace continued all day, and as the sun began to retreat off the starboard side, LaRue gave the orders to maintain their speed with all urgency through the night.

Despite his best efforts, the reality of the oppressive conditions was not to be denied. Late in the evening of December 24, tempers began to flare among some of the younger men among the refugees. The refugees had been and were grateful, but even grateful people needed food and water and accommodations for basic life, and right now the *Meredith Victory* had precious few such luxuries. LaRue heard a disturbance just outside the bridge and the next level down, where the seamen lived.

He stepped off the bridge and down the ladder, and then down one more ladder to the general quarters, moving down the passageway toward the noise. The first sights and sounds were angry gestures and angry voices. Seven of his crew held a defensive position in the passageway. In front of them were at least two hundred Korean men. LaRue didn't understand them, but the message was clear: they wanted food and water and better conditions, none of which LaRue could offer.

LaRue feared the confrontation could spark into an uncontrollable riot that would kill them all. *How do you control a riot onboard a ship of fourteen thousand?* He cautiously confirmed that his sidearm was still available and regretfully rested his hand on the butt of his pistol—just in case. But instead, LaRue stood back and watched something astounding take place. One by one, his men took their own small meals and turned them over to the Koreans. There seemed to be real surprise on the faces of the men when they realized what LaRue's crew was doing. LaRue watched closely as the hungry Koreans looked somewhat apologetically at the crew, and then—without taking the meals— slowly turned and walked back to their families. As hungry as they and their families were, they would not take the little food their rescuers had for themselves.

LaRue tried his best to rest at night, but sleep escaped him again. He opened his captain's log and wrote, "The nearness of Christmas carries my thoughts to the holy family—how they, too, were cold and without shelter. Like the crucified Christ these good people suffer through the actions of guilty men."

* * *

At dawn on December 25, fatigue set in for all the crew. Countless hours tending to thousands of refugees made the situation difficult. Sleep was rare for the young crew and often interrupted. Their burden wore on them.

But in spite of their fatigue, the crew rejoiced to find that all had survived the night at sea. They were famished and thirsty, but they were alive and reasonably healthy.

On the bridge, LaRue struggled against the fatigue to stay focused on his ship and the safety of its cargo. He would swing back and forth between two competing thoughts. On one hand, he marveled at the lives onboard his little ship. On the other hand, he dared not think about the great risk.

As LaRue worked to maintain his focus on the mission, his concentration was interrupted by Chief Mate Savastio as he stepped onto the bridge.

"Captain, how many did you say we have aboard?" he asked, catching his breath and wiping sweat from his brow.

"Dino, you know very well what the count is: fourteen thousand," LaRue answered.

"Well, Captain, you can make it fourteen thousand and one now!"

LaRue turned to Savastio and smiled apologetically with a realization he had not yet pondered. Of course, many pregnant women had come aboard. A baby had been born, and more would no doubt be on their way. He shook his head, smiling.

"I see my Chief Mate and medical officer has been busy. Did you have any assistance?"

"One of the Korean women must be a midwife or something. She helped me deliver the baby. That was really fantastic, Captain. I mean, they don't train us for that in our first-aid class. I think I'll remember this for a long time," Savastio said, beaming. "Captain, what should we name this one?"

"Name? I suppose that's the mother's job."

"Maybe, but I got the idea the mother wanted us to name the baby. It's your ship, Captain. What do you say?" Savastio asked.

LaRue smiled and thought for a moment. "Do you remember that dish they like so much? kimchi, right?"

"Yes, Captain, kimchi."

"Okay, let's name the first one Meredith Victory Kimchi #1."

"If there's more? I've got several more women down here who may give birth in the next few hours."

"Really? Okay. Meredith Victory Kimchi #2, #3, and so forth.

How's that, Savastio?"

"Well, it's not very original—but it's highly functional. Consider it done, sir. I'm off to check on those others now." And Savastio bounded off the bridge en route to check on the other women. Before the voyage was over, the crew used names one through five: five babies were born en route with their only medical attention being that of Chief Mate Savastio and a native midwife.

* * *

After two days without proper facilities, food, or fresh water, the *Meredith Victory* drew close to the Pusan harbor and dropped anchor a few miles offshore. She was met by a smaller craft carrying the commanding naval officers at Pusan. The crew lowered ladders and helped the Navy officers aboard. Chief Mate Savastio escorted the officers into LaRue's private quarters.

Savastio started to leave, but LaRue invited him to stay. "Gentlemen, I see you've met Chief Mate Savastio. You men are a sight for sore eyes. Believe it or not, I've got fourteen thousand people aboard and instructions to discharge them here at Pusan."

The officers looked distinctly ill at ease and reluctant to speak. "Well, I've got bad news. That's not approved. We simply don't have room here. We've got over a million refugees in Pusan right now, and we just can't bring any more into the city."

Captain LaRue looked stunned at the revelation. He rubbed his furrowed brow and tried to make sense of it. "No room? I don't understand—we had clear directions to bring these poor people here. I've got ten thousand people below deck, four thousand more on top. I don't know what I'll find when we get them out of the cargo holds. You can certainly imagine that the conditions are impossible. What are we supposed to do with them?"

"Captain, I understand the dilemma. I can't even believe how many you've got out there on the deck. I hate to see what you've got down below, but we've got one *million* refugees here in Pusan. We just can't take any more. It's simply not possible. If so much as a mouse got off your ship, I think the whole city would slide into the sea. We've sent the last few incoming ships to Koje-do. That's where you really need to go. It's only fifty miles or so, and they'll take good care of you and your refugees down there."

LaRue resisted further, but eventually the logistical, military, and red-tape reasons won out over reason. LaRue resigned himself to one more day at sea. Koje-do it was. LaRue felt the weight of crushing disappointment on his crew and the refugees. He could only hope that no riots would be sparked when the refugees figured out they wouldn't be getting off at Pusan.

"Captain, if I may," Savastio said before the Navy officers left. "Is there any way you fellas can spare us some rice, maybe a little fresh water, blankets, anything of the sort that can help us over the next twenty-four hours?"

The Navy officers pondered the request and looked at each other for a moment. "I think we can do that, and maybe one better. I've got a couple of men who speak Korean and a few military police. Maybe some interpreters and a few MPs might help you keep order until tomorrow. Will that help?

"Absolutely. We'll take whatever you can get us," LaRue gladly answered. "Work out any of the details with Savastio here, and he'll make it happen."

Within a few hours some rice, fresh water, and blankets had been put aboard. Three interpreters began to make their way among the refugees, along with a half-dozen MPs to help maintain good order on the ship.

A bit of peace washed over LaRue. He watched the interpreters comfort his refugees, and for the first time since their departure, he saw relaxed smiles on their faces. LaRue began to understand the magnitude of it all. He now felt the assurance of full confidence that no matter what, this ship would deliver her cargo of souls safely to Koje-do. While they regrettably had another day at sea, the supplies would be invaluable. So with a little bit of food and fresh water, the *Meredith Victory* weighed anchor and pressed on.

The *Meredith Victory* sailed again the afternoon of December 25. The few hours to Koje-do passed quickly. As she slowed to a stop outside the harbor, the harbormaster, Frank McKenzie, peered through his binoculars to identify the incoming ship.

"What ship is that? I can't identify it from here," he asked his colleague, Clarence Worth.

"Radio indicates we're looking at the *Meredith Victory,* sir. We just got some paperwork on her a little bit ago. Apparently she's coming out of Hungnam. She tried to unload in Pusan, but they sent her here."

"Typical Victory ship—but what in the world is she carrying? What's on her deck? I can't make it out from here, but her deck is completely covered. Here—you take a look. What is it?" McKenzie handed the binoculars over to Worth. He peered through the binoculars, twisting the focus to bring the image into sharpness.

"McKenzie, you're not going to believe it, but what you're looking at is people! Every inch of that deck is full of people. They look really miserable too."

"People? She's a cargo ship. Unbelievable! They must have used her to take more of the refugees out of Hungnam." McKenzie whistled. "They must have been really desperate up there to press her into service. Well, I'm sure they're eager to dock, but you're going to have to give them the bad news. All the docks are full. Tell them to anchor out there overnight, and by morning we'll figure out a way to squeeze them in somehow."

"Yeah, thanks, McKenzie, let me give them the bad news,"

Worth said.

"Can't think of a better man for the job, my friend," McKenzie said with a smile. "Seriously, be sure to tell them we'll get them in first thing in the morning without delay. Tell them their long journey is nearly over."

* * *

The *Meredith Victory* spent Christmas night at sea, ever so close to port and yet an eternity away. On the top deck, her huddled masses clung tightly to each other, preserving what little mutual warmth they could share. With morning came the call that LaRue longed to hear: clearance into the port of Koje-do had finally been granted. LaRue enthusiastically gave the order to engage the screw, and the *Meredith Victory* sprang to life. In a manner never seen before or since, she slowly plowed her way into the harbor to unload her precious cargo. But even with the delay, there was still no room at the docks to berth the *Meredith Victory* and her human cargo.

After a short consultation on the available options, the military dispatched two LSTs to offload the refugees—"landing ships, tanks" in the formal language of the military. They were normally tasked with unloading tanks from ships and taking them on shore. Pressed into service in this fashion, they could hold about seven thousand people each. The prescription was just what LaRue needed.

The LSTs made a slow approach and then gently nestled on each side of the *Meredith Victory*. Crewmen on all three ships tossed large lines back and forth and lashed the three ships together. Unfortunately, the seas were not particularly cooperative. The swells and billows strained the moorings as the three ships danced together in the waves. They repeatedly tested their moorings, separated a foot or two, and then slammed together with a deafening crash of steel on steel. But there was no delaying the next phase. LaRue gave the orders to begin offloading the refugees.

Those on the top deck departed first. The refugees happily scrambled over the side of the *Meredith Victory* and down into the waiting LSTs. LaRue watched nervously as the swells caused the ships to stretch apart and then crash together again. If a person slipped between the ships, he would be crushed instantly.

As those on the top deck scrambled into the LSTs, the *Meredith Victory*'s crew set their attention to opening the deck hatches and starting the process of emptying the holds of their human cargo. Removing each of the deck covers, the crew wondered what they would really find down below. Despite the cold temperatures, the rising stench poured out of the holds as each cover was removed. It burned the eyes and noses of those on deck with pungent bitterness. The loading platforms were lowered into the hold, and refugees excitedly, but without pushing or shoving, clambered onto the wooden platform. Fathers, who were hoisted up, untied the sashes around their waists and lowered them down into the hold to retrieve their children. Little hands clasped tightly to the linen sashes and scrambled up into the sunlight.

The cranes continued to hoist the wooden platforms delicately out of the hold and then swung them around and lowered the refugees onto the deck. From there, the refugees scrambled over the edge of the ship and into the waiting landing craft.

* * *

In the darkness of the hold, Dong-hyuck sat weakly with his father. Exhausted by the conditions and desperately thirsty, they sat in the dark. They leaned on each other, unsure if their voyage would ever end. For days they had suffered in the oppressive conditions down below. They had been vaguely aware of a stop that had been made somewhere—they thought it was a day or two ago. In the oppressive darkness, time had little sense of reality. And then they had realized they were moving again. Now they were aware of a second stop. To both father and son, this one seemed different. There was more noise and stirring above them. The loud metal clanging of steel against steel reverberated through the inner chambers of the ship. Slowly, the noise of the work above them became clearer and obviously closer in proximity.

Suddenly, a razor's edge of brilliant white light pierced the darkness as the edge of a wooden cargo hatch was jostled from its position. Then the razor of light exploded into a sky of immeasurable brightness and flooded into the dark hold. All below winced and shut their eyes tightly against the blinding pain of the light. It was thirty seconds before they dared to pry their eyes open again. When they did, they saw the faces of men looking down. They saw ropes being lowered. They saw cranes lowering a loading platform to them. They saw blue sky, and they realized they had finally arrived.

Men and boys grabbed hold of the ropes and were hoisted to freedom. All in the cargo hold pressed away from the lowering pallet so that it could be placed on the deck below their feet. When it settled into place, women, children, and a few men clambered onto the pallet and held on tightly as they were hoisted into the blue sky above.

About twenty minutes passed as more and more were hauled out of the depths of the cargo hold. Then it was time for Dong-hyuck and his father to leave. They excitedly grabbed the makeshift ropes and scampered up and out. Finally, they emerged onto the main deck and into the full brilliance of the sun and the fresh air.

Still squinting hard against the extreme brightness, Dong-hyuck asked, "Where are we, Father?"

Byung-soon looked around, spinning quickly in three hundred and sixty degrees—surveying the landscape around them.

"I don't know, son, except that we are in the south. Look at the greenness of the hills. It is warmer here. Feel the warmth, my boy." He smiled deeply at his son, and for the first time in several days, permitted himself to relax. "Son, we've made it," he said with a huge smile on his face. He embraced his boy tightly and wondered what this new place would hold for them.

Dong-hyuck and his father quickly followed a line of refugees to the edge of the *Meredith Victory* and scrambled over the edge and into the waiting LST.

CHAPTER SIXTEEN

Lost

The military ship carrying Jack Stiles also carried nearly a thousand other bruised and bloodied soldiers and Marines. Each of them had a story to tell about combat, and death, and things no man should see. But no one talked. It was the first step in a long process of burying the memories alongside their fallen colleagues.

Onboard medics tended to many of the men, patching them up and keeping them as comfortable as possible. The worst of the wounded had been gathered into a makeshift hospital on deck three. But for a few men, the desperate desire to not die in North Korea, to make it out of Hungnam and onto a ship, was all they had left. For those few men, the cold storage near the ship's mess served as a makeshift morgue.

Jack slumbered deep in sleep on the second bunk of a four-bunk unit as the ship maneuvered into position against the dock at Koje-do. Soldiers and Marines began to slowly stir, retrieve their belongings, and hobble their way to the nearest ladder to disembark.

"Hey, fella—you leaving, or are you just gonna sleep all day? This ain't some motel, you know." Jack didn't stir. The young Army private came closer, raised his voice, and jostled Jack with his boot. "Come on, boy, up and at 'em—everybody's leaving, let's go!"

Jack startled from sleep in an instant, shot upright, and smashed into the base of the unoccupied bunk above him. The loose wire mesh supporting the thin mattress clanged loudly, and the combined shock sent Jack into action. From his frozen foxhole, he looked into the eyes of his Chinese foe. He lunged at his attacker and instinctively reached for the private's neck. They tumbled to the deck as Jack secured his hand and started to squeeze with all of his remaining strength.

"Arrrrrrrrrggghhhhh," the private groaned with the little bit of breath he could force out through his throat. He balled his hands into fists and landed brutal blows against the side of Jack's face until finally Jack released his death grip on his throat.

The young man scrambled for safety, coughing and sputtering and trying to breathe again. When he finally could talk, he spat, "You idiot! I was just trying to wake you up. Figures I'd make it through Korea and then some crazed Marine tries to kill me . . ."

Jack's head spun. He looked around, struggling to remember where he was and how he got here. He was in a foxhole at Chosin. He felt the cold of frozen dirt biting against his face. Then abruptly, his reality changed. It was the cold steel of the deck that he felt. He turned onto his back and could see that he was on a ship. Realization of what he had done flooded his mind. "I'm sorry, I just thought you were . . . I just thought you . . . never mind. I'm sorry. I didn't mean to hurt you."

The Army private was on his feet as Jack unsteadily climbed to his. "Just stay away from me," he muttered, waving his arm at Jack and disappearing into the adjacent passageway.

"I'm sorry, man!" Jack hollered after him, but he was gone. Jack stood for a second or two in silence, ashamed. In a moment, Jack noticed that he was alone. There was no sound of combat, no noise of conversation, no sound of human activity. Flickering lights in the crew quarters hummed and cast stark shadows among the empty bunks. The entire area was empty—just the bunks and a few scattered personal effects someone had left behind. It was an uneasy feeling. Jack straightened his tattered and stained uniform and hobbled to the passageway. He slowly climbed two ladders and joined a line of men leaving the ship.

In just a few minutes, Jack passed outside into brilliant sunlight. He squinted at the bright blue, cloudless sky. He couldn't remember the last time he'd seen blue skies. He noticed the gentle ocean breeze carrying warm temperatures. The long line of men inched forward as he and the others crossed over a wide gangway and were suddenly back on solid ground.

Jack stood still for a few minutes as his eyes adjusted to the brilliance of the day. He breathed deeply and savored the salt scent of the coastal breeze, a stark contrast to the damp, oily smell of the Navy transport ship. His eyes took in a sight that reminded him of a few days earlier in Hungnam, in what now seemed almost a dream. He struggled to shake the sleep from his mind as he tried to process what was before him. Something wasn't right. Something was unexpected. Thousands of huddled people, men, women, children. They carried bundles and babies. They moved as one away from the docks toward some unseen destination. And then he knew. *Refugees!*

Jack quickly spun and saw a group of MPs directing soldiers just a few hundred feet ahead. He limped as quickly as he could to their position and interrupted their conversation.

"Hey, what's up with the refugees here? I thought they were all going to Pusan?"

"Yep. *Were.* Pusan's full. They sent them here. Lovely, huh?"

"Who'd they send here? How many? Do you know what ships?" Jack fired his questions as fast as they occurred to him.

"Slow down, slow down," the MP chastened. His voice was terse. He looked Jack square in the eyes. "No clue."

"They were from Hungnam, right?"

"Yep. Hungnam. That's all I got for ya."

"Thanks," Jack replied sarcastically as he drifted away from the MPs. "Sorry to bother you."

His heart beating wildly, Jack scanned the throngs of civilian refugees and realized that maybe there was hope. Maybe she was here. He promised himself that this time, if he found her, he would not let her go again.

* * *

Loading cranes continued their delicate ballet as they plucked wooden platforms full of mothers, fathers, and babies from the blackness of the cargo holds, swung them perilously above the three rocking ships, and lowered them onto the deck of the *Meredith Victory*. From there, the refugees scattered and crawled over the ship's rail and slid down into the waiting LSTs.

Despite LaRue's fears, the offloading went very well. After five hours, the LSTs were completely filled and the *Meredith Victory* had been emptied of her human cargo. Suddenly, it was over.

LaRue stood on the deck of his now-empty ship and gazed at the sea of faces crowded into the LST on the port side of the *Meredith Victory*. The Koreans didn't normally show much emotion. But in this case, their faces revealed overflowing relief and joy. LaRue was all the more stunned when several thousand refugees on the LST looked up at him and gave a half-bow, bestowing upon him an honor he had never expected.

He choked back a growing tightness in his throat and knew it had been worth it all.

"Final count, son?" LaRue asked the young man assigned to the duty.

"Fourteen thousand, five souls, Captain!"

Internally, LaRue reeled at the accomplishment. Somehow, his voice held steady.

"Very fine. A job well done. Finish up your duties, and we'll see if we can't get a little shore time."

"Yes, sir," the young man replied.

Content that all had disembarked safely, LaRue felt it was his duty to make one final round through his ship. He roamed across the deck where thousands had once huddled. The masses of humanity had left behind little evidence: a few scraps of clothing, bits of blankets, and other waste. But apart from such indications, it struck LaRue as almost unbelievable that just a short time ago the deck and every hold below had been full of humanity.

He made his way to a metal ladder. He didn't really want to see the stark reality down below, but knew he must. He descended into the still-putrid atmosphere of the ship's holds. On each deck he examined his ship, with only a small flashlight as his guide. The evidence of her cargo was manifest. The holds reeked of sweat, urine, and human waste. In each corner of each hold, he found the same evidence of the journey: feces piled at least three feet deep.

As LaRue examined the farthest corners of cargo hold two and the lowest deck of the hold, he noticed a strange sight tucked against one of the bulkheads. He approached cautiously. As he drew closer, his heart raced and then nearly stopped. His eyes saw it, but his mind could scarcely process the sight. Piled neatly in the hold was a small pile of grenades and automatic machine guns, including a Chinese burp gun. For the first time in the voyage, he felt a rising sickness in his stomach. He glanced at the nearby drums of jet fuel. He glanced back at the weapons cache. The combination of deadly firepower and jet fuel chilled his blood. He staggered at the thought of what would have happened if someone had wanted to destroy his ship. A cold sweat gripped him around the neck, and he fought back nausea.

Had the weapons been in the possession of some of the refugees? Or had soldiers come aboard, posing as refugees, perhaps intending to destroy his ship? If they had been saboteurs,

LaRue wondered if perhaps they had been moved by their mutual peril and laid their weapons aside. Whatever the circumstances, LaRue was grateful that *somebody* for *some reason* had chosen to lay the weapons down. He would ask his crew to retrieve the cache and turn them over to the Army.

Content with the security of his ship, LaRue worked his way up the ladders and returned to his cabin with one more official duty to perform. He retrieved the logbook from his desk and made an entry no other captain in history has ever made:

"Five births, no deaths, en route. Disembarked 14,005 persons safely."

Captain LaRue put the pen down and closed the logbook. A knock on his door interrupted his thoughts. "Come in."

Dino Savastio stood in the doorway. He was normally all business, attentive to every detail of his duty, but now relaxed and at ease. "Captain, nice work," Savastio offered.

"Hey, Dino. Same to you. Be sure to tell the crew that I appreciate all their work on this one."

"Will do, Captain. Any word on our next port?"

"Well, I'm hoping we might be able to give the crew a few days rest here, but then I'm guessing we're back to Pusan. We'll obviously need to get the ship cleaned up a bit. I would encourage you not to go down into the holds unnecessarily," LaRue said, smiling. "From there—I suppose we'll just have to see where the wind blows us."

"Yes, sir. That's what keeps this job exciting," Savastio said as he lingered near the door.

"You can say that again. Anything else?"

Savastio straightened. "Captain, I hope you won't mind me saying, but it was a real honor to serve with you on this one. This trip was unique. We did something very special out there," he said as he looked out the portal at the masses of people still trailing away from the docks. "This wasn't just hauling cargo. These were lives. Fourteen thousand of them—or to be precise, fourteen thousand and five," he recalled with a smile.

LaRue smiled in return, feeling a swell of pride in his crew. "I appreciate that, Dino. It's a privilege to have you as my Chief Mate. You're a fine officer. I know you'll continue to do well with the Merchant Marine. You'll probably get your own ship someday. Whatever caused you to want this job, anyway? I don't guess you ever expected you'd be hauling thousands of people on an old cargo ship."

Savastio smiled as he rewound faded memories. "No, sir, I didn't. But I love this job. See, I grew up in Italy. My parents got us out just as Mussolini was really coming to power. I still remember kids in my neighborhood starting to wear the outfit of the *Balilla* group—the black shirts, black cap, and black shorts. My folks had enough foresight to get out and come to America. When I turned eighteen, I tried to sign up for the US Navy. I really wanted to serve on the subs. But they said they didn't want first-generation Italians on the subs. They even said I wasn't fit for a life at sea. So, here I am, funny enough," Dino laughed. "That's my story. Hauling cargo or hauling people, I'm just happy to be here, sir."

"Thanks for sharing that. Somebody told me you had been interested in submarines, but I hadn't heard the full story before. The Navy made a mistake with that decision. But frankly, I'm glad they did. I'm glad you're here."

"Thank you, sir. Have a great rest of the day. Catch up on a little sleep, huh?" Savastio said as he turned and left LaRue's quarters.

"You too, Dino."

* * *

On the docks at Koje-do, Jack waited hopefully. He hoped

desperately that Tae-bok had decided to come—and that she was here, not in Pusan, though he had no way of knowing that either. *If* she had left her home, wherever she had been taken, he hoped she and the children had arrived safely. Even if they had come to Koje-do, how would he ever find them? Tens of thousands of refugees flooded the city, and now he watched as unbelievable thousands disembarked from the *Meredith Victory,* the last refugee ship to have left Hungnam. This, he thought, was the only place he might find them. If only she had made the choice to leave.

Jack wandered among the refugees. He scanned thousands of faces of young women with children. They all shuffled along, half-dragging their bodies and their burdens from the difficulties of the voyage. Many had babies strapped to their backs and bundles perched precariously on their heads. Men moved alongside the women as they carried heavier burdens and the remainder of their families' possessions. He waded into the crowd and circled around, looking at those whom he could not originally see. Jack was bumped and jostled repeatedly, and he apologized frequently as he would nearly trip over some small child. He felt lost anew in this ocean of humanity as he desperately searched for Tae-bok.

He continued wandering for more long hours, searching for her. His determination increased with each passing hour. If he found her, Jack decided, this time he would tell her how he felt. This time, he wouldn't let her go. He saw other ships arriving in the harbor. Most were military, but Jack continued to walk from one end of the docks to the other, up and down different piers, clinging to hope that perhaps she had decided to come.

Finally, Jack saw her. There she was, holding the baby with the older boy beside her. Jack called to her and moved excitedly through the rush of refugees. He closed the distance quickly as he thought of all he would say to her. This time he wouldn't be such a fool. This time, he would make it count. The crowd passed between them, and he lost sight of Tae-bok until the crowds parted again . . . and he looked into the eyes of a strange woman. The woman glanced at him, pushed past him, and continued on her way with her children. Jack's optimism was draining away as the sun continued its race toward the horizon.

With hope mostly gone and daylight quickly retreating, he rested on a small half-wall near the docks and watched the crowds stream by. The faces blurred together. Thousands passed him. The flood of people finally shrank to a small trickle of stragglers. Jack wrestled with reality. Either she had not come, she had been taken to Pusan, or she was here but simply could not be found among the tens of thousands of people.

The long day pressed upon him, and he grew drowsy as he rested. With deep regret, he finally convinced himself it was time to abandon the search. Jack got back onto his weary legs and walked away, dejected and tired. His hopes had been for naught. Yet, despite the fact that she had not come or could not be found, he felt grateful for the small amount of time he'd had with her and the children. He could not recall exactly how many days he had been with Tae-bok and her family since the attack on the road, but he was thankful for however long it had been.

Jack muttered aloud as he walked, "Well, that's it. Give it up, Jack, you're not going to find her. Get your head on straight, Marine, and get back to work. You did what you could."

When he had finished trying to talk some sense into himself, Jack walked the long length of the pier one last time. A military transport truck was gathering up Marines near the main road. Jack hobbled up to the truck as a few soldiers climbed aboard.

"Hey, fellas, where you headed?"

The driver responded, "There's some temporary barracks a couple miles from here. We're supposed to meet up there, and then they'll get us back to Pusan in a day or two. Got room if you want a ride. Jump in the back."

Jack thought for a second and decided it was indeed time to go.

"Yeah, if you've got room, I think I will. Thanks." He walked to the back of the truck and awkwardly hoisted himself into the transport. The soldiers already onboard slid down the wooden plank just a bit to make enough room for him. He dropped his body down hard on the wooden bench as he continued to try to tell himself it was time to get back to reality.

Jack glanced up and nodded at the Marine seated across from him. The driver cranked the diesel engine, and the whole transport rattled to life as the engine sputtered and rattled before blowing a black cloud of soot behind it.

"Name's Alejandro Martinez. What happened to you, buddy?" the Marine asked, taking note of Jack's swollen and bruised face and extending a war-weary and battered hand across to Jack.

Jack laughed halfheartedly and shook his head. "Long story, man. Better not to ask. Jack Stiles is the name. I was up at Chosin, got wounded, got a little detained along the way."

"Stiles? Did you say *Jack* Stiles?" Martinez asked.

"Yeah—Jack Stiles. What's it to you?"

"Well, we picked up a woman alongside the MSR on the way to Hungnam. She was carrying a baby, and she had a little boy walking with her. She had this note pinned to the baby—it said to take her to Hungnam. We did. The note had your name on it. Are you looking for her?"

"Absolutely." Jack started to stand. "Where is she?"

"I don't know, but when we got to Hungnam, she and the two kids got into the line for the last ship that was leaving—I think it was the *Meredith Victory*. If you're looking for her, she's got to be around here somewhere. What's the deal with that woman, anyway?"

"Too long of a story. Thanks, man," Jack shot back as he flung himself out of the already moving transport. He landed hard on his bad leg and groaned as a shot of pain raced up his right leg. He collapsed onto one knee and tried to shake off the searing pain.

Martinez stuck his head out the back of the transport and hollered at Jack. "You owe us one, Stiles! I'll find you in Pusan, and you're gonna buy me dinner!" Jack acknowledged the laughing Marine with a quick wave of his hand, but he didn't look back. He regained his balance and quickly spotted an MP directing traffic away from the docks. Jack limped his way up to him.

"Hey, where's the refugees from the *Meredith Victory?* Do you have any idea where they went?"

"*Meredith Victory?* Not exactly, buddy. I think she unloaded into two LSTs—they disembarked them here an hour or so ago. Crazy ship had like fourteen thousand people on her. Good luck with that. I think most of them started walking into town—down the main road there." The MP pointed toward a busy road away from the docks. "There's a whole line of them still walking."

"Thanks," Jack blurted out as he took off half-running, half-limping.

Jack struggled along on his bad leg for about fifteen minutes as he slowly caught up with the stretched-out line of refugees. He hobbled parallel to them at a trot, turning to inspect every face he possibly could. He processed them all as quickly as he could, racing through the first thousand or so within another fifteen minutes.

"Tae-bok!" Jack shouted. "Are you here?"

Several women turned to look at the strange American shouting at them. Jack realized he had found *a* Tae-bok—or more than one—but not *the* Tae-bok. He pressed ahead with his frantic visual search along the long line of refugees. Breathing hard and with pain now shooting through his leg, Jack passed several large clusters of refugees walking together and sorted through them

the very best he could, checking faces, clothing, children—
anything that might identify Tae-bok.

The sun had completely sunk below the horizon, and yet Jack
had sorted through maybe only a third of the long line of
refugees streaming into the city. The darkness made it nearly
impossible now to see the faces of the people. He breathed hard
from the exertion and finally forced himself to pause and catch
his breath. He bent over to rub his cramping leg. The pain
radiated both down toward his foot and upwards to his hip,
twisting on the inside like a hot poker cruelly applied to the nerve.

After a moment's rest, Jack determined he could press on a
little farther. A line of passing trucks provided an extra bit of
illumination on the river of faces. Jack took advantage of the
dancing light as it played off the refugees. It flickered among
them and cast long, disconcerting shadows both to the left and
right of the long line of people. A flash of light from a quickly
passing jeep momentarily illuminated the faces of a small group
of women walking together. It was then that Jack looked directly
into Tae-bok's eyes.

The light flashed away as quickly as it had come, and he again
saw nothing.

He resigned himself to defeat once more. The lights and
shadows had conspired to distort the faces and given fertile
ground for his exhausted mind to play its tricks yet again.

"Jack?"

He jerked back to attention when he heard his name called.
He glared at the line of refugees through the harsh light. There
she was again, not more than twenty yards away. She stood
motionless with the baby strapped to her chest, a torn and
tattered note still pinned to the little one and Yong-ho holding her
hand by her side. It was surely not real.

Tae-bok stepped out of the crowd and weaved her way
through the masses of men, women, children, families, parcels,

and bundles and approached Jack silently, but with a vivid smile on her face. Jack dared not move. She stopped just ten feet away and looked Jack directly in the eyes. She smiled. *It is her, it really is her,* Jack dared to allow himself at last to believe. She really had decided to come.

Tae-bok's dark eyes showed few signs of weariness from three days in the impossible conditions at sea. Instead, they glimmered with a sparkle of hope as she looked up at him. Jack looked intently at her and decided he had never seen anyone quite so beautiful. He didn't know what to say or even how to begin to say it. But she did.

Tae-bok knelt down and whispered something to Yong-ho, never shifting her eyes from Jack. She then closed the remaining few feet. Yong-ho reacted with a massive smile and reached up and took Jack's right hand. He held it tightly. Jack looked down at his rough, war-torn hand as it embraced the little boy's soft, innocent one. Then Jack felt greater warmth as Tae-bok slipped her delicate hand into his left hand and squeezed it tightly.

Jack never let go.

CHAPTER SEVENTEEN

Funeral

The perfectly polished black Lincoln Town Car gently slowed to an almost imperceptible stop at Rose Acres Cemetery. An expanse of still-green grass rolled out across the field. Its continuity was interrupted by countless grave markers. Meredith Stiles painfully swung her trembling legs to the right so that she might step out of the Lincoln. Her family carefully steadied her by her frail arms and eased her from the backseat to her feet. Fighting back against the ravages of the arthritis, she had insisted on walking. She steadfastly refused the funeral director's suggestion of a wheelchair.

Thirty yards ahead was a solemn arrangement of folding chairs positioned neatly on a small surface of artificial grass. Meredith's walk was a struggle across the uneven ground. Strong arms on either side gently eased her along the way.

Meredith had been here before. She recognized a place just to the right where a few years back she and Jack had assembled with friends and family to say good-bye to an old friend. She knew that each grave marker told a story—a story of life and struggles, of successes and failures, and ultimately of final defeat by the cruel hand of death.

Those who followed Meredith across the grassy cemetery matched her slow pace with respect. They followed slowly but patiently as she made her way to her chair in the front row of the graveside service.

When she sat down, she turned to see the preacher standing resolutely near the hearse, his black suit coat without so much as a wrinkle, his red tie cinched neatly around his neck, his well-worn, leather-bound Bible clenched firmly in his hands. Before him stood the Marine Corps Honor Guard. They stood motionless. It was difficult to tell if they even breathed. The group was led by a young man, younger even than her children.

The formation commander waited patiently for the preacher's signal. When all had been seated, the preacher nodded, and the lead man began his duties in a way that spoke honor with every move. Every call was crisp. Every response from the honor guard was precise. They first turned and formed two lines. The two lines approached the hearse. The formation commander positioned his hand on the rear door of the hearse and respectfully paused.

Meredith heard only silence.

With military precision, the commander opened the hearse, did a crisp about-face, walked ten paces, and then did another about-face and stood silently. His barked order spurred his men to action. They moved as one. They mechanically placed their hands on the flag-draped casket, slid it out of the hearse, and then held it silently with perfect stillness.

The commander gave more orders, and the men pivoted. He looked at the preacher; the preacher nodded and began a slow walk toward the graveside. The six strong young men of the honor guard carried the casket with precision and respect for their aged, fallen colleague. They followed the preacher precisely across the cemetery. Meredith observed the military team's subjection to a civilian, a preacher, and remembered that was how it was always supposed to be—first to a president, and then in death to a preacher. The honor guard gently placed the flag-draped casket on the rails at the graveside. Each man moved deliberately and in perfect timing with each other and saluted their fallen comrade.

The preacher paused for a moment as those assembled rested in the silence of the occasion. Then he began. He spoke softly about the fact that on this day, they had come as far as they could go. In the preceding funeral service, they had remembered Jack in death. They remembered his service to a grateful nation. They spoke of their fond memories of him. They spoke of his service in Korea. Now, the preacher said, they must leave Jack's body and allow it to return to the dust, "from whence it came."

With a few concluding words, the preacher opened his Bible and began to read.

"The Lord is my shepherd, I shall not want . . ."

As the final words of Psalm 23 fell across the assembly, the preacher led the gathering in a simple prayer, asking blessings upon Jack's family.

With the final "amen" and at their commander's direction, two men of the honor guard respectfully lifted the flag from the casket and began a series of thirteen precise and perfectly regimented folds until the flag was formed into a perfect triangle. It was handed to the formation commander as though it was the most precious item on earth—as though it represented the blood of an entire generation's sacrifice for freedom, as indeed it did.

The formation commander, looking to be no more than twenty-five years old, respectfully approached the grieving widow and bent on one knee in the damp grass. He held the sacred flag waist-high, with the straight edge toward Meredith, and gently leaned toward her.

"Meredith Stiles, on behalf of the president of the United States, the commandant of the Marine Corps, and a grateful nation, please accept this flag as a symbol of our appreciation for your loved one's service to country and corps." Meredith's feeble hands took the crisply folded flag and pressed it tightly to her chest. She closed her eyes gently, and for a moment, just barely a fleeting moment, she held him again.

The young man returned to his feet and directed his Marines to move deliberately and formally across the funeral lawn to a point about sixty yards away where they had previously laid their rifles against a tree. One Marine retreated about twenty yards further and stood rapt at attention with a bugle at his lips.

Then, penetrating the still silence, the lead Marine barked orders to his men. Seven Marines stood at attention, turned ninety degrees, and loaded a round into their rifles.

"Ready," the commander barked.

"Aim."

The Marines raised their guns in perfect unison toward the late-morning sky.

"Fire!"

The crack of the simultaneous rifle rounds broke the crisp autumn air, raced across the valleys, and echoed back from the hills. As the men reloaded and continued firing in unison, Meredith jumped with each shot, the very sounds taking her back to a time and place long faded in her memory, but never forgotten.

When the final shot echoed across the cemetery and with rifles held at attention, the bugle began its sad, lonely cry. No one moved. It seemed as though all of nature, save the gentle breeze, deferred its business as the old, sad song played. The final note of Taps echoed across the little cemetery in New Hampshire. Perfect silence let the last note find its resting place in the hills and valleys. For a moment, the only sound was the gentle caress of the trees by the light autumn wind.

With the final note played, the Marine Corps team methodically retrieved each brass shell from the grass and then approached the family one final time. There was one more action to follow through.

Each member of the honor guard approached the family and saluted the four soldiers who had attended the graveside service

243

with their mother. The four stood in full military dress, just to the side of Meredith: Colonel Yong-ho Stiles, United States Marine Corps; First Lieutenant Kyung-chan Stiles, United States Marine Corps; Second Lieutenant Mary Beth Stiles, United States Air Force, and Staff Sergeant Leonard LaRue Stiles, United States Army.

The men of the United States Marine Corps saluted their colleagues, then turned and walked in formation to their vehicle. The preacher greeted the family, shook the hands of those in attendance, and offered a few parting words of comfort to Meredith. The assembled crowd began a slow dispersal across the cemetery lawn.

Meredith's family helped her rise from the metal folding chair. As she rose to her feet, she noticed a man in a gray sport coat standing twenty or thirty yards away under a tree, not really belonging among her friends. Meredith motioned to her son Kyung-chan.

"Yes, Mother?"

"That gentleman over there . . . do you see him?" she asked, pointing at the man standing awkwardly alone.

"Yes?"

"Ask him to come see me, please," Meredith said with a little smile.

"Do you know this man, Mother?"

"I believe I do. Please ask him to come."

Kyung-chan walked in the brisk formal strides of a born Marine to the stranger under the tree. A few words were exchanged. Kyung-chan turned to walk back, and the man tentatively followed.

"Mother," Kyung-chan said as he presented the man, "This is Mr. Pierce."

Meredith raised a trembling hand. "Mr. Pierce, it is so nice to finally meet you."

"Thank you, ma'am. Mrs. Stiles, correct?" he asked as he gently took her hand.

"I am. Or you may call me by the name I knew long ago: Jang Tae-bok. But I'm a bit partial to Meredith." She smiled.

"Very well, Meredith. Please accept my sympathies. I didn't know your husband, but I am sorry for your loss and grateful for his service. Anytime this nation loses one of its men, it is a great loss for all of us. Thank you very much for inviting me." Jonathan Pierce turned and nodded at Meredith's son.

"Mr. Pierce, may I ask a favor of you?"

"Yes, of course. What can I do for you?"

"My husband read your book on the Korean War a few years ago. He enjoyed it very much. It is, as you have said, the forgotten war. Everyone remembers World War II. Everyone knows Vietnam. No one remembers Korea. But you know this, of course—I'm sorry for prattling on. Anyway, he was impressed that you lived so close by. Thank you for coming. He would have appreciated it."

Jonathan Pierce looked at her with some confusion—this old, grieving woman standing feebly before him. "You're very welcome. I'm glad my schedule permitted me to come." He softened his voice, tender as though he was speaking to his own grandmother. "Meredith, you were about to ask me a favor. Is there something I can do for you?"

"Mr. Pierce, what you can do for me is to write another book."

Perplexed, Pierce looked inquisitively at Meredith. "Yes, ma'am, I will probably do that . . . but I don't have anything more to write at the moment about the Korean War. I've been asked by my publisher to write some other things . . . some things about Vietnam." He grimaced apologetically.

"Yes, Mr. Pierce, I understand."

Meredith smiled slightly and then stirred a bit in her handbag.

She held her flag carefully between her arm and body, gently retrieved a small leather-bound notebook, and handed it to him.

"Mr. Pierce," Meredith whispered, as if to be heard only by him, "may I tell you my story? It is not so much a war story, Mr. Pierce. It is a *love* story. I thought I should write it down before it is too late. I ask again: may I tell you my story?"

Jonathan Pierce glanced at the book and then at Meredith. He gently turned the leather cover and began to skim through the pages of her memories. He stood motionless, save for the gentle rustling of pages. The perfect handwriting was easy to read, and it filled his mind the way new leaves fill a barren landscape in the spring. A few moments passed as Pierce took in the world on her pages. He closed the leather book gently.

With a look of full understanding, Pierce choked past a growing tightness in his throat. "Yes, ma'am, you certainly may. I would be honored to read your story."

"Well, Mr. Pierce. I hope you don't just read it. I hope you'll consider writing my story. Write something, Mr. Pierce. Write something so that they will all know just how much they all did."

Pierce looked deep into the grieving widow's eyes. He saw a world far away, a world of memories, of love lost and love found.

"Yes, ma'am. Yes, ma'am, I believe I will."

Epilogue

After rescuing more than fourteen thousand souls with his small cargo ship, Captain Leonard P. LaRue continued as master of the SS *Meredith Victory* until her decommissioning in 1953. In 1954, after being hospitalized for the removal of an infected kidney, LaRue resigned from a life at sea with the Moore-McCormack lines. His resignation letter read, in part:

> My stay in the hospital proved to be climactic in that it resolved me on a course of action to settle two absorbing questions: 1. What is the real purpose of life? 2. What am I going to do about it? Going to sea had many enjoyable facets but each of us in his own manner must walk the Road into Eternity alone and I feel certain that for me the Road stretches onward from here.

LaRue chose to enter a Benedictine monastery: St. Paul's Abbey in Newton, New Jersey. He wore a new name until the time of his death: Brother Marinus. He would later reflect, "I think often of that voyage. I think of how such a small vessel was able to hold so many persons and surmount endless perils without harm to a soul. As I think, the clear, unmistakable message comes to me that on that Christmastide, in the bleak and bitter waters off the shores of Korea, God's own hand was at the helm of my ship."

In later years, Rear Admiral J. Robert Lunney asked LaRue what prompted him to attempt such a great rescue. He said, "The answer is in the Holy Bible: 'No greater love hath a man, than to lay down his life for his friends.'"

In the final years of LaRue's life, St. Paul's Abbey fell into decline. When word reached Korea, members of the order there sent men to St. Paul's, and soon leadership of the abbey transitioned to the Koreans. They explained, "Captain LaRue saved us, now we will save him."

LaRue remained in service at the monastery until his death on October 12, 2001. Men would later say of Captain LaRue, "He was exactly the right man, in exactly the right place, at exactly the right time."

History surely agrees.

* * *

At the age of fourteen, Won Dong-hyuck left his mother in North Korea. He and his father walked to Hungnam and were evacuated on the *Meredith Victory*. They lived and worked on the island of Koje-do for two years. To secure an education, Dong-hyuck worked two jobs during the day and attended high school at night. In 1956, just before he graduated from high school, Dong-hyuck's father died. Dong-hyuck married in 1966 and has one son, who works as a missionary, and two daughters. He has two grandsons and two granddaughters. He looks forward to even more. In 2012, he moved from South Korea to Ohio to be near one of his daughters.

Dong-hyuck was recently privileged to reunite with three of his rescuers from the SS *Meredith Victory*: Robert Lunney, Burley Smith, and Merl Smith. He remains in contact with them today.

In the intervening sixty-plus years, Dong-hyuck has never heard from his mother or the rest of the family he left behind in

Korea.

He believes his mother died in North Korea in 1964.

* * *

Rear Admiral J. Robert Lunney of the NY Naval Militia, a WWII Navy veteran, served as the Staff Officer aboard the *Meredith Victory* during the Korean War and during the rescue operation from Hungnam. He graduated from the Cornell Law School in 1954 and served as an Assistant US Attorney in New York and later formed his own law firm. He is a former president of the Naval Reserve Association and former president of the Sons of the Revolution.

In 1997 and 1998, Lunney became one of the few Americans to return to North Korea. The Department of Defense sent him back to North Korea to serve as an observer of Joint Recovery Operations, an operation that seeks to recover American war dead from the Korean War.

* * *

Dino S. Savastio served as Chief Mate during his time on the *Meredith Victory*. With the aid of a Korean midwife, he delivered the five babies born en route to Pusan and Koje-do. In 1957 he became captain of his own ship. In 1978, Captain Savastio became assistant vice-president of the Moore-McCormack Lines. He retired from the Moore-McCormack Lines in 1983 as vice-president of operations. He died in 2008.

* * *

Burley Smith served aboard the *Meredith Victory* during the Hungnam evacuation as her Junior Third Mate. As one of the three watch-standing deck officers, Smith was in charge of the eight to twelve watch on the bridge. He vividly recalls dangling above a raging sea as he clung to one of the vertical stanchions on the bridge wing during the *Meredith Victory*'s encounter with Typhoon Kezia. Burley Smith lives in Florida with his family.

* * *

Merl Smith was an Engineering Officer aboard the *Meredith Victory* during the rescue mission in Hungnam. He later served on ships serving South America. He now resides in Kinderhook, New York.

* * *

The SS *Meredith Victory* was retired after the Korean War. Recognition for the amazing accomplishment of the ship and her crew would develop over the next few years.

In 1958 the South Korean president, Syngman Rhee, awarded the officers and crew of the *Meredith Victory* the Korean Presidential Unit Citation. The citation read in part: "The arrival of the *Meredith Victory* in Pusan after a three-day voyage through dangerous waters was a memorable occasion for all who participated in this humanitarian mission and is remembered by the people of Korea as an inspiring example of Christian faith in action."

In 1960, in recognition of the incomparable role she played in history's most astonishing humanitarian mission, the *Meredith Victory* received recognition as a "Gallant Ship" by a special act passed by the United States Congress and signed by President Eisenhower. In part, the commendation for her and her crew read as follows: "The courage, resourcefulness, sound seamanship and teamwork of her master, officers and crew in successfully completing one of the greatest marine rescues in the history of the world have caused the name of the MEREDITH VICTORY to be perpetuated as that of a Gallant Ship."

She was the only Merchant Marine ship and crew serving during the Korean War to receive such a citation.

She again served her country when hostilities in Vietnam flared. After the Vietnam War she was again mothballed in the reserve fleet. On October 1, 1993, the *Meredith Victory* was sold for scrap, and in the ultimate stroke of irony, is reported to have been cut into pieces in China.

She still holds a Guinness World Record: "The SS *Meredith Victory* performed the greatest rescue operation ever by a single ship by evacuating 14,000 refugees from Hungnam, North Korea in December 1950."

The Eisenhower administration hailed the rescue operation as "One of the greatest marine rescues in the history of the world."

* * *

Many ships from the US 7th Fleet played a critical role in the evacuation of the one hundred thousand civilians from Hungnam. In particular, the USS *Saint Paul,* USS *Rochester,* USS *Missouri,* and other ships fired more than twenty thousand shells into the hills around Hungnam in order to hold back the Communist forces.

Many men risked their lives so that others could live free.

* * *

The United States suffered the loss of more than thirty-six thousand men in the Korean War. More than ninety thousand men were wounded. Tragically, some eight thousand men remain missing in action. The United States, as well as South Korea, technically remains at a state of war with North Korea. More than twenty-eight thousand US troops remain on duty in South Korea today.

* * *

The one hundred thousand Korean civilians who were evacuated from Hungnam on Christmas Eve of 1950, and their descendants, live on today. As refugees, they risked all to escape Communism. Their lives are a tribute to the men who risked everything to take them to safety: the men of the US Merchant Marine, the US Navy, the Marine Corps, the Army, and the Air Force. Most importantly, their lives are a tribute to the power of hope.

Unknown to us are their countless stories, accomplishments, and contributions to society.

They are the subject of what was, and remains today, the greatest naval evacuation in all of human history.

Made in the USA
Coppell, TX
18 September 2024

37452500R00152